A t 7:41 A.M., the little clock carried home its mission and the bomb exploded on the window ledge of Homer Wayne DuPree's bedroom. Eula Jo had heard the blast five blocks away, instantly exhilarated with the knowledge that Homer Wayne had been blown all to Hell. As she ran joyfully back to the mansion amid a throng of others drawn by the noise, she began screaming.

"Call the Goddamn police. They done kilt mah husband."

Homer hadn't been blown all the way to Hell, however, only part way—about 22 feet as well as they were able to later calculate. The black powder had, predictably, "low ordered". The two separate cardboard boxes had been the first problem. One box, the one with the blasting cap, had fully blown. The second, insulated by the cardboard wall of the two boxes, had merely spewed raw black powder all over Homer's bedroom and the ground outside.

MURDERING HOMER

A Nights on Fire Novel

by Gary Clifton

CHAPTER 1: OLD FACE, WRONG PLACE

The sparse crowd of hardscrabble patrons at Tubby's Fine Food froze in horror as the Giant Pink Rabbit sprang to his feet, his glassy eyes as wide in horrified shock as 1905 silver dollars. "Glub, glub, arrrgh." He choked, spitting a wad of half-chewed cheeseburger down the back of the long haired, tattooed man in the next booth.

Kobok and Bush watched somberly. This was it. Too many cholesterol stuffed grease burgers, and rancid, foot long cigars had finally rung the bell. The Giant Pink Rabbit was about to drop dead on the floor of Tubby's from rancid grease ingestion poisoning.

Always ready to Serve and Protect, Kobok asked, "You want I should call an ambulance."

"Holy double Hell, Kobok," the Giant Pink rabbit gasped, pointing at the door.

The Giant Pink Rabbit was not real. Everyone knows—or should know—that Giant Pink Rabbits rarely appear in broad daylight. He was Dallas Detective Harrison "Bull" Hooper who physically resembled the posture and body movement of a lowland gorilla—except Hooper was tougher.

They had waited an hour for Monroe "Squatty" Crockus to appear. Squatty, an avowed skinhead, had firebombed an African American church, claiming two victims. A reportedly reliable snitch had provided them some of that reliable information that Squatty was in love with Heavy Hilda, the waitress at Tubby's greasy spoon on South St. Paul Street, on the south fringe of Downtown Dallas. Squatty was purported to appear for lunch daily at 11:30 A.M.

The capture Squatty plan was hatched the evening before at

Adair's Tavern. ATF Special Agent Kobok and Dallas Homicide Detective Bull Hooper were on their fifth beers. ATF Special Agent Randall Bush nursed a Dr. Pepper."

Bush had just revealed the strategery.

"A what kinda Goddamned suit?" Hooper had roared, expelling his ever-present cigar stub halfway across Adair's Saloon. All three watched curiously as the nasty remnant danced along the worn wooden floor.

Bush held up the pink rabbit costume. "Bull, the white ears and tail are particularly fetching."

"Jesus Christ, it's Christmas. Why not rent a Santa suit?"

"All rented. Only thing left was this and they only had it in two extra-large." Kobok took a long pull on his beer and waived to the bar for another round.

Hooper stood and held the costume against his chest. A rousing round of applause sounded from the predominantly cop-crowd. "Screw this," Hooper growled.

Kobok said, "Bull Hooper, it's your turn in the barrel. You know damned well, if me 'n Bush hadn't lied like wet rats when you shot that doper last Spring, you'd be in the joint."

Hooper tossed the costume on the table. "Yeah, and you two comedians in adjacent cells. Pig Rhodden needed killin'. When he pulled that damned Barlow knife, I accommodated him. I shoulda got an award from the garbage removal department."

Bush said, "You know the problem. We put a man on foot outside of Tubby's and if Squatty makes him, he's gone back to Arkansas. Visibility from inside is so poor, we can't see him before he sees us waiting and he's still gone. We need a decoy actor."

Kobok drained his glass. "Hooper, I know you wanna catch this toad as bad as we do."

At 11:00 A.M. the next day, Hooper, a foot-long stogie donating to the pollution situation, stood in front of Tubby's waving a tin cup labeled "Help the Homeless."

By 12 noon, Kobok ordered Hooper a burger, stepped to the door, and motioned the Giant Pink Rabbit inside. So much for reliable information. Hooper had just started on his first large bite of grease when a familiar face strolled in.

"It's him!" The Giant Pink Rabbit spat the last glob of semi-chewed burger into an adjacent booth. "Well maybe that's not Squatty, but I know that sumbitch from someplace."

Kobok, seeing the Giant Pink Rabbit was not dying, followed his eyes to the door. The scrawny guy entering carried the look of death alright, but he wasn't Squatty Crockus. Kobok instantly recognized the acne scarred, evil mug. Holy mother of nightmares, the surprise wouldn't have been greater if a DART bus had crashed through the door.

"Jesus Christ," Kobok gasped. "It's not Squatty. That dude is the friggin' Prince of Draconia."

"Get your eyes checked, Kobok. He's in the joint," Hooper grunted, inadvertently incriminating half the shady crowd in Tubby's. "We sent that sucker away for sixty-five years. He can't be in no damned greasy spoon in by-God, Dallas, America."

"Don't look over there, Bull. He shoulda already made me. I'm gonna grab the little rat before he gets outside."

Bush said through a mouthful of soggy salad, "The Prince of Draconia? Draconian is an adjective. There's no such word as Draconia."

Too innately stupid to recognize Kobok or Hooper immediately, His Highness caught sight of the pink rabbit get-up. He called out, "Hey, Homey, yo' purse don't match yo' outfit."

Kobok's anger exploded to critical mass. Because of the Prince, Kobok had beat himself up regularly for five years for what he perceived as failure to complete an elementary follow-up investigation of a nickel and dime firebombing near north Dallas. To his mind, his laxity had caused the grisly, retaliation murder of a ten-year-old girl and repeated attempts to murder a sixty-year-old Waste Management executive.

The self-blame monkey for failures, real or self-assessed, perched on Kobok's shoulder every waking hour and in a thousand dreams. They shared dinner, sex after dinner, traffic jams—no instant went unattended. Like the bully's big brother, his burden grew larger at the end of each day. Now, for Christ's sake, there he stood, alive and well at Tubby's counter. The Prince had been born on Halloween. Each October 31st twisted the aggravation screw down a notch or two. Kobok had convinced himself he should have let the air out of this miserable piece of humanity the first time he saw him—or the second—or the third.

The Prince looked away, then sharply back at Kobok.

"He's gonna run!" Kobok kicked back his chair and lunged at the little man as he slithered out of the doorway. He managed a grip on the lapels of the fleeing man's silk shirt. With the desperation of a trapped rattlesnake, the Prince delivered a glancing knee to Kobok's groin and a mini bite on his right wrist. Frantic, the fugitive first ran north on the crowded sidewalk. Then he veered across one of two solid lanes of wall to wall southbound one-way traffic into the center lane of South St. Paul Street, squeezing inches from instant death. Kobok duplicated the move, cutting across a lane of traffic and running north between lines of traffic. A symphony of blaring horns marked their progress.

At 41, Kobok chugged along, thirty feet behind. The Prince was nearly twenty years younger and had a thirty-foot lead, but Kobok had caught him before and intended to again. A guy fresh out of the joint might be hardy from chopping cotton, strong from lifting weights in an air-conditioned prison gym, or pliable from being some alpha con's wife, but track and field had not been added to the Texas prison system curriculum. Kobok would wear him down unless an inattentive motorist did the honors.

Kobok had been a Special Agent, Bureau of Alcohol, Tobacco, Firearms and Explosives for eighteen years that mid-December day in 1989. He'd been transferred to Dallas from Kansas City four years earlier following a shots-fired incident. Slender, fairly fit, he wore his gray flecked, black hair in the federal agent approved preppy style. Unmarried, he did well with the ladies, plentiful in the Dallas area - sometimes too well. A flawed man, like all humans, Kobok, on balance was a very competent, street wise federal cop.

Hooper had one upped Kobok, knocking over the table, burgers flying. Bush, bewildered, was on Hooper's heels as they ran into the chilly, north wind. "Who we chasing?" Bush shouted.

"A guy Kobok and I put away forever four years ago," the giant Hooper puffed over his shoulder. "You weren't on the job yet, kid. I'm thinkin' we gotta escaped convict here."

Twenty years older than Kobok and a head shorter, Hooper was no longer a candidate for the Dallas Police Track team. Life had left him husky, tough, and bald with a half inch rim of silver hair circling the back of his head like a misplaced tiara atop a cantaloupe. Bull Hooper was well known among a wide swath of the Dallas criminal element as an extremely poor choice of folks to piss off. Squad room banter said that Hooper had been in Homicide since before color T.V. He'd cleared more homicides than most police department's entire personnel.

Bush, who jogged daily, quickly passed Hooper. On seeing Kobok pivot after the fleeing man into the center lane against traffic, Bush followed.

The Giant Pink Rabbit, attempting to pull out his badge from his fanny pack to interdict traffic, came up with a .38 revolver instead. Waving a pistol was more efficient than a badge. Traffic stopped and let him cross to the center. The volume of car horns multiplied tenfold.

Randall Bush had been an ATF agent for just over three years. Kobok had been his training officer for nearly a year while Bush considered using the degree he'd earned at an exclusive eastern law school. Several Dallas law firms had reached out to him. Two years earlier, much to the consternation of his father, a well-known Dallas psychiatrist, he had opted for the pay cut and life in the fast lane by staying in the often-chaotic circus of ATF. At 26, tall, fit, and boyishly blond handsome, he was now Kobok's regular partner.

The weird parade threaded north toward the heart of even heavier downtown noonday traffic. They ran in a narrow row, vulnerable for a head on collision with the chain of oncoming traffic. The sound of Christmas music wafting from utility poles further downtown gradually grew louder. As they crossed Wood Street, St. Paul traffic missed the light. The fugitive avoided being killed by brake-screeching, westbound Wood Street motorists. Skidding tires and blaring horns preceded a double lane of multiple car rear-enders. The pile up instantly gridlocked traffic in both directions. He continued north in the center lane.

Kobok dodged through tumbled parked cars in the intersection. Bush, passed him, zig sagging across Wood Street following the Prince in the center lane. Drivers' were collectively mesmerized by the spectacle of a fleeing man, two men in suits pursuing and a Giant Pink Rabbit waving a revolver lumbering along behind. Trapped in an impassible traffic jam, none had the wherewithal in those pre-cellular days, to report the unbelievable procession. But plenty had called from somewhere. The Dallas Alarm Office switchboard instantly became a sea of red lights.

The Prince crossed eastbound one-way Jackson street, this time catching the light. Dancing with what brought him, he continued to run between lanes of cars into oncoming traffic. Bush had gained ground, now only fifteen feet from contact.

The Prince caught the light at Commerce Street, turned right in front of another brake screeching, southbound St. Paul motorist. He ran between lanes on eastbound Commerce. The momentary stop in the left-hand lane of St. Paul allowed Bush, two steps behind, a window to cut into the narrow opening between vehicles. As he made the turn, he saw from the corner of his eye Kobok was about a car length behind. Hooper was about forty feet in the rear.

Kobok made the last second of the temporarily closed intersection and followed Bush between lanes of traffic. Hooper, still in his pink getup and waving his .38, had no problem making the turn, just as eastbound Commerce caught the light. The lesson learned here was, of course, what better way to clear traffic than have a 240-pound Giant Pink Rabbit wave a revolver as he ran—lumbered perhaps—along between lanes of traffic with floppy white ears whipping in the wind. The situation was similar, but now different. Oncoming traffic was coming from behind, exposing all four runners to the possibility of being blind-sided by a motorist changing lanes at the wrong moment.

At the intersection with South Harwood, diagonally across from the Police and Courts Building, Bush reattached himself to the silk shirt. They landed on a manhole cover at street center.

Kobok piled on. Then the Giant Pink Rabbit rumbled up gasping for breath, still waving his pistol. Traffic came to a chaotic halt.

The good news: fifty feet from the building full of cops meant plenty of assistance. The bad news: The Dallas Police switchboard had already received about a hundred "911" calls, which combined with all the guys looking out the window to see the commotion, meant half the cops in Dallas arrived to restore order. Who says you can't find a cop when you need one.

Hooper stuck the pistol back in his fanny pack and pulled out his badge to ward off eight or ten eager young uniforms intent on using Bush or Kobok's heads as sounding boards.

Hooper pulled back the hood of his costume, making his bald head readily recognizable to the glut of cops who flooded the intersection.

Kobok gained breath and motioned Bush aside. He dropped a knee in the cowering Prince's back and spat between his teeth, "How the hell did you get out?"

"Early release," the now sobbing prisoner sneered, the left side of his face pressed against the asphalt. Kobok briefly pondered pulling off his head, but quickly backed off in view of the extensive police presence.

One slender graying uniformed sergeant sidled up to Hooper. "Nice outfit, Bull."

"Finally coming out of the closet, Hooper?" A blond officer in plain clothes chided, making certain that in the crowd of cops, Hooper couldn't spot him making such a suicidal statement.

"Boys," Hooper held court, amidst a background of car horns and angry shouts. "This here is strictly a high-level government operation. I've been forced by the high command into service as a secret, U.S. Government, undercover operative. Y'all must know that Federal building down there is ass-bust full of folks wearing stuff like pink rabbit creations. Hell, Kobok's supervisor goes around all day in a chicken suit." His words fueled a round of laughter and additional caustic comments about Hooper's rabbit outfit and the Federal Government.

As Hooper chatted away, Kobok wondered what percent of the DPD would be wiped out by a single runaway cement truck plowing into the massed police presence. The crowd of cops began wandering back to the Police and Courts Building or to one of the eight or ten squad cars parked willy nelly in the intersection. Most walked away cursing at the shortcomings of the criminal justice system that would allow trash like the Prince back on the street.

Kobok was queasy from the foot chase. He vowed for the umpteenth time to drink less, sleep more, and find his way home earlier regularly. He'd started the morning's activities with a slight hangover, not an unusual practice for Kobok. He'd earned the nickname "Agent McScruff" in the ATF squad room.

Kobok, Bush, and Hooper dragged the sniveling prisoner diagonally the fifty feet to the Police and Courts Building. Hooper was puffing on a new stogie like a steam calliope invading Dealey Plaza. The Homicide office was in that building at the time which allowed Hooper to go upstairs to lose the rabbit suit.

Kobok wrestled the whining prisoner down the stairs to the Records and Book-in Unit in the basement about twenty feet from the spot where Jack Ruby shot Lee Harvey Oswald. Kobok filled out a criminal records request.

The clerk, a slender black lady of fifty with rose tinted glasses waited quietly. Her disinterested expression announced she had already seen everything come through the door down there which could possibly be of surprise or interest to her including the Prince, the pink rabbit, Kobok, Lee Harvey Oswald, or the ghost of Elvis.

Presently, she tossed a computer printout on the countertop. The information was enough to make an undertaker vomit. The Prince had been paroled back to Dallas three weeks earlier via an early release. Newspapers had been filled with headlines announcing a Federal Judge had arbitrarily decided the State of Texas had too many prisoners in the Department of Corrections.

Via the arrogance of an appointed bureaucrat, the judge had ordered the State to release several thousand. The Prince had served less than four years of sixty-five for attempted capital murder. He had been responsible for multiple additional crimes, including one of the most haunting, revolting offenses Kobok had ever encountered. But only the attempted murder made it all the way to a jury.

The Prince, taking strength from the presence of so many witnesses spat out a serenade of profanity and threats. "You can't fuck with me, puta."

"Puta? Get lost while you can dirtbag," Kobok shoved the Prince away, concerned his anger would overcome reason and cause him to summarily execute the loser in front of the glut of spectators in the Records and Book-in Unit.

"I'm gonna sue, Kobok," he snarled the well-used line. Ten minutes in custody had allowed him to remember Kobok's name.

Angry to the edge of murder, the comment tripped the safety-switch in Kobok's "go nuts" mechanism. Kobok pushed the Prince out the door of the Records Unit and into a small, unoccupied restroom in the basement hallway. The Prince squealed, piglet style. The sound called up newer, vivid recollections of little Sherry Kincaid in full color. Exhaustion from the foot chase and the residual hangover headache amplified the screeching already working overtime between his ears. Bush, rapidly gaining a grip on the reality of the business he had chosen, stepped into the small room and turned the door lock.

Kobok threw the Prince bodily into a commode stall. The Prince assumed a fetal position around the commode, eyes sick in terror. Somehow, he seemed to belong there, expecting what he had inflicted upon others.

"I shoulda finished you when I had the chance." Kobok leaned down to whisper in his rat-ear. "Sue! Tear your ass boy. Sue away. Who's your parole officer?"

"I...I ain't sure," he stammered, sobbing.

Kobok reached over the commode for a better handful. "Charlie something." The Prince covered his face. "No man, Charlie Mitchell...that's it."

Kobok knew Texas State Parole Officer Mitchell. "You lie to me and I'll find you and let the air outta you," he said softly, still bent over the commode.

"Please man," he sobbed. "In the name of God, lemme go."

"Is that what Sherry said, scumbag, while you burned her naked little body with cigarettes...strangled her with her panties?" Kobok was once again flooded with the vision of her mutilated body. He backed out of the stall, leaving the huddled man full length between the commode and metal divider. "I wonder if Sherry's father knows you're out. I'll bet he'll wanna know where to find you." Then, for the sake of rehabilitation, Kobok stepped back into the stall and delivered a kick—only a medium one shielded by the toilet—in the ribs.

The Prince vomited down the imitation silk shirt, choking. He had a history of losing his stomach at the slightest fear. Kobok turned to Bush, still on guard detail. "Thanks, partner," he smiled. Bush unlocked the door and stepped into the hallway. A uniformed officer stood staring curiously past them into the restroom. He wore a red shoulder patch signifying he was attached to the Traffic Division.

"There's a sick man in the commode stall over there, Officer." Kobok pointed.

"Probably another wino," the officer shrugged, continuing to peer into the commode area.

"Probably much worse," Kobok suggested as Bush and he started for the elevator.

A crowd of normal riffraff accumulated in the foyer, attempting in some way to better their lives by requesting what public information was available regarding their sorry arrest records. Kobok had no way of knowing whether someone had been watching and had witnessed the entire chase fiasco. He didn't really give a damn.

Bush and Kobok took the elevator up to Homicide. "Damn, partner," Bush said softly. "Like you've told me, be careful what you do in the presence of hostile witnesses."

"Randall, the Prince chapter happened while you were still in college. I tell you the story, you're gonna want a piece of him."

Hooper had changed from the ill-fitting rabbit suit to an ill-fitting, brown polyester suit. Kobok explained the early release status of the Prince.

"What a crock," he grunted as he took the chair behind his battered desk. Kobok and Bush sat across from him in plastic chairs "Got any idea what we oughta do?" Hooper asked. "About the Prince...or Squatty Crockus?"

Kobok sighed. "A loser like the Prince can't stay out of trouble. He'll turn up again soon...with his ass in a sling."

"You're right." Hooper tossed Bush the rabbit costume. "Y'all want me to have a squad car run you back to the Federal Building?"

Kobok said, "Naw, we just ran it, we can walk six blocks as a cool-down."

As they walked down Commerce, Christmas music drifting down on a cool, but comfortable December day, Kobok was surprised not a soul recognized them from the wild, traffic stopping foot chase of less than an hour earlier. They stopped for lunch—Tubby's cuisine had been lost in combat—in an Italian restaurant adjacent to the Adolphus Hotel. From a lobby payphone, Kobok called Tootie, the group secretary. She assured him the current Arson and bomb Squad supervisor, Cummins Klaster, called Short Cummins, was out of pocket for the next couple of hours. Kobok was not in the mood for supervision.

Bush had not been on the payroll when the Prince episode went down. Kobok spent a half hour briefing Bush on the parameters of the Prince episode. Then Bush and he spent another hour reading the 1984 investigative file and the transcript of the subsequent 1985 trial. Bush agreed, the Prince needed killing ala the Hooper theory.

Kobok called Kincaid Motors, a low rent used car dealership in Denton, Texas, 35 miles north of Dallas. Kincaid, with a history of involvement with car thieves and other unsavory characters, was the father of Sherry Kincaid, the murder victim Kobok felt he had failed five years earlier. When told Kincaid was out of town, Kobok told the secretary to tell Kincaid the Prince was out of prison. He sat studying the ceiling, reflecting on what a hell of a mess the Prince incident had been.

CHAPTER 2: HOMER WAYNE AND EULA JO

Homer Wayne DuPree was born in Terrebonne Parish, Louisiana, eleventh of eleven children in a tar paper sharecropper's shack mounted on Bois D'Arc poles to stay above the swamp and avoid being eaten by 'gators.

His ol' daddy, Pierre, dabbled at sharecropping, a highly difficult vocation when the top three inches of soil were water. Pierre sometimes dabbled at hunting 'gators in the vast swamps and made an occasional dime or two, day dabbling on the shrimp boats which permeated the area.

Then one day, Pierre dabbled with a whore he met at *Sam Johnny's Roadhouse* and managed to get into a row with her pimp. Pierre continued to live two days with his guts cut mostly out. He was buried by Parish employees in a wooden box at Parrish expense in a watery grave at the edge of Swamp Felicity.

Homer Wayne, the youngest of the children struggled through many hungry nights and penniless days until his mama died when he was seventeen. Mama gone meant the welfare check was gone and shortly, so was Homer Wayne.

Homer Wayne stuffed everything he owned in a *Benoit Brothers* number two grocery sack and beat it the hell out of the territory. He rode a Greyhound bus as far as $7.25 would carry him which happened to be the downtown Dallas bus terminal. Homer Wayne never fully admitted, even to himself, as he was leaning on the dumpster behind the station on Jackson Street, that he intended, when no one was looking, to dive for a morsel of anything edible.

A friendly, African American garbage truck driver beeped his horn to move Homer Wayne and snag the night's dumpster haul. The big, robust kid from Terrebone Parrish moved accommodatingly. The two struck up a conversation, the driver gave him the last half of his bologna sandwich. Homer Wayne hitched a ride back to company headquarters on South Industrial. Management hired the husky, amiable kid from the swamps of Louisiana and put him to work wheeling a garbage rig from 9:00 P.M. until 6:00 A.M., six days weekly, Sunday nights off.

Forty years later, Homer Wayne was still wrestling that rig down narrow alleys, still six days a week. However, he now owned the whole sixty-acre operation on South Industrial, 37 state of the art trash compactor trucks, more dumpsters than he could count, with 79 full time employees, a multiple bathroom mansion on Newmanshire Drive in far north Dallas, and a hundred million dollars of downtown Dallas real estate. Homer Wayne DuPree, who still couldn't read worth a nickel, was indeed a genuine American success story. A shy redneck, who had begun life with an outhouse and two paths, was now tricked out in a very large house with no paths and twenty-two baths.

Soon after arriving in Dallas, Homer Wayne met Sally Lou Rogers at an ice cream social in the Church of the Lamb. They shared a double chocolate sundae, then shared a loving household which bore four daughters through 38 years of marital bliss. The idyllic life was grand in all capitals.

Early on a February 1984 Sunday morning, Sally Lou was frying up a mess of eggs, onions, and hash browns for Homer Wayne before church. She suddenly looked skyward, gasped twice, and dropped dead on the floor of the kitchen of the spacious mansion.

Homer Wayne was, needless to say, lost and distraught. His four daughters and eight grandchildren formed a herculean effort to help: visiting the mansion, inviting grandpa over for dinner, stopping by to vacuum the carpet even though Homer Wayne had a full-time maid. The kids did their damnedest, with a view of course at all times to confirm that if Grandpa Homer Wayne croaked of grief, they'd protect their chunk of his millions, hopefully each manipulating to screw the others however possible.

Meanwhile, Homer Wayne continued to wheel—or occasional ride shotgun on—a six-ton garbage compactor Monday evening until Sunday morning, and grow richer by the day. Some of the municipalities in the Dallas area owned and operated their own equipment. However, many did not and Homer Wayne was always there to fill a need. But the Homer Wayne DuPree saga was not destined to end up a one trick pony.

Enter Eula Jo Ragsdale. Eula Jo's mama, Sally Mae had been a whore. Born in Ellis County, south of Dallas, she'd plied her trade in the oilfields of southeast Texas while her product was still marketable as she gradually depreciated to third team status. Sally Mae contacted syphilis, spread the dreaded ailment to many unsuspecting "johns", and finally returned to the old family homestead in Ellis County to wither and die.

The men in Eula Jo's life: her father Elrod, and two brothers, Cleo and Claude worked at menial jobs or more often at no jobs at all when they weren't locked up. They were mostly burglars, an occupation at which they were not very good. When Eula Jo was 14, brother Cleo was shot and killed by a Texas Highway Patrol officer while fleeing after robbing the Drover's Bank of Kemp, Texas. Daddy Elrod and brother Claude got arrested for the same robbery. Both got life without parole—at a time when life meant life.

Eula Jo was screwed when mama passed, literally. Already fully equipped with forty pounds of pure Ellis County boobs, she caught the eye of many a fellow who otherwise would never have wavered into temptation. Dumb, lazy, dependent, and as clingy as a garden slug, Eula Jo's employment horizons were limited. Partly sliding along the easiest path, plus being overly physically equipped to pursue her mama's trade, she saw no reason to break Ella Mae's mode. Eula Jo had been a non-virgin since she'd lain with her brother Cleo when she was nine. Eula Jo became a whore. Actually, she always had been; it just took her until age fifteen to find herself. Whoring beat hell out of waiting tables at the local truck stop or burglary and other crap which brought cops who hurt people.

With boobs like melons, solicitation was rarely necessary. Men, far and wide, lasered in on Eula Jo's chest like moths to a mercury light. The rest pretty much took its course.

Before her sixteenth birthday, Eula Jo had lain with half the men—or so it seemed—in Ellis County. Having been busted a half dozen times by Ellis County cops for prostitution, she was well known. The culmination of her young career came when a reporter walked into the office of the chief of police in one of the small towns in the area and "discovered" Eula Jo on her back on the chief's desk, with the cop himself riding atop in what the newspaper described as a "very credible Bronco Billy imitation."

There was never a scene like in the Frankenstein movies when the villagers pursued her through darkened mountains by torchlight. Nobody had any torches and besides, Eula Jo had already drifted north forty miles to the brighter lights and greater anonymity of Dallas. She labored in Big D for 12 years, doing business in back seats, pickup truck beds, behind dumpsters, in an occasional motel room, and twice atop a wobbly Harley Davidson in that damned cemetery on Oakland in South Dallas, a pistol shot from Fair Park and the Cotton Bowl.

Life in the whore bidness is akin to the use-cycle of racecars driven in Saturday night dirt track competitions all over north Texas. A family jalopy might be coaxed and coddled to run for many years, but those race track contraptions crashed themselves either into a wall or on the rocks of hard use in a fraction of the time. Whoring was the same. If a hooker wasn't butchered, strangled, beaten to death by a pimp, or lost to some form of ailment which medical practice couldn't cure, natural wear and tear filled the gap. Hard use equated exactly to driving one of these cars around that dirt track.

So at twenty-one, cheerleader age at the University of Texas, Eula Jo was already beginning to fade. To score a real jackpot, she found more and more need to operate in dim light, then dimmer still. At 27, Eula had gone through 33 arrests, five pimps, three husbands, seven abortions, a complete hysterectomy, and two additional female surgeries to correct plumbing damaged in the pursuit of her livelihood.

Horrifyingly aware she was well on the way to whoredom

injured reserve, Eula Jo was beside herself. Dammit, she might have gained five pounds and looked a little hard around the eyes, but in reduced light, Eula Jo, by God, Ragsdale was built like a brick shithouse. Life just was not fair, no way, no time.

Those who believe in miracles, particularly high mileage ladies of the night, would be better served to play the Power Ball Lottery. Blessed benefactors are as rare as two headed cats. Then, when cruel fortune seemed lowest, Eula Jo had endured a miserable, cold Tuesday night. She had been scoreless until nearly 3:00 A.M. before she hooked a chiseler in an old Dodge pickup on Skillman Avenue. After two hours of him pawing and pinching like a hungry goat—he also smelled like one— he'd summarily dumped her out on South Industrial Boulevard without ponying up a nickel. It was just before dawn when she watched the trick drive away.

Stiff, cold, broke, hungry, and a hopeless victim of life's inequity, she surveyed her surroundings. She stood at curbside in front of the main entry to the sprawling *DuPree Waste Management* Complex. The office lights were fully ablaze at 5:00 A.M. A good place to panhandle some change, or otherwise walk all the way to East Dallas. Instead, she walked in the front door. An ugly, smelly, pudgy old man walked in the back door just as she arrived. He was sixty going on death warmed over, had a large mole on the end of his long nose, but he smiled at her.

"Howdy young lady. Ahm Homer Wayne DuPree. Can we hep ya'?"

Now Eula Jo couldn't read worth a damn, but she could recognize that the name the old man had just given was a match to the company title on the sign out front. At least she was pretty sure it was the same.

"Uh, I'm sorta lost. Got abducted by this horrible monster of a man. He abused me and tossed me out on the street." She gestured back toward Industrial Boulevard.

"Well you poor little girl. Could you do with a cup of coffee? We usually have plenty of doughnuts if you're hungry?"

Eula Jo bent hungrily over the doughnuts, showing Homer Wayne more cleavage than he'd imagined in two lifetimes. She wolfed down sticky sweet pastries, intently perceived Homer Wayne's lonely lust, and in thirty-seven minutes and six donuts was hired on the spot as an employee in good standing of *DuPree Waste Management*. Homer Wayne had not a clue as to what the hell she would or could do, but any heifer that sexy, with those boobs as big as a fat boy's head, just couldn't be tossed back into the great sea of passing humanity.

That Eula Jo tricked with several of Homer Wayne's drivers and maintained regular business with four or five long time customers, never reached Homer's ear. Homer Wayne, plenty smart in some ways, was always a tad slow in others.

Eula Jo, equally as thick between the ears in matters like adding two plus two, was a long time, street-smart grifter with the morals of a diamond back rattlesnake. Within two months of Sally Lou's death, she had encroached far enough to accompany Homer Wayne to his mansion in North Dallas most mornings after the night shift of both of them had ended.

A veteran pleaser of horny old men, she showed Homer an exotic menu of bedroom delights he had never remotely imagined. Homer Wayne, enraptured to the max, promoted Eula Jo to Director of Public Relations, bought her a brand-new silver Corvette, and equipped her with every credit card Homer's labor could afford.

Her duties were to drive around in her Corvette and cultivate business. She did just that—cultivating a wide spectrum of men she picked up in local dives. Bedding them in various low rent motels courtesy of Homer Wayne's cornucopia of plastic money.

But, she saved the best lovin' for Homer Wayne and in another month, she'd moved, chest first, into the DuPree mansion, sleeping in the same bed Homer Wayne had shared with his loving wife of 38 years. Eula Jo had not yet won the Power Ball Lottery, but the winning number was within arms' reach.

Homer Wayne's family mustered a desperate quorum and attacked from several directions. The actually hired a private detective who provided info which, when presented to Homer Wayne as proof positive Eula Jo was a no-good hussy, bounced off his tough hide like bullets off Superman. Direct appeals from the kids, then from grandkids, then from his sister Emma Ruth who rode a bus all the way from Terrebone Parrish went unheeded. The old man was tough, resolute, and besides, he was being subjected each day to a new sexual activity, the likes of which he frankly had not even dreamed.

To an old man in lust, Eula Jo's criminal record and reputation were only youthful errors. After all, she told him at least 87 times a day how much she loved him. Nobody would say that if they didn't mean it—would they?

Ten weeks from the day Eula Jo swayed into *DuPree Waste Management,* Homer Wayne and Eula Jo were married in a private ceremony before a Justice of the Peace in the Oak Cliff Courthouse Annex. Homer tipped the judge a hundred and handed twenty-dollar bills to a pair of passing clerks who agreed to stand up as witnesses. Eula Jo now not only slept in Homer's long-time marital bed, she owned that sucker—at least part of it.

Eula Jo was resurrected. Them damned kids could pound sand. Homer Wayne, paunchy with about a year's hair left, had breath of sewage quality, smoked cigars which smelled like buffalo crap, slept all day, and tended to break wind at inopportune times. But he had more money than Bulgaria and he was now hers.

CHAPTER 3: ROSIE BECKMAN AND MARILYN CRAWFORD

Kobok had no inkling that the Homer Wayne and Eula Jo DuPree combo existed when Howdy tossed him the lead sheet of a firebombing on Knox Street, just north of downtown. For that matter, Randy Bush was in law school back east far from the ATF payroll. He'd miss the entire Prince performance.

Accompanied by a just-average hangover, he drove out to the firebombing in a Plymouth he was assigned at the time, arriving at just past 8:30 A.M. It was mid-June, 1984, a time in North Texas when summer had essentially obliterated any semblance of mild temperatures without passing "GO". Spring or Fall were rarely in the mix; only hot wind replacing cold. This beautiful, sunny morning promised a 90-degree afternoon.

In a few weeks, the murderous heat and relentless sun would stifle much outdoor activity. The sun would force thousands to the nearest swimming hole or air-conditioned relief, and kill the requisite quota of souls via heat prostration.

The Dallas Fire Department had cleared the scene, but the burned hulk was prominent in the apartment parking lot. Unburned splotches low on the doors showed the Cutlass had been dark blue before the fire. Kobok jotted down the license number of the charred vehicle, legible through blackened soot. After radioing in the license number to his group clerk, Tootie, he examined pieces of shattered glass strewn around and under the car.

Tootie responded in two minutes that the license was registered to *Jerry W. Kincaid* with an address in Denton. The information, which would eventually prove traumatic, was meaningless to Kobok. The firebombing victim's listed apartment address was on the second level.

She answered the door on the first knock. He suspected she'd been watching him through a window. Leaving little to the imagination in a light green semi-transparent robe, she was early twentyish, her long dark hair combed back over her ears. Shapely, but moving slightly to tubby, her figure forecast obesity at thirty. She was about a seven by Dallas standards where nines and above were abundant.

"Rosie Beckman?" He showed her his credentials.

"You here about my car?"

"Yes ma'am, if you're Rosie Beckman?"

"Yeah, c'mon in," she stepped back into the apartment. "Can I make you a cup of tea, Mr …?"

"Kobok. No thank you."

"Sit down, please," she offered, taking a stuffed chair opposite the door. The burst of nipples through the thin robe hinted of readily available sexuality. Kobok was unable to block a brief flash of this nubile girl standing naked at room center.

"Ms. Beckman, the report here says the Dallas Fire Department received the fire alarm call on your car at 2:35 A.M. Were you here when the car was burned?" he carefully avoided eye contact with the nipples.

"Yes."

"In bed?"

"Yes."

"Was anyone else here?"

"No, I was alone," she answered too quickly. He should have recognized the body language but didn't.

"Who is Jerry Kincaid?"

"Uh …who?"

"Jerry Kincaid. The license on the Cutlass is registered to him in, uh … Denton," he looked at his notes.

"Oh, he's the guy I bought the car from," she again spoke quickly. "He's kind of a car dealer, I think."

"How did you buy the car? I mean how did you learn it was for sale?"

"Um…answered an ad in the newspaper."

"How long have you had the car?"

"Er, just since yesterday. He delivered it."

"Is it financed?"

"No, I paid cash. My mom gave me the money."

"Is it insured?" Many car fires were owner generated insurance frauds.

"Yeah, I guess," she nodded intently.

"With whom, please?"

"I don't understand…"

"What insurance company?"

"Oh, uh, my mom would take care of that. I don't know the name of the company or anything."

"Can I have your mother's name and telephone number, please?"

"She lives in North Dallas. It's 214 555-0171. Her name is Virginia Beckman."

Kobok wrote down the information. "Do you have any idea who would want to burn your car?"

"Well, I think maybe it could have been Gilberto Rincon." Her body language again hinted hesitation which danced unnoticed past his hangover.

"Why him?" He jotted down the name.

"Uh, well, I stiffed him on a dope deal. He sold me some grass, you know marijuana, and I never paid him the $300.00. He called me and threatened to burn me out." The brown eyes appeared thoughtful.

"Where could we find him?"

"His brother runs a Mexican restaurant down on Lemmon Avenue. He kinda hangs there sometimes. It's called the 'La Margarita'".

"Rincon, how did you … I mean did you date him?"

"Met him in a bar on Greenville Avenue. Dated him a few times. Beto, that's his nickname, was such a hothead and so possessive, I broke it off about six weeks ago."

"But you did the dope deal after that?"

"Yeah. Please don't tell my mom," the eyes reflected mild alarm.

"Okay, I wouldn't say anything to your mother about anything. I'm sorry to ask, but did you sleep with Rincon?"

"Yeah, a few times," she studied the floor. He pondered the

probable numbers of partners with whom this young lady had shared her bed.

In those days, cellular telephones were an idea only in the Dick Tracy comic strip. He picked up the telephone and dialed the number she'd given for her mother. There was no answer. "Do you have an alternative number, maybe at work for your mom?"

"Oh, she's in Europe."

"Your father?"

"Dead. Heart attack two years ago."

"How will you file an insurance claim on the Cutlass?"

"I, I'll have to wait for her to come back from Europe. Maybe her lawyer..." Again, something wasn't right in her tone, but Kobok rationalized that most people are nervous when interviewed by the police, particularly the Feds.

"The lawyer's name?"

"I, I don't remember."

"When will she be back...your mother?"

"Maybe a month or so."

"You met Rincon in a bar on Greenville? Which one?"

"Uh...don't recall," she lied.

"Try harder."

"Big Daddy's"

"A titty bar. Are you a dancer?"

"You're gonna tell my mom. I just did it a couple of weeks." She studied the closed door at the edge of the room.

"We gather information, Ms. Beckman, not give it out. I'll tell no one anything."

She looked back at the closed door.

"Somebody in there, Ms. Beckman?"

"No, no."

"I guess I could look. Safety, you know?"

"No...no. Don't you need a warrant or something?"

He terminated the interview and took several Polaroid shots of the burned cutlass. He stuffed several shards of wine bottle glass into an unused paint can from the trunk of the Plymouth. Paint cans are the standard evidence containers for fire debris. The petroleum base of plastic bags tended to distort laboratory analysis if used to transport burn debris evidence. Hence, metal cans. The remnants of glass were greasy with gasoline. No fingerprints would survive the oily wash job.

Inquiry could be made to gas stations in the neighborhood to try to determine who bought gas in a wine bottle. But since sale of gasoline in a glass container was illegal, the chances of finding someone to admit the sale, even if inquiry accidentally found the right clerk on the right shift, were slim to none. In the most often used method, the perpetrator had drained small amounts of gas from shut down pumps at closed gas stations, and no witness could usually be found.

But Kobok already had four or five similar cases on his desk which he had little chance of solving or "clearing." Most vehicle fire-bombings died at the onset because human bodily injury seldom resulted; the dollar amounts were small by both insurance and police standards; the offense often was owner-generated as insurance fraud; and suspects beyond the owner were a rare as armadillos in winter. He had no doubt this one would suffer the same fate.

To avoid any accusations of lack of effort by his goofy supervisor, H.D. "Howdy Doody" James, Kobok needed to make a token attempt to find and sweat the suspect Rincon and interview Rosie Beckman's mother.

Although Rosie had said her mother was in Europe, experience dictated double checking. He herded the Plymouth up Hillcrest toward the swanky address in North Dallas. By radio, he called Tootie and asked her to "crisscross" the telephone number Rosie Beckman had given to find the street address where the phone was installed.

He found the spacious, palatial residence among others in the tree lined "don't-show-up-without-a-few-million-bucks" neighborhood of the elites. He parked the Plymouth in the front circle drive and worked on the doorbell for several minutes with no luck. Walking across the neatly trimmed lawns, he tried the house on the west, again unable to raise any inhabitants.

The mansion on the East was a red brick, two-story with white pillared columns supporting a tall, graceful porch. An African-American lady in a black maid's dress with white lace-trimmed collar answered. Kobok flashed his credentials.

The maid turned and shouted, "Ms. Crawford, the police are at the door."

After a brief wait, Ms. Crawford appeared in a totally unexpected form. Instead of a matronly socialite, she was thirty-two or three, blond, tanned, and strikingly beautiful in white tennis shorts with matching Polo shirt. The outfit was rather sparse and fit her figure well.

"I'm Marilyn Crawford." The voiced carried the poise of those secure in their splendor.

"I'm trying to locate Mrs. Beckman next door," he held up his credentials.

"Why?" Her credentials flashed nearly a foot off her chest. Her tone suggested she was used to her demands being obeyed.

The normal response would have involved telling her he'd ask the questions, but he needed information, not a complaint from a trillionaire. "Her daughter's car, a Cutlass, was firebombed last night. I'm assigned to investigate." The young victim's silky, semi-transparent bathrobe reminded him to maintain eye to eye contact. Mrs. Crawford was armed with many assets which tended to distract concentration.

"Oh, how terrible," she responded, blue eyes calm. "Would you care to step in out of the heat?"

He followed the lovely figure down a hallway, admiring the shapely backside and a pair of beautifully tanned, tennis-firm legs of fashion model caliber. He sat on a leather sofa in a library with more books that any human could read in four lifetimes. The elegant homemaker sat beside him, carelessly allowing a lovely knee to brush against his. Was she...? Naw, not possible. For the first time in years, he declined to pursue the lead. A complaint from this chick and he was gone to the dope wars in and off battlefield Miami, ATF's current dumping ground for agents who stumbled.

"Ms. Beckman told me that her mother was out of the country. Do you know if she has a caretaker or someone looking after the place? I was hoping to locate the insurance carrier involved."

"Well, her maid comes in two or three days a week, and I

don't recall which days. A lawn service keeps the grounds in order and I have no idea how to reach either one. Sorry," she smiled radiantly.

"Perhaps the family has a local connection…maybe a lawyer who might…?

"Harless Androvski," she said quickly. "We use the same lawyer."

He jotted down the information. When he looked up, she was watching him intently.

"Yes, well anyway, Kobok, I'm sorry I'm not of much help. Was Rosie … hurt? I mean, I hadn't

heard." Her face reflected concern.

"No."

"Why would anyone, I mean, was it intentional?"

"It's still under investigation," he evaded, handing her his card. "If you happen to see the maid over there, could you ask her to call me, or call me yourself, please, and I'll drive out."

"Of course," she smiled easily through glistening white teeth. He wondered if life was easier if you looked like that and lived in a zillion dollar house. He'd never know. "Uh, would you have time for a drink, Kobok?"

He read the familiar signal. Time to tread lightly. "A little early for me." Then lust interceded.

"Maybe a rain check?"

Her smile was exquisitely inviting. "I didn't know Rosie had a car. What, exactly is a 'Cutlass'?"

"A poor person's ride," he thought. He said, "An Oldsmobile. Ms. Crawford, have you seen any problems over at the Beckman's? I mean, have they been the target of any violence, or had domestic problems or anything like that?"

"Not that I know of Mr. Kobok. I mean, Rosie has come over from time to time since she was a child. In fact, she has stayed temporarily in this house while her mother and father…that is, before he died, were traveling. But I don't really know much of a personal nature." Over two weeks would pass before Kobok would realize that "not knowing much of a personal nature" was subject to interpretation.

He thanked the winsome Ms. Crawford and walked to his

Plymouth. The strange sensation that she was watching him walk away was magnified when he glanced back as he reached the car. She was still standing in the wide, opulent doorway studying him intently. Years of chasing ladies caused him to wonder if her intense stare was a sign of availability. Or maybe she was just going to report him for the appearance of the Plymouth, unwashed for a month. He sure as hell wasn't going to make any overt advance to a lady who wore hundred-dollar tennis shoes. He made a note to wash the Plymouth and do his damnedest to stifle any carnal thought in Marilyn Crawford's direction.

CHAPTER 4: GILBERTO RINCON

In the fifteen-minute drive from the palatial abode of the lovely Ms. Crawford to Lemmon Avenue, the socioeconomic strata changed from penthouse to outhouse in little more than the twinkling of an eye.

The *La Margarita Restaurant* was wedged into a strip shopping center about halfway between Oak Lawn Avenue and Love Field. The time was 10:50 A.M., a statistic made significant by a sign taped inside the front door-glass advising that the restaurant didn't open until 11:00 A.M. Kobok banged on the front door for several minutes before it was opened by a fat Hispanic man of about thirty. He wore a greasy, white apron over a white shirt and bowtie. Kobok guessed he probably doubled as head waiter after cooking the day's fare. His face read tired. The odor of cooking food wafted out the crack of doorway. It smelled greasily good, possibly just the cure for Kobok's hangover.

"Don't open 'til 11:00," he warned through the crack.

"I wanna talk to Gilberto Rincon," Kobok pushed inside, waving his ID.

"What's that little turd done now?" the fat man asked expectantly, retreating into the entryway.

"I'll ask the questions. Who are you?"

"I, uh, I'm Caesar Rincon," he looked intently at the out-held credentials, obviously a man to whom little good could come from any confrontation with the law. "Beto, I mean, Gilberto Rincon is my younger brother. I own this restaurant," he bowed slightly, again retreating a step or two.

"Is he here?"

"Oh, Hell no, he ain't … here." The pudgy face reflected an

expression as if a cockroach had crawled out just as the health inspector arrived.

"Where can I reach him?"

"I, I ain't sure," the brown eyes lied.

A small liquor bar was tucked along one wall adjacent to the front door. Both Federal and state law stipulated any licensed liquor premise could be inspected by appropriate officers of the law at any time during business hours. Kobok looked around and not finding an official more appropriate than himself, decided that 10:55 was close enough to business hours for government work. He stepped behind the bar and began examining liquor bottles.

"Whatcha doin'?" Rincon objected, his comment more plea than question.

"Like I said, I'll ask the questions. Since I don't got nothing' else to do except wait for your brother, I'm gonna inspect this bar. Looky here," he held up a worn bottle of scotch. "The seal is gone from this bottle. Where's the phone so I can get the liquor board out here to shut this place down for a week or so." Kobok scrutinized the back-bar with mock intensity.

"Seal? Liquor board? Hey man, sheeit," he wailed. "Please man, don' gimme no trouble."

"Gee whiz, Mr. Rincon, if I knew where to find Gilberto, I wouldn't have time to shut this joint down, now would I?" Kobok still held the scotch bottle.

"He's prolly at home man," he surrendered. "Prolly layin' up on his ass asleep." He gave an address and telephone number.

Kobok set the scotch on the bar, scribbled the info in his notebook, and started out the door. "If I get there and you've called him, I'm gonna come back and run my foot in your ass, then walk down to the corner." He nodded toward Love Field.

The fat man paled, shaking his head vigorously, "Probably wouldn't get up to answer the phone anyway." Kobok left, confident that no call would be made.

Kobock made the ten-minute drive to Bachman Lake Park and parked beneath a tree. Incoming jets arriving at Love Field roared a hundred feet above at one-minute intervals. He called Tootie and requested she see what her computer had to say about Gilberto Rincon, Hispanic male in his early twenties.

Shortly she reported three possible in the absence of an exact date of birth.

"Any report an address north of Love Field when they got arrested?"

"Yes, Gilberto Ibarra Rincon showed an address on Lemmon Avenue. Got popped for shoplifting two months ago. Shows his date of birth as 10-31-62, in Laredo. A Halloween baby." He wrote the address on his pad. It was the location of the La Margarita, where he had just visited.

Chances were good that the address Caesar Rincon had given for his brother was valid.

The address was north of Love Field five minutes away on a side street off Webb Chapel Extension. It was actually an old house, re-done to make four apartments, wedged in behind rows of low rent apartment complexes.

The name "Rincon" was scribbled on a scrap of paper taped to a box marked "Unit D" on the front porch. Kobok found "C" and "D" at the rear stoop with only one outside door. Of long practice, he walked up the three outside steps and tried the door. The outer door was only an opening to two apartments at the head of the stairs. Walking as quietly as a big footed man could, he eased up, rapped on the door marked "D" and waited.

The unmistakable crashing inside told him the occupant was fleeing. He kicked the door and rushed in, only to find the premises empty. Sitting on a small table was a full quart of the cheap wine of the same manufacture as the fragments he'd had picked up at the firebombing.

"He's gotta snake hole somewhere." Kobok made a quick search.

Then a snitch came forward and identified the escape route. A small, black and white, fuzzy terrier with a black patch of hair across his nose squatted, looking upward in a small bathroom, transfixed on a trapdoor in the ceiling.

Kobok bounded down the stairs, hustled to the front door just in time to hear footsteps running down toward the front door. The door crashed open and a scrawny, sleazy little man with a scraggly mustache stumbled out. Kobok extended a foot and the man sprawled down the two concrete steps onto an unforgiving front sidewalk.

The scratched-up suspect made a move as if to get up and run again. Kobok, the master of understatement bluffed softly, "Run and I'll shoot your ass."

That very persuasive argument caused the man to remain on the ground.

"Gilberto Rincon," Kobok said. "We know you firebombed Rosie Beckman's car and I don't like your ass." He was well aware he had nothing more to go on.

"Ain't did shit."

"You learn that line in fuck-up school?"

"Huh?"

"Gilberto, we're gonna have the surveillance unit watch you 24/7. You even spit on the sidewalk, it's your ass." There was no such unit and if there was, they wouldn't waste time on a dime bag marijuana dealer.

"How well you know Jerry Kincaid?"

This time, Rincon sprang to his feet and was in full panic mode running west toward Marsh Lane. Incredibly, Jerry Kincaid, Denton car dealer, was no stranger to Gilberto Rincon. He had only rousted Rincon to create a file. He had no reason to chase. He said under his breath, "Got his attention. Let him run, dope dealers rarely get enough exercise."

He'd watch the sheets. He assumed a low rent loser like Rincon would stumble soon enough and he'd have another go at him. He didn't stop to consider the old adage of how "assume" segmented tended to make an "*ass*-of-*u*-and-*me*".

CHAPTER 5: JERRY AND SHERRY KINCAID

Kobok watched Gilberto Rincoln flee and calculated the situation. The routine firebombing of Rosie Beckman's Cutlass would quickly hit the dead pool. To avoid management criticism, i.e. a row with dumb butt supervisor Howdy Doody James, he needed to add at least one more nuisance inquiry. His hangover was waning, and he recalled an excellent little Mexican food diner on the service road of I35 halfway to Denton.

He called Tootie and asked if she could phone Denton and see if Kincaid was around and if so, to tell him ATF was coming by at 12:00 P.M. She called back in minutes and said Kincaid would be waiting.

Tootie said, "Kobok, he sounded scared shitless. What are you into, dude?"

"High crimes and disobedience, kid. It's intense." He chuckled and headed north.

Stuffed with enchiladas and salsa, he found Kincaid Motors one street East of I-35, tucked behind a convenience store. The sign, badly in need of paint declared "Gerald Kincaid, owner,". A quick once over of the twenty cars on the lot indicated some of the inventory could stand a bit of paint also.

A thirtyish man with a thin combover and a pencil mustache, wearing a red polo shirt stood in the open doorway of a small, metal office building. As Kobock approached, he saw the man was skinny enough to stand under a clothesline and avoid rain.

"You the ATF guy?"

Kobok showed his badge and credentials. "If you're Jerry Kincaid?"

"I am," he extended his hand. Kobok noted it was soft, the

palm damp. "Step inside, please." Kincaid settled behind a small desk. Kobok took a seat opposite.

The small structure was twelve feet square with a commode visible through an open door in a corner. A small air conditioner chugged away in a rear window. Kobok's suspicious mind instantly locked onto the possibility that selling enough cars to make a living from a dingy little operation like this would be difficult. Kincaid could very likely have an ancillary occupation.

"How can I help you, Kobok?"

"Rosie Beckman…"

"Who?"

"Rosie Beckman. A cutlass she says you sold her yesterday was firebombed last night…on the parking lot of her apartment complex on Knox just north of downtown."

"You're kiddin'. We jes took that car down there yesterday. I didn't recognize the name. Sorry. And some sucker burned it. Firebomb you say?"

"We?"

"We? Oh me 'n a guy who helps me from time to time. He followed, and I dropped it off."

"She says you toted the note," Kobok lied.

"Uh, no…well, sorta. She ponied up a few hundert and I agreed to carry a note."

"So you have the title. Can I see it, please?"

Kincaid slid back his chair and retrieved a folder from a nearby cabinet. He tossed it on the desk in front of Kobok. Kobok had interviewed countless persons from all levels of society and from varying connections to crimes. Kincaid wasn't quite "right".

The title showed ownership of the Cutlass had been transferred by the Texas Department of Public Safety to Jerry Kincaid two weeks earlier. The address of record was the street address Kobok had seen on a post at the edge of Kincaid Motors.

"Kincaid, normal practice usually means when a dealer takes in a car, he leaves the title open, so it can be transferred to the next buyer without the need for an extra DPS transfer. That way, the previous owner's name shows up on the current title, not the dealer's. I've never seen a dealer title a vehicle to himself. Why…?"

"That Cutlass was a repo. I'd sold it to one of those dopey strippers down in Dallas and kept the title. She didn't pay and we went down to repo it off the lot of the Green Bull Topless Club there on Northwest Highway."

"Yeah, but why title it in your name?"

"I gave it to my wife as an anniversary present. Jes' went ahead and titled it to us."

"You mean to you?" Kobok thought the story unlikely. What was Kincaid hiding? "Then you sold it less than two months later?"

"Engine hadda funny noise. Got rid of it." His smile was used car dealer oily.

"I'll need to talk to your 'man'. Was the helper who assisted in delivering the Cutlass to Rosie Beckman the same guy who helped repo it."

"Er, yeah, but he left early this morning to visit his mother in Montana."

"This file show who the previous owner was. The stripper you spoke of?"

Kincaid turned the file around. The slight tremor in his hands was subtle but visible.

"Uh...Stephanie Jane Manner."

Kobok snapped instantly that if the previous owner of record on the title was Stephanie Jane Manner, that transfer was also convoluted. If Kincaid had sold the Cutlass to Stephanie on a tote the note transaction, then the owner who had originally sold it to Kincaid should be on the title, not the name of the financed owner, Stephanie.

"I need a copy of this file."

Kincaid was copying the four-page file at an old machine when a pretty blonde girl of about ten skipped in the front door. She held a canned soft drink in each hand. Her pierced earlobes were adorned with small star-shaped gold earrings.

"My daughter, Sherry," Kincaid craned his neck. At her name, Sherry smiled at Kobok.

"Hello, Sherry. Skipping school, today." Kobok grinned.

"School's out for summer vacation," she replied.

"Her mom had to go to Dallas," Kincaid tossed four copies

on the desk. "Sherry is helping me around here. She just made a soda run to the store next door. She always stops to play some of them games when she's over there."

Kobok stuffed the copies in his folder and rose to leave. "Any idea who'd want to firebomb Rosie Beckman's car, Kincaid?"

"Uh, not a clue."

Kobok held Kincaid's gaze. "Maybe Gilberto Rincon?"

Kincaid, an accomplished used car dealer and apparently a small-time thug locked on his "I ain't done it" face. "Rincon? Never heard of him." Kobok had seen through lying countenances so many times, he could have sketched Kincaid's reaction on his folder.

The Denton Police Department was housed in an old warehouse building on the south edge of downtown. A smiling records clerk printed out a three-page sheet and tossed a mug photo atop the pages. Kincaid had been arrested twice for misdemeanor narcotics possession, both resulting in fines and no jail time. Interestingly, a copy of his FBI rap sheet showed an old arrest by the Oklahoma City Police Department four years before. The case showed no disposition. He'd have Tootie contact the Oklahoma City ATF office and see if more info was available.

Kobok asked for and was introduced to a Denton narcotics officer. Shortly he sat across from a bearded young officer in a pink T-shirt and dark plastic rimmed glasses. His desk nametag read "A. Gammon".

"Kincaid is part of a half assed group of five to eight couples who get together, get stoned out the ass, and are widely reported to deal smaller quantities of grass, meth, and whatever, to support their habit. This is a university town, with all the incumbent dope problems that go with college kids. Kincaid and his friends have sort of managed to stay under the radar. Frankly, they are such small potatoes, we just don't have the manpower to screw with them."

Kobok tossed the FBI RAP sheet on Gammon's desk. Gammon said, "Yeah, I dunno if I've seen this or not, but Kincaid is a small-time car dealer. Only one prior entry is surprising. Prolly means he just hasn't got caught...yet."

Kobok explained the Rosie Beckman firebombing and the irregularity in the handling of the car title.

Gammon shrugged. "Who knows. No law is broken. Maybe Kincaid is just a dummy."

"Says he repoed the car from a Stripper at the Green Bull Topless joint, Stephanie Manner. I forgot to check that with your records clerk."

Gammon dialed his desk phone, spoke briefly, and hung up. "Nobody who hits exactly. Stripper? I'd say phony name possible, but where there's a car involved, it's probably a good name."

As Kobok drove back south on I35, he radioed Tootie and asked her to call DPS, Austin and see if they had an address for Stephanie Manner. In view of the limited potential of the case, he opted not to bother Tootie with calls to ATF, Oklahoma City, to check out the listed arrest for Kincaid. He'd call later when he checked with the Department of Motor Vehicles for a title search on the Cutlass.

As he threaded the Plymouth through suburban Carrollton traffic into the Dallas city limits, Tootie radioed him back. DPS reported the last known address they had for Stephanie Manner was on Webb Chapel Extension just off Northwest Highway. He noted the address was not far from where he'd encountered Gilberto Rincon. He took the Northwest Highway exit off I35.

The address for Stephanie Manner was on the second-floor rear of a two-level apartment complex squeezed in among many of similar disrepair. Kobok estimated the parking lot ratio of cars that would function was about equal to those that would not.

After a knock brought no one to the door, he walked around front to a door marked "Manager." The address, typical in the area, proved to be not only the office but the residence of whoever was down enough on their luck to be stuck there.

The door was opened by a bleached blond of fifty or so, with about an inch of white roots revealing her level of give a damn factor.

"Yeah," she said. He saw that a cereal box top would have made equal impression as she glanced casually at his credentials. Cops at the door were a common business in that neighborhood.

"Stephanie Manner in 209. She still up there?"

"We can't," she snapped as she tried to slam the door. Kobok caught it with a size 14 and stepped inside.

"Warrant?" She yielded ground.

"I get a warrant, you get an interference charge. A simple question between us will remain there."

"Okay, she still stays up there. Lives with another chick. Both strippers, dunno where, but maybe over at that Green Bull place on Northwest. Both dippy young broads who dance nekked on a bar." She lit a filter tip, hacking for a full sixty seconds on the first drag.

The Green Bull was just cranking up for the day, although the ear-splitting music could be heard a block away. Kobok flashed credentials at the door guy and asked to see a manager.

"I'm Freddie Maroney, day manager." The slender man approached and extended a hand. "Let's talk in my office. Presence of the law runs off customers." He was fortyish, slender, with a three-day growth of dark beard.

Maroney closed the office door, dampening the crescendo of deafness-inducing music only slightly. He slumped in a battered chair behind a more battered desk and gestured to a chair opposite. "What brings the feds to us today, mister uh…?"

"Kobok. Looking at the firebombing of an old Cutlass just north of downtown last night. Title chase shows the car might have belonged to a dancer here, Stephanie Manner. I show an address on Webb Chapel Extension around the corner."

"Stephanie? Lemme see." Maroney dug in a desk drawer. And pulled out a typed list of names which bore signs of numerous names scratched out and replacements penciled in.

Kobok thought of a baseball lineup card. The stripper business changed batters more often than a last place ballclub.

"Oh, hell, Stephanie? You're lookin' for Sparky. She don't come in 'til around four."

"She doesn't answer her door."

"Hey, man. Maybe stoned, maybe in a motel with some punk she picked up in here, maybe fled to Canada. Stability is not a factor with these chicks. I say she'll be in around four. She may be in Philadelphia at four. You never know. That's why we have a flexible roster." He held up the list of names.

"Did she have a Cutlass repossessed off the lot here? Maybe within the last couple of months."

"Prolly, man, but in this atmosphere, I couldn't say for sure who stepped in what. Can you come 'round after four and see what she has to say?"

CHAPTER 6: SQUAD SUPERVISOR H.D. "HOWDY DOODY" JAMES

Kobok glanced at his watch as he merged into Northwest Highway traffic. It was just past three thirty, a good time to ease on home and act like he'd worked on the Rosie Beckman firebombing until dark. But if he could go by the office and knock out a report, he could justify that the matter was sufficiently investigated to push to the dead file. Perhaps so late in the day, his idiot supervisor, H.D. "Howdy Doody" James had himself disappeared early and could be avoided another day.

He wheeled the Plymouth into the parking structure a block south of the Earle Cabell Federal Building and hoofed it over to the ATF office. About a half dozen agents were scattered at manual typewriters across the squad room in those mid-eighties, non-dictating machine days.

He should have gone home. Howdy stuck his combover out of his glass man cave and hailed him as he walked in. Fortyish, plumpish, and stupidish, James had been transferred into Dallas from the Internal Affairs Division in D.C. six months earlier. He'd spent the first five or six mornings radioing in for directions to the office. He seemed to have mastered the trip at present.

"Well, Kobok, have we cleared your latest assignment. As you know, you need a couple of solid cases filed. It's nearly time for the Summer re-location program. They could use you in Miami."

"This little firebombing is not going to clip a tentacle off the nefarious arm of organized crime, James. It appears to be a either a jilted lover or a spite deal over some un-paid-for marijuana. May even be another insurance fraud. No real witnesses, limited suspect pool, no injuries. Got one possible witness to interview. Stripper at a club on Northwest Highway. Doesn't come to work until four. I'll catch her on the way home."

Howdy placed hands on hips like a petulant suburbanite addressing the paper boy. "Well, another excuse for you to end up in a beer joint cozying up with some hussy."

Kobok saw the glimmer of lust in Howdy's expression. He figured if the junior executive had enough sense to find Northwest Highway and/or pick up a female, he'd be on the way as they spoke. But a man who couldn't find the office would not fare well on Northwest Highway.

"That about it? Gotta report to type." He turned and walked to his desk. He typed his report but slid it in a desk drawer. Best to see what Sparky had to say before he made his cancel-the-case report prematurely.

By half past five, the number of vehicles on the Green Bull parking lot had increased to around twenty, with a heavy preponderance of pickup trucks. The bouncer waved him through. When he found Maroney's office, the day-manager was leaned back in his chair. A nude girl appeared from beneath the desk and fled.

"Oh, hell, Kobok," he stammered as he pulled up his trousers. "Just, uh, conducting an audition. Sorry, man."

"Is she hired?"

"Uh, already works here. You know how it is." He chuckled nervously.

Kobok certainly did.

Maroney zipped his fly. "Surprise, Sparky is alive, well, and so far, not too stoned to stand upright. I'll call her in. Y'all can use my office. Be sure and tell her twice you're a cop or she's liable to try to sell you some lovin'."

Stephanie "Sparky" Manner was twenty with a long dark ponytail and the words "hot" and "cold" tattooed respectively below each nipple of her fried egg sized breasts. The ink was visible because she was wearing only a pink band aide sized G-string. Kobok had taken Maroney's seat behind the desk. She sat on a plastic chair opposite and plopped her spike heeled feet on the desk like a drugstore cowboy. Kobok estimated she had an I.Q. about dead even with room temperature.

"Stephanie Manner?"

"Yeah…uh, they call me Sparky."

She turned up both arms, elbows down, and said, "I'm clean, dude. See, no tracks. You can strip search me if you want?"

Kobok chuckled at the irony of the comment. "I understand you had a blue Cutlass repossessed off the lot out back within the last couple months. "

"Repo? You mean stolen. That prick Beto forged my name on the title and sold it to some sumbitch. They towed it right off the lot."

"Beto? What's the full name?"

"Uh, Gilberto…last name Rincon, I think."

"Who towed it?"

"Damned if I know. It was a present from my mom for finishing high school."

"Too bad. A graduation present."

"Oh hell, dude, I never graduated. She jes' bought me the car cuz she was tired of tryin' to get me to go to school. Gimme that cutlass and kicked my ass out."

"Did you report it stolen?"

"Yeah, called the Dallas cops. They said I'd just sold it to buy dope. Nobody's gonna believe a toked-out whore, dude."

"Beto. Your boyfriend?"

"Yeah, sorta. He was. Just a small-time marijuana dealer. He slept in with me n' Melinda for a couple weeks. Found my car title in a dresser drawer, stole it, and I'm shit outta luck."

"He still around?"

"Yeah, I've heard he's around. I ain't seen him or I'd poke out his Goddamned eye."

"You know a guy named Jerry Kincaid?" Kobok tossed the mug photo from the Denton Police Department on the desk.

"Yeah. High roller. Comes in here sometimes. Got a damned fake Rolex. Too arrogant to know the chicks who work here can knock off a fake watch pretty easy."

"You and Kincaid ever…hook up?"

"Well, Mister Fed, I guess you could say that. I gave him a freebee out back in his Cadillac once, then the next time was supposed to be for a hundred bucks. He stiffed me. Not long after, I met that turd Beto and I ain't seen Jerry since."

Kobok worked his way up Central Expressway to his Spring Valley Road Apartment. Spring Valley was the border between Dallas and the City of Richardson, the north side, where he lived being inside Richardson.

As he eased the Plymouth into a parking slot, Tad, the nine-year-old son of his lady-friend across the courtyard came running with two gloves and a well-worn baseball. Tad's mother, Anne, was a vivacious blonde with whom Kobok enjoyed a more than neighborly relationship.

Anne laughingly described herself as "dumb happy," and appeared to be willing to go with the flow of Kobok's heavy drinking, irregular hours, and suspected involvement with low rent chicks he met at Adair's or the Dallas Police Association Bar. Shapely and personable, she was 12 years younger than Kobok, twice as smart, and couldn't cook much beyond spaghetti. Kobok often spent the night with Anne, but still maintained his own apartment. A slightly removed relationship was apparently good medicine for her, too.

Kobok had developed a very common ailment among street cops, a defensive mindset. The shrinks called it paranoia— becoming convinced permanent emotional attachments tended to morph to transient in his universe. When someone referred to him as "tough", he tended to be annoyed. He remained wedged on high center, convinced he did what he had to do in a world that was more hard than tough. Hell, maybe he should propose marriage to Anne? He flushed that thought immediately. Physical only was just fine.

The two men he'd killed needed killing, the shrinks had counseled. They'd expostulated in expansive, naïve confidence from squeaky chairs and psycho-decided blaming himself for those two incidents was hubris that needed to be put behind him. Why then could he not go a full day without seeing their faces in the freeze frame? Repeated, half-drunk examination of his rapidly hardening face in the bathroom mirror created crystal clarity. The shrinks were nuts and he was just a little tired. Maybe a few more beers would help.

Following a long game of catch with Tad in the quickly

advancing June heat, Anne slinked down the stairs in her most popular get up, short shorts and a bikini top. She handed him a cold beer. If she worked at the Green Bull, he reasoned, she'd be unable to carry the weight of all the currency customers stuffed into her G-string. He had spaghetti, several beers, and Anne that night, ultimately dozing in her bed while dreaming of dead men and burned Cutlasses.

By 6:15 the next morning, wrapped in a towel, he had crept across the courtyard and was in the Great American Central Expressway Road Race in company with a hundred thousand other fools who hadn't managed to inherit a million bucks. As he crept along, he pondered ways to drop the Gilberto Rincon, Rosie Beckman, Jerry Kincaid triad so he could pursue a couple of more significant, "avoid Miami" investigations in his slush pile. Like many best laid plans, it wasn't going to work out that way.

CHAPTER 7: THE PRINCE OF DRACONIA

As the Summer heat quickly accelerated to unbearable misery across the area, dry rot in the Homer Wayne/ Eula Jo mansion was spreading like fire ants after a July rain. Eula Jo had been Homer Wayne's wife for nearly two months. His schedule had not changed. Six nights a week, he worked a garbage route. Each morning, he whizzed in the front circle drive of the residence between 6:30 and seven, then detoured on a concrete extension around the house, parked his pickup in the rear near the pool, and came home to mama. In deference to his first wife, he'd had a rear porch glassed in, complete with a window air-conditioner and propane wall-space heater.

Homer Wayne would ease in the back-porch door, get himself a cold beer from a fridge he kept there, then use a corner shower to rid himself of any musk the night might have brought him. Eula Jo, more often than not, had barely beat him in the door after a hard night out. She'd be waiting, nekked as sin, in the master bedroom bed just inside the house, adjacent to the porch.

Eula Jo had found a form of paradise. With no real duties at Dupree Waste Management, she was blissfully free to pursue her old occupation. Only now, money was of no consequence. She could screw who the hell ever she pleased. Homer Wayne lacked the acumen to examine her credit card bills, and the office staff, cognizant of Eula Jo's shady pedigree, were too fearful for their jobs to drop a dime on her.

On his morning arrival, Eula Jo who had heated up the juices of many a tepid man's system, would commence work— the homemaker-bedroom kind. Homer Wayne, only sixty, was nonetheless well into the long inevitable decline in male libido.

In short, he had trouble getting it up. Often Eula Jo would spend an hour, offering her best before he could produce. The complete failure rate was frequent.

The effort quickly rubbed the lifelong prostitute raw. Her frustration was quickly tail-gated by resentment, then disgust. Hellfire, she'd been up all night, too. And when she occasionally did succeed in lighting Homer Wayne's fire, then afterward, she'd move to the den sofa to grab some sleep. Homer's snoring, exacerbated by wheezing, coughing, and spitting, was too much, even for Eula Jo. Suddenly, one sleepless afternoon, the realization occurred that the old fool had to die sooner or later. Blessed relief. Homer Wayne would be out of the picture and she'd own everything—or so she thought. She'd enjoy both her freedom of the night, and one day her freedom from Homer Wayne DuPree.

In May, a month or so before Kobok caught the Rosie Beckman firebombing, Eula Jo was working a club on Greenville Avenue. Decked out in one of her scantier whore costumes, she was draped across the bar, trolling for new fulfillment. And there HE was, across the bar, dark-eyed handsome, smallish, and sullen, with a cruel, masterful twist of his mouth. He would eventually affect, then dominate, then ultimately destroy her. But he sure as hell looked good in dim light.

She began by giving him a full dose of whore eye-contact and cleavage across the bar, which he ignored. Eula Jo moved around the bar to the stranger's side and embarked on a direct, frontal attack. She sipped her vodka Collins and offered to buy him a drink. He wasn't interested.

Casually, he turned enough to give her an up and down. "You got some kinda tits on you bitch. Whorin' pay pretty good?"

Any stud with that kind of cutting, witty tongue was too ruggedly macho to let get away. Only after fifteen minutes of her best hustle did she decide to mention to this newly exciting hunk of little, dark skinned loser that all services provided by her would, of course, be free of charge. He still wasn't interested. The light in the place was probably a trifle too bright to cover the flaws in Eula Jo's fading face.

Finally, in desperation, she offered the man a lift, in the event he was on foot, in "her" Corvette. He casually inquired as to the year and condition of the vehicle, probably with some intention of stealing it. She led him proudly to the curbside explaining that she had a "sugar daddy", who could provide plenty more of whatever she needed.

And so, the romance began. Eula Jo handed over the keys of the Corvette to her darling new friend and they roared away down Greenville Avenue on a route which would eventually destroy lives and property with equally carnivorous ferocity.

They had sex that night in the front seat of the Corvette, no easy task. He was rough, abusive. During the heat of passion, he confessed that he was an Arab prince in hiding from political enemies of his family in the homelands, a small dukedom in a place called Draconia.

Eula Jo, who had never learned to read all the words in the newspaper or to spell even Ellis County from where she had come, didn't care if Draconia was a suburb of El Paso. She had always thought all Arabs came from New Jersey, anyway. The apex of his passion came when he whispered hoarsely that he'd kidnapped and tortured little girls. Not only was she not alarmed by the implied threat, his comments only enraptured her further.

She dropped him that night at a convenience store on Northwest Highway at Webb Chapel Extension, not far from the Green Bull, where Kobok would interview Sparky Manners about the Rosie Beckman firebombing. She, however, had no idea such a joint existed. In those pre-cellular days, surreptitious contact was tricky. She gave him the DuPree mansion home number with instructions to call only after 8:00 P.M. When he called the very next night, she was pleasantly surprised at her exhilaration. Confident now, she would soon have him in her web of perversion and lust, she'd soon learn the relationship would spiral in another direction.

She picked him up at the same convenience store. This night, she opted to bring him to the mansion where he sated his lust in the very bed she shared with Homer Wayne. Again, he mentioned the danger he faced from his political enemies.

The criminal, Gestapo FBI, in cahoots with enemies back in the Middle East who were also looking for him. Life was a bitch and so was she, he added. As passion developed, he became even more sadistically aggressive, slapping her several times, pinching, biting, inflicting pain. She endured his abuse stoically, only crying out when she fainted from exhilaration.

She drove him back to Northwest Highway, various intimate parts of her body painfully aware of the night's rough games. When she returned to the mansion and studied her nude body in a mirror, she was stunned at the marks he'd left. No problem, Homer Wayne's credit cards had supplied her with enough expensive make up to cover anything short of an appendectomy.

As she tenderly powdered and painted her battle wounds, she realized with a sort of morbid fascination that Eula Jo Ragsdale, sociopath, grifter, who had never in her life felt an emotional attraction to a living soul besides herself, was hopelessly in love with this twisted little man. He was only five or six years her junior.

In the next week, he called her once. In an hour she was posing nude in various pornographic poses in the master bedroom just behind the wall to the rear glassed in porch. He snapped photos with a Polaroid he'd stolen somewhere. Then he found Homer Wayne's bathrobe. He bound her hands behind her with the cloth belt so tight the pain instantly became intense. He beat her with a leather belt he'd filched from Homer Wayne's closet, then burned several places on her body with a lit cigarette. The nipples of her oversized breasts were a particular target. Again, he derived the greatest high while describing atrocities and murders perpetrated against little girls. Mother of heaven, she achieved the greatest sexual high she had ever known. When he finally removed the robe-handcuffs, her fingers were blue, the ligature marks on the verge of oozing blood.

That night, after she had been released, he dozed in Homer's bed. She was in far too much pain to sleep. She found and swallowed a half dozen aspirin and wandered the big house slugging from a quart of vodka in dire agony—glorious suffering of love. She noticed an open match book cover in the pocket of his shirt tossed in a corner. Visible was the initial "S" with a telephone number. She removed the matches and moved to Homer Wayne's desk in an upstairs study. The matches bore a logo. She could decipher the words "topless club" but not the name of the place.

She penciled down the number but did not record the name of the club. She replaced the matches in his shirt pocket, woke him, told him she loved him, and drove him back to Northwest Highway. He made her give him oral sex on the fringe of the brightly lit store parking lot, then exited and walked away without a word.

He went a week, then ten days without calling. She died a hundred deaths, then a thousand. She spent several nights trolling the area of the convenience store on Northwest Highway, but no Prince showed. My God, he was in the clutches of that shameless hussy from the matchbook cover. She called the number several times from payphones but received no answer nor was there an answering machine. If she found that slut, she'd murder her ass out of hand.

When Homer Wayne came home that morning, he downed three beers, and spent an hour fondling, probing, grasping her battle-love damaged parts, trying to achieve the ultimate act. When he finally dropped off from sheer exhaustion, she slipped into the kitchen and dialed the match book number. A youngish female answered. Loud music played in the background.

"You're dead, bitch," Eula Jo hissed "Leave my Prince alone!"

The young female sounded amused. "Piss off, honey. Dunno nobody named Prince." She hung up. In the days of no caller ID, verification of the death threat was lost forever.

That afternoon, HE called. Heavenly music filled her ears. She'd answered in the kitchen with Homer Wayne snoring and coughing in the next room. But that damned, impotent old fool wouldn't wake if a bomb went off beside his head. That such an occurrence could be remotely possible was beyond her imagination. Piss on Homer Wayne, her Prince was ordering her to duty.

That night, after some very good grass he'd brought and a quart of wine she purchased, the sadism scene was act II or III or what the hell ever. She managed to convince him that if he'd forgo the rope handcuffs, she'd lie perfectly still for whatever cruelty he desired. That way, she said, she had greater flexibility to cooperate and show her undying love. He ignored her suggestions.

Her after-sado mirror inspection revealed some serious burn marks and bruises. No matter, a little make up would satisfy the deception. Besides, Homer Wayne was so enraptured with her circus of sex tricks, he wouldn't notice if she was coated with yellow porch paint.

Eula Jo set about the dual task of developing romances with two men on entirely different planes of existence. Her time with Homer Wayne DuPree was limited mostly to a few hours in the early evenings before he began towing garbage or a snatched hour or so at his mansion after he came home in the mornings just past 6:30.

The remainder of her time was available for her Persian prince, but he didn't always cooperate. In the months of their relationship, she never really learned exactly where he lived. She knew the general area well enough. She picked him up and dropped him off at several locations near Northwest Highway and Webb Chapel Extension during that time, but his address was never entrusted to her.

A semi-reformed whore knows better than any person alive that a little outside use of the sexual parts seldom ruins the equipment. Therefore, she always remotely suspected, but never allowed herself to dwell upon, the distinct possibility that her new Royal lover had another woman, or women, available in the neighborhood where she dropped him off. The matchbook cover incident fortified the reality. She would hope upon hope that someday his affections would become totally directed toward her. It just had to be, that was all there was to it.

Homer Wayne didn't require nearly as much persuasion to be drawn into the inner web. His simple Louisiana background and nearly 40 years of monogamous sexual relationship had left his sexual education at a level barely above kindergarten. Eula Jo, having acquired more than a slight amount of experience along sexual lines, was able to quickly introduce Homer Wayne to a certified PhD. of horizontal delight, and perpendicular, and sub-perpendicular, and an infinitely endless combination of the same.

Homer Wayne DuPree, who had lain with only one woman before Eula Jo, who had never seen a porn movie, had been catapulted into outer space of sex-land. That his love would share her favors with another was beyond his imagination.

CHAPTER 8: An Easy Kill

Homer Wayne and Eula Jo: The very sound of the combination rang of ominous, low-class poetry. The lovebirds had settled into Homer Wayne's little twenty room bungalow, he with the intention of living there happily ever after, she with the intention of forming up a program for Homer Wayne wherein he would get a good screwing for the screwing he was getting.

Homer relentlessly continued his work schedule of early evening until daybreak, six days weekly, Monday through Saturday. Eula Jo developed the habit of allowing Homer Wayne to be clear of the door each evening about seven minutes before she turned her world to her Prince. Often, he'd brazenly call with ol' stupid Homer Wayne asleep or wide awake, to order her out early. She'd zip out to Northwest Highway to find him at various locations he had pre-selected. But gradually they settled on meeting at the convenience store at the corner of Northwest Highway and Webb Chapel Extension.

They'd worked out an elaborate code to exchange daytime phone calls. He called her. She never had his number. But such precaution wasn't necessary. Homer Wayne, in their way of thinking, was dumber than a post, totally naïve, and as trusting as a newborn calf.

They would then spend the evenings either lingering over an expensive meal at one of the several posh North Dallas restaurants or taking in a movie at Eula Jo's (nee Homer Wayne's) expense, of course. Then came the inevitable sadism session in, on, and around Homer Wayne's bed.

Homer Wayne continued to lavish her with assets. By this time, she had all the major credit cards ever issued, a credit account at each major department and ladies store in North

Dallas, and a checking account that seemed to magically fill faster than Midas' stash. Homer Wayne never questioned that Eula Jo, even tending slightly to plumpish, would have difficulty eating a hundred bucks worth of spaghetti by herself. Sometimes she had dinner bills after she had already had dinner with Homer Wayne. He simply paid the bills—or more correctly his staff paid them—and didn't consider the possibilities. Meanwhile, her nude examinations in the mirror disclosed marks that might be permanent. No matter, when she and the Prince were together, the marks would be love trophies. When they were apart, the pain was a reminder of her passionate love.

The DuPree mansion had a whole other, other. Eula Jo endured the stiflingly uncomfortable token visits from each of Homer Wayne's daughters in silence. Pompous, self-righteous bitches dragging squalling brats behind them. All they wanted was Homer Wayne's money and by God she wasn't going to stand for that outright theft of *her* property. Her mind was always with the Prince .

One morning, following an hour-long session of Homer Wayne fondling torturously sore body parts and an unsuccessful attempt at sex, he broke wind and told her his birthday was the following weekend. He intended to take Friday night off and on Saturday, have his children and grandchildren out to the mansion for a pool party and a catered barbeque. Great God, a full day of those unbearable daughters and grandchildren was more than a put- upon homemaker should ever be expected to endure.

That afternoon, the Prince called her. She'd learned to answer daytime telephone calls in the den. Homer was an idiot, but no sense tipping their hands. She'd solidified the deception by yanking Homer Wayne's bedroom phone out of the wall. When she told him about the upcoming weekend delay, he'd called her vile names and hung up. Her heart nearly froze. She was going to be trapped with riffraff while her Prince would drift to another woman. Great mother of God!

Homer gave her a list of family names to call and invite. She studied the calendar, then called every name on the list, providing each with a date for the Saturday following Homer

Wayne's birthday. That would settle that bunch, by God. Of course, each relative knew Homer Wayne's birthdate. They called among themselves, agreed the date was a result of Eula Jo's lack of literacy, and all showed up on the correct blessed day. Homer Wayne had ordered his secretary to arrange for the caterer. Eula Jo endured the disgusting spectacle, the screaming kids in *her* pool, and the separation from her Prince.

Her only consolation came when she appeared at poolside in a bikini. Although a tad fleshy, with her forty pounds of chest, sore as hell from the Prince's abuse and Homer Wayne's niggling follow up, she was the envy of those dumb ass daughters. That they sniggered behind her back, she knew damned well was pure petty jealousy. If any of those fools had the *cajones* to ask about numerous bruises on her body, she'd tell them to piss off. But it never happened.

She endured one of the longest separations from her love in some time, five days. She also endured increased holiday sexual demands of Homer, whom she despised, solely because he wasn't the Prince. The problem was partly because Homer Wayne took a couple of extra days off from the garbage business making her time more difficult to juggle. But the main reason, she suspected in horror, was that the Prince might have another woman. But call he did, eventually.

Eula Jo couldn't live without the Prince. She also realized that she couldn't resume life without the refinements and wealth of Homer Wayne. At least she certainly didn't intend to. She was his wife and what was his was hers. She just needed to wait until the old fool croaked. Toleration of her gross husband drifted gradually from disgusted tolerance to intolerance, to dislike. By mid-June, she had finally reached the apex of outright venomous hatred.

One day just after the birthday disaster, the U.S. Postal Service provided an opportunity which notched Eula Jo up several rungs on the ladder of progressive thinking. The mailman delivered a package from a large life insurance company known to her because the company frequently advertised on daily TV soap operas.

Eula Jo casually opened Homer Wayne's personal mail while

he slept, just as she had done on numerous occasions before. The brochure inside offered the company's insured, Mr. Homer Wayne DuPree, the opportunity to purchase additional life insurance in increments of $50,000 with no physical examination required. From the brochure, Eula Jo also learned for the first time that Homer Wayne had $50,000 in life insurance with the company. The form went into considerable verbiage, much of which evaporated above her head. "Beneficiaries" a word followed by an entire half page of explanation, had no meaning to a junior high school dropout from Ellis County, Texas.

Eula Jo's limited reading skills required several hours studying the brochure, the enclosed life insurance policy, and the possibilities. She knew vaguely from watching the soaps, and from years of talking on street corners with other ladies of the night, that if her husband died, the wife inherited some of his possessions—or something like that. The intricacies of wills, probate, estate laws, and as stated, beneficiaries, were light years from her comprehension.

Unknown to her, secreted in his safe-deposit box, was the will Homer Wayne and his lawyers had drawn up, leaving the vast majority of his holdings to his children and grandchildren, including the $50,000 package she was holding in her hands. He had provided an annuity set up which would pay Eula Jo a generous monthly pension for life. She would not, however, receive a sizeable chunk of cash or anything similar. Homer Wayne, slow but practical, saw Eula Jo's weaknesses along those lines as surely as he failed to comprehend her traitorous nature or her complete lack of moral fiber.

She gradually concluded that the premiums on the $50,000 policy were paid from DuPree corporate funds which in all probability were not reviewed by Homer Wayne. An increase in coverage would be routinely accepted by the company bookkeepers.

The form was annotated by convenient yellow marker in two places, with a red "X" beside each. The space for any added coverage was blank. In her crude scrawl, she added two zeros to $50,000 and wrote $500,000 in the space. She dug through his home-desk until she found a document with his valid signature.

As close as she could imitate, she forged his signature in the two yellowed spaces. She sealed the application into the enclosed, stamped envelope, strutted out to the curbside mailbox in her see-through robe, stuffed the new-found fortune in, and raised the red flag.

As she walked back up the wide sidewalk, a passing delivery truck driver spotted the transparent robe and ample chest and honked, nearly driving through a neighbor's yard. Eula Jo, the queen of class, shot him the finger. To hell with him, she was in line to become rich. Eula Jo couldn't possibly comprehend that if the 50k of life insurance went to Homer Wayne's children as beneficiaries, so would the 500k.

She re-entered the house and opened a tall boy. She sat at the kitchen table and rationalized; Homer Wayne was constantly exposed to dangerous equipment in the garbage business. Surely he'd be killed one day in the immediate future. Perhaps some Samaritan would murder him in an armed robbery. She would think on the possibilities before telling the Prince.

Then after more Prince-absent days, she gradually realized a situation was growing which forced Eula Jo into another gear. First, the Prince's demand for money increased incessantly while his time spent with Eula Jo slid relentlessly downstream. He had regularly skipped days calling her but demanded more and more cash when he did surface. He hadn't talked to her since the Friday before Homer Wayne's birthday. Eula Jo began to sense in horror that he was slipping away.

Desperation became the devil's playground. Gradually, she realized the futility of the situation because Homer Wayne hadn't been killed in a hundred years or so on a garbage truck, he probably wasn't about to cooperate in doing so in the foreseeable future. At best, he wasn't going to croak in time to save her life with the Prince. She reasoned that if she had full time to spend with the brown skinned beauty and unlimited funds to spend on him, then he would certainly become solely her property. God, let it be so. She would deal with that bitch in his shirt pocket match book when the time came. Homer needed to die, sooner rather than later.

She'd had a friend, also a hooker, who married one of her

tricks, then fed him rat poison. She was in the joint for murder—she'd copped a plea for a reduced sentence. But screw that. Them dumb damned cops would figure that out pronto. She needed advice, and quick. She had a second friend who was in the joint for shooting her pimp, but that was a different deal.

Then, he called, again in daytime. He ordered her to pick him up at around eight—neither were very good with exact times—at the convenience store on Northwest Highway. He slithered onto the seat and informed her he needed to use the Corvette. The Prince had ridden in the Corvette many times by now, often insisting on driving. On this evening, she noticed he was unusually nervous, sweating profusely. She drove back to the rear of the mansion. Since she knew nothing of his affairs and was totally attuned to his every command, she handed him the keys and he whizzed away.

As the evening passed midnight, she began to worry again. Had his political enemies, or the demon FBI gotten hold of him? If he wrecked the Corvette, she would tell Homer Wayne some wild tale which he'd believe. She'd cross that bridge when necessary. Was he using the Corvette to service another woman? When he swerved into the back yard at nearly 3:00 A.M. the flood of relief at just seeing him safe was overwhelming.

When she bedded him in Homer's bed, he reeked some sort of machine—oil, perhaps. He was wringing wet with perspiration and shaking with nervous anxiety. It took two hits of cocaine and a half quart of wine to calm him to sexual readiness. Then he commenced his perverted routine. He was particularly rough that night, biting, slapping, and brutal. She endured, laying with hands free but behind her in Faux confinement. When she climaxed, she fainted again.

They didn't get started back to Northwest Highway until past five A.M., barely time enough to make the round trip and beat Homer Wayne home. The Prince drove. On the way she made a decision—not an easy process for Eula Jo. She accelerated the trek over the bridge of conspiracy and murder by leaning over and whispering the details of the $500,000 life insurance application in his ear.

"A half million, baby," she purred

Always wary of his moody disposition, she waited for a smack. Instead, she got acceptance. The Prince, whose specialty was consuming the fruits of another man's labor was instantly on board. He looked across at her, twisted his mouth in an evil smile, and declared the old bastard was a dead man. "He'll be an easy kill, bitch, an easy kill."

It was the first time she'd ever seen him smile. She knew that worthless chunk of crap Homer Wayne was a dead man... soon.

His smile included a final plan. If that bitch could come up with a half mil when the old fool croaked, he'd kill Homer Wayne alright...then he'd finish off this whining sow and keep the whole wad.

CHAPTER 9: INDECISION: THE CONSPIRATORS' GREAT ENEMY

The next evening, he called at just past eight. Homer Wayne had just cleared the door. Then the routine—she picked him up at the convenience store, he ordered her to proceed to the DuPree, Newmanshire Drive palace. As she drove the Corvette to and from Northwest Highway that night—twice—she noticed the car reeked of gasoline. Damned thing probably had a leak or something. No problem, Homer Wayne could afford to fix it.

While he snorted a couple of lines she'd spread on the massive dining room table, she quickly stripped and emerged from the bedroom in all her glory. High and vicious, he arbitrarily slapped her around, causing a minor nosebleed.

As she stood, sobbing and bleeding in the dining room, he snarled, "Wait and do what you' told, bitch."

"Thank you, baby, it's what I deserved." Eula Jo, who had operated on the street for years without a pimp, certainly had one now—or at least the relationship existed.

He marched her into the master bedroom, ordered her to clasp her hands over the top of the door, and whipped her with one of Homer Wayne's wide leather belts for fifteen minutes. The bloody welts would be too much to hide from old stupid Homer Wayne. She'd need a subterfuge. When he'd finished, he ordered her to put on a robe. In pain, she was disappointed he had offered no sex after the whipping. Eula Jo had no idea he had simply been using her suffering and his violence as sexual stimulation when he kept a date for another chick later in the night. She'd gotten all she was going to get from his twisted psyche that night.

But he had other important business to discuss with her. How to off that useless lump, Homer Wayne. She toweled blood off her back as best she could, donned one of Homer's work shirts—no sense in ruining a fine robe—and sat next to him at the dining table. After two lines and a couple of glasses of that cheap wine she kept around just for him, her pain subsided enough so that she could concentrate on a life and death situation—Homer Wayne's' death and her new life as a millionaire and her Prince forever.

They spent an hour cogitating various methods of the final elimination of her totally unnecessary husband. All the while, Eula Jo, her cocaine and wine soothing her pain, had difficulty concentrating, even more than her uninventive mind usually could summon. She anticipated the "normal" violent sex session to commence as soon as her Prince made the final decision. Her system already ramped up, she could actually think of little else.

"Bitch, you could jes' shoot his ass. Say it was an accident. A burglar was trying to get in and you let him have it."

Christ, she thought, Homer Wayne had a shotgun in an upstairs closet, but she had no idea how to operate it. And hell fire, she didn't have it in her to gun down another human being, even a skunk like Homer Wayne.

They discussed arsenic. She related the tale of woe of her friend who done in her husband with rat poison. The cops would figure it out and she'd never get the insurance money. In the end, although she could never have deduced it, he was just about as short between the horns as she. Loaded up with sadism and treachery, his powers of innovation were limited to whips, sexual abuse, and apparently a taste for murdering little girls.

When he stood abruptly from the dining table, ordered her to drive him back to Northwest Highway, she was devastated. No more whip for the night, no burns and violence. Good God, he was slipping away again. She begged him to take her into the master bedroom and use her as he wished. Her dirty talk might have further stimulated him for his next chick, but Eula Jo was not going to get any that night.

"Whut about the bloody welts on my back."

"Bitch, call the cops, tell 'um some dude broke in and whipped your ass with that belt." He walked into the bedroom and carefully wiped clean the bloody belt he used to mutilate her back an hour before. He understood the science of fingerprints.

As her back was so painfully injured she couldn't lean against the car seat, he had to drive the Corvette back to the convenience store. Leaning forward she rode in silence. She drove back home in tears, agonized from having to make contact with the car seatback.

She initially prepared to shower. The water would wash away blood and possibly provide some pain relief. Sudden revelation canceled the shower plan. If an imaginary burglar had marked up her back as the Prince had suggested, why not mesh an intruder into a plan to convince Homer that she really was being harassed and threatened. Her wrists bore ligature marks, a faint, but residual condition from the rope handcuff treatment the Prince had inflicted earlier. She'd say he'd tied her hands over the top of the door and had his way with her. Damn, a path to the end of Homer Wayne was just around the corner. She found Homer Wayne's' leather belt, the weapon the Prince had used on her back, and washed it in the kitchen sink.

The Dallas Police Channel six dispatcher directed a unit to the mansion. Since the initial 911 call had suggested possible sexual assault, they found a female officer in the area and directed her to the location as a backup. While she waited, Eula Jo called Homer Wayne's company dispatcher and reported she'd been raped and beaten.

Eula Jo's charade dragged bottom at the jump. The female officer, Patti McIntyre, had worked Vice for a year early in her career. Her duties often required posing as a decoy prostitute along Harry Hines Boulevard, Skillman Street, and other locations where hookers congregated. She'd been surprised at the atmosphere. Although rancor sometimes developed among ladies over customers and minor stretches of territory, the general relationships had been friendly, protective, amiable. Lost sisters of the night had few allies outside their own kind. Officer McIntyre's eyes on the street, plus becoming familiar with books full of mug shots, had left her able to ID many, many hookers on sight.

McIntyre pushed her way into the kitchen where Eula Jo

sat, naked, displaying her bloodied back to the male officer who'd already arrived. Eula Jo, whose percentage of time spent naked with men rivaled almost any woman in the world, had unashamedly shucked off so the first officer could examine the havoc the "burglar" had wrought.

"Mrs. DuPree, I don't think you'll need hospitalization, but I've got E.M.T.'s on the way to take a look. Perhaps you might want to slip on a robe. Can I find one for you in a closet somewhere, ma'am."

Eula Jo, showing off her 44 what-the-hell-evers, leaned back in the straight-backed chair ignoring the pain of contact with the hard wood. She actually enjoyed having men ogle her assets. Still horny from the earlier let down at the Prince's early departure, she rather wished he'd reach out and touch someone—her.

McIntyre studied Eula Jo's face. "Hey, kiddo. Long time no see. Lemme think, I know you from…Skillman."

Eula Jo looked up, dumbfounded. "How…who…?"

"I worked the street down there, but I can't recall your name?"

"Worked the street? Honest?"

"Sure did."

"My God, you made it from whorin' to bein' a cop?"

"No, hon, I always was a cop…a least when I worked the street. What's your name again?"

Suddenly Eula Jo's brazen display of mammary flesh didn't seem so sexy. But what the hell, she'd made it with chicks before, either as paying customers or to entertain some male pervert who had cash to watch the show. She left 'um like she'd had 'um. "Eula Jo Ragsdale…uh now DuPree," she gestured at the opulence surrounding them while still sitting stiff backed.

"Patti McIntyre," the officer shook her hand. "What's happened to you here, dear?"

The male officer who'd made a cursory search of the house to see if anyone else was present, walked in, holding out Homer Wayne's terrycloth bathrobe. He draped it over her shoulders. It had no belt.

Eula Jo spun her yarn of a Hispanic male suddenly

appearing in the den as she was watching T.V., then ordering her into the master bedroom at knife point, stripping her, and administering a beating with one of her husband's belts while her hands were tied over the top of the door. Hellfire, the real assailant had been Hispanic, after all.

"Did he sexually assault you?" the male officer asked.

Good God, they could take her to the hospital and examine her for sperm. "No," she blurted. He made me do it…uh, airily."

"Orally?" the officer asked.

"Yeah, orally." Surely, they wouldn't pump her stomach. She was instantly on the verge of panic. What else had she screwed up? Them damned cops, they just always knew stuff.

McIntyre asked casually, "What were you watching on T.V., Eula Jo?"

Oh Jesus Christ. She hadn't watched evening T.V. in years. "Uh, Johnny Carson I think. I'm too upset to recall."

Both officers knew the Carson show had gone off the air an hour before Eula Jo had dialed 911. The male officer stepped back into the master bedroom and returned with the belt. He carried it on a ball point pen stuck through the buckle. "Maybe we can raise prints off this," he said.

"Oh, he wiped it clean," Eula Jo said quickly.

"Had you gotten loose from the door when he wiped it?" McIntyre asked.

"Uh, yeah. He'd already untied me. I saw him wipe it off."

"Did he take anything?" the male officer asked. "Maybe he left prints…"

"He was wearing gloves."

McIntyre asked, "Wonder why he wiped the belt if he was wearing gloves. Did you see where he left the belt, you say… when he untied you?"

"Uh, he mighta tuck it with him." Where the hell was Homer Wayne. A damned uniformed beat cop, one that told a tale about working the streets as a decoy prostitute, had just burned her story to the ground.

Meanwhile, several miles away, a major cop-brain trust was having their second beer.

Kobok had spent the day before and the early part of the

current day interviewing and reporting on the Rosie Beckman Cutlass firebombing. Later in the second day, he and Dallas Homicide Detective Bull Hooper had spent the afternoon interviewing a suspect in an arson murder in the Lew Sterrett Justice Center, the spiffy name for the Dallas county jail. The interview, which had dragged on until after midnight, had gone nowhere.

Kobok and Hooper had dropped by Adair's Saloon for a quick one. As is often the case, "quick" had roman numerals after it. It was nearly last call. Kobok was just about to order a third round when the bartender hailed him. "Kobok, your answering service is tryin' to reach you."

Kobok had dutifully left Adair's number with the service and was now paying the price. He answered the wall phone, then turned and motioned Hooper over. "Hellfire, ATF's answering service must be wired into Internal Affairs. It's you they're lookin' for."

Hooper spoke briefly, scribbled in his notebook and returned to the table. "Dunno why the hell they need Homicide, but I gotta go look at some kinda unusual sexual assault out in North Dallas. Lemme pick up my pickup and you can follow me out there if you got time."

"Hell, Bull, it's damned near time to get back up. I wouldn't miss it for the world."

"I think they called me 'cuz the homeowner is that 'ol boy who owns DuPree Waste Management over on Industrial. His wife called 911 to report a break in and assault. Money talks and bullshit walks, as you know."

Kobok and Hooper entered from the front door after squeezing past emergency vehicles with lights flashing and several neighbors in nightclothes standing outside the yellow barricade tape. Eula Jo, again proudly nude was standing in a side drawing room, bent over a sofa, while a young E.M.T. applied a medical salve to her back. A husky graying man in a yellow rubber suit stood by, watching.

McIntyre pulled them aside and explained what she knew. "Hey, aren't you an ATF guy?" she asked Kobok.

He nodded.

McIntyre said, "She says her husband works all night. That's him. He owns the company. Dunno why the hell he'd work all night. Her story don't ring quite true. Hispanic assailant so she says. Musta slipped the back-door porch lock, hung her hands over the bedroom doorframe, whipped the crap outta her back then made her give him head. I know this chick used to turn tricks down on Skillman. Now she's married to more money than all the gold in California."

Hooper peered into the small room at Eula Jo standing nude with her husband and two other men in the room. "Her back's banged up, but she'll live. We sure hubby and her weren't playing grab-ass and it got outta hand? She sure as hell isn't bashful."

"Not sure of anything. Just thought you might want to look in."

Hooper motioned Homer Wayne out into a hallway. Both Kobock and he flashed ID's.

Homer Wayne, angrily asked, "Why the hell is the federal government out here? Who's looking for the Mexican who done this to my wife?"

"Where were you when she called 911?" Hooper asked.

McIntyre said, "The 911 call came in at 12:50 A.M."

Homer Wayne roared, "I was out earning tax money to pay y'all's salary."

"Has either one of you had threats or have you had any prior prowlers or other problems, Mr. DuPree?" Kobok asked.

"No, but the streets are full of crooks."

They saw McIntyre walk past, a rope belt in her hand. She stepped into the drawing room where an E.M.T., gently slipped the terrycloth robe back over Eula Jo's nakedness.

Kobok and Hooper heard McIntyre say, "Is this the belt he used to tie your hands?"

"Uh," Eula Jo stammered. "Where'd you find it?"

"He untied your hands. Where did you see him throw it?" McIntyre asked.

"Uh...I didn't see."

Hooper and Kobok talked on the front porch.

"Something stinks here," Hooper said. "Wonder if she had

set up shop to turn a trick and the John got outta hand. That damned bathrobe belt was in a dresser drawer. He wipes the belt although he was wearing gloves, then take time to stuff the restraint in a drawer, then doesn't steal a damn thing. Suppose she wiped the belt?"

Kobok said, "Did you see all the bruises on her body. Looked like she'd played a football game nekked."

"Or playing with some dude while nekked," Hooper added.

Kobok said, "Is it possible her husband, Homer Wayne is a wife beater and she's too scared to tell us?"

Hooper said, "That old chick gets too roughed up, she'd kill his ass."

Hooper said, "I'll open a case number and go through the motions. This is gonna end up unfounded."

Kobok and Hooper went their separate ways. But they'd made initial contact with Eula Jo and Homer Wayne DuPree. As often happens in the big city, contacts often recur in the strangest ways.

CHAPTER 10: THE PLAN

The Prince and Eula Jo would spend the next few days plotting, conceiving, conniving, scheming, and preparing for the murder and final elimination of Homer Wayne DuPree, expendable garbage man. The old ass didn't deserve to live. Homer Wayne died a hundred horrible, mysterious ways in the minds of the plotters. He was shot, strangled, buried alive, drowned, stabbed (with several instruments), crushed in vehicle accidents because of pre-arranged mechanical failure or other means, poisoned (four different ways), bludgeoned and tossed into a garbage truck compactor, and finally, run over with the silver Corvette. However, each method died on the vine of the planning stage for varying reasons.

Eula Jo descended daily more deeply into the dunk tank of self- pity and despair. She developed a loathing for Homer Wayne which required increasingly more effort to suppress and keep hidden. Surprisingly, during one of the mornings he opted to fondle and probe her anatomy, she didn't impulsively grab a kitchen knife and drive it into his heart. She would have liked to do just that, but simply lacked the will.

When they weren't wrestling around in Homer Wayne DuPree's bed, the plotters plotted almost non-stop. It was a sorry bed at that, old and out of date, lumpy, and prone to roll occupants to the center.

A weekend passed. On Monday evening, she'd fetched him to the mansion. They'd scarcely had time to feel the effects of their first line. Eula Jo, terrified of his ability to alter moods like changing socks cowered when he suddenly exclaimed, "Godddamn, we can do it tonight."

Eula Jo's heart swelled with joy like Christmas past. Her

Prince, a genius, had done it. God has answered her prayers. He laid out the plan to rid the world of that worthless twit Homer Wayne like an old Persian rug. That damned glassed in back porch would be the scene of the glorious event.

The porch extended the full width of the house. Entry to the kitchen was only possible by walking across it, passing the refrigerator, the shower, and the propane heater. Dummy Homer Wayne, mindful of hiding his old pickup from neighbors, didn't even have a key to the front door. He'd have to come in the back door. The previous Mrs. DuPree had hired a contractor to cut a second door from the porch directly into the master bedroom. For many years, Homer Wayne slept days there, running a window air conditioning unit to block outside noise. He loved the old, lumpy mattress, refusing requests of both wives to replace it.

The plan was the most bizarre and complex the love birds had discussed. Most convenient, it did not require laying hands on the victim. They'd kill him with a gas explosion, the Prince declared. All the materials required should be right on the premises. He ordered Eula Jo to set about the house finding pliers, plastic tape, a book of matches, and a length of string. She quickly complied, scurrying through the house raiding drawers and cubbyholes. String seemed non-existent until she found the former Mrs. DuPree's knitting basket in an upstairs sewing room. As she found a book of matches in a kitchen drawer, her mind drifted to the matches she'd filched from his shirt pocket. Terrified he'd know what she was thinking, she quickly dropped the thought.

The deed itself, as said, wasn't simple. Before they left, the Prince would disconnect the propane line running from the outside tank where it connected to the back of the small heater inside the sun porch. The room would fill with deadly, highly explosive fumes.

He then pulled most of the matches from the package, taped them into a circular bundle, then stuffed three or four individual matches into the circular bundle. He taped the end of the string to the individual matches. When the string pulled the individual matches free, the entire packet would flame. He taped the bundle of matches to the baseboard, then opened the refrigerator door and tied the string through the handle. He told Eula Jo that when Homer Wayne responded to her calls for help, he'd see the refrigerator door open, slam it shut, the matches would flame, the propane would explode, and Homer Wayne's useless ass would be blown over the moon.

The Plan was marvelous. Eula Jo using the fake burglary and assault report of a few days earlier as bait, would call Homer Wayne's dispatcher and report threatening calls and a man prowling the back yard. Homer Wayne would rush home, enter the porch, and trip the invention. Homer Wayne's ass would be history. Eula Jo and the Prince would have five hundred grand, the Corvette, the furniture, and whatever else they could pilfer from the place.

He neglected to disclose the true conclusion—she was last in line, right after the day he got his hands on the swag.

As soon as he got access to the half mil, he'd bury the bitch in a shallow grave in far south Dallas County. He thought to himself he'd need to find a shovel, so he could force her to dig her own grave. The thought of using a whip while she dug gave him a sexual urge. Would an idiot like Homer Wayne keep a shovel around the place? Damned details.

For the present, Eula Jo, to avoid being blown over or about the same general area, would assume a position in her Corvette parked nearby. The dumb-assed cops would conclude that she had gone there to sleep because of continued threatening telephone calls. The bulk of the big house would break the force of the explosion, allowing her to escape the holocaust uninjured.

They giggled on Homer Wayne's worn out mattress, curious if enough parts of the old fool would be left around to prove the life insurance claim. Then he used her brutally, leaving bite marks that a physician really should have treated.

She treated her wounds with antibiotic salve and walked out the back door—after the Prince used Homer Wayne's pliers to loosen the connection on the back of the heater. The hissing sound was like heavenly music as they slammed and locked the door behind them.

The study of exploding materials is an inexact science

even on the most predictable of days. The Prince's plan would work. It just wasn't going to quite work as expected, a common occurrence in bombings.

From the parking lot of the well-visited convenience store, Eula Jo made the requisite call to Homer Wayne's dispatcher. She knew the man who answered. She'd made mad love with him on the rear parking lot just before the Prince came on the scene. She spun her tale of horror and fear and returned to the mansion. Dawn was tickling the eastern sky. Trembling with excitement, she parked the Corvette in the driveway to the rear on the opposite side of the house Homer used for access. She sat in her bucket seat, genuinely frightened. What if the damn blast knocked the house over on her? Homer Wayne deserved to die, not her. Twice she started the Corvette and inched it a few yards further from the house. Damn his eyes.

After an eternally long quarter hour, she ducked below door level as Homer Wayne arrived in a trash compacter truck, pulling as usual into the backyard on the far side from her hiding place. He ran across the backyard in his over-the-knee rubber boots and turned the sun porch door lock. A pungent, foreign odor reached him before he entered the porch. He was still wearing his garbage uniform jacket. The outside tank had long since emptied into the porch. He unlocked the porch door and entered. In his haste, he did not close the glass porch door, nor did he notice as the back door swung back wide after he entered.

He approached the ambush cautiously. Homer Wayne DuPree may have ridden in that morning on a garbage truck, but he owned the damn thing and several more. When inside, he recognized the odor as Propane. In panic, he did not notice the open refrigerator door or the knitting string.

First, he hustled around the room throwing open the windows. Once the door and windows were open, the air in the porch was mixed with the outside elements in less than a half-minute. Fresh air quickly thinned the propane. Seized with fear for his loving wife, he ran frantically through the big house looking for her.

After several minutes of futile search, he concluded that she had been abducted by the same lunatic who had been making threatening telephone calls and who had subjected her to the inhuman whipping the week before. Instead of telephoning for the police, in his excitement he ran back toward the backyard and his garbage truck to call the dispatcher.

His reverse trip carried him back through the sun porch. Passing through the now well-ventilated room, he observed for the first time the open refrigerator door. He instinctively shoved the door closed as he passed, pulling the string line match device through the abrasion, alerting him to a sudden flame on the baseboard.

The Prince's device worked, sort of. However, the plan had begun to slide off center from the outset. Propane gas is heavier than the atmosphere. Much heavier. The ratio is 1.55/1. Allowed to blend freely, it rarely rises more than eight to twelve inches off the lowest level available. Homer Wayne had ignited a propane explosion, diluted with air, which was less than a foot tall.

The explosion was only a muffled last gasp which consumed the small quantity of propane remaining, all at floor level, in a single whoosh-breath. The noise was clearly audible to Eula Jo forted up in the Corvette in the circle driveway. She fired up the Corvette, raced the few blocks to a nearby payphone, and dialed 911.

After blurting out the address, she was just briefing the dispatcher on the gory details of her beloved husband eradicated in a blazing inferno, when Homer Wayne reached the same operator from a neighbor's telephone. Homer asked the dispatcher to send a fire engine to his residence to put out a small grass fire that propane had ignited in the yard next to the sun porch. After requesting the apparatus, Homer then told the dispatcher that his wife had been abducted by a monster.

The dispatcher advised Homer Wayne that his wife was quite safe and was on her other line. She then advised Eula Jo that she had better hook 'um for home—pronto. Eula Jo cranked the Corvette in panic. When she skidded into the mansion back yard, mother of Christ, there stood the idiot Homer Wayne by the pool in his yellow garbage suit. Not only was he not dead, he was smiling at her. At first, she vainly hoped she might be seeing a ghost until he said, "Hey, babe, I ain't hurt."

The Prince had said Homer would be such an easy kill. Damnit, an easy kill. Dirty old bastard, an easy kill. Now they'll have to kill him all over again.

Great God, she needed to reach the Prince.

CHAPTER 11: More Damned Cops

Kobok had spent the evening at Anne's, playing a hot game of Monopoly with Tad who kicked his ass the entire time. He considered spiriting the Monopoly Monster out to the dumpster after the kid dozed on the sofa. He'd demurred, then carried Tad to his bed and spent the next hour attending to Anne's needs.

Dutifully, he'd phoned the answering service with Anne's number early in the evening. At just past five A.M., he was already awake for the day, sitting on the edge of her bed when his answering service brought him news not particularly unexpected.

"Kobok, Detective Hooper says he needs your assistance at an explosion at the DuPree mansion. He says you know the address."

He knew the address alright. Last week, he'd responded there to a not so convincing burglary and assault case with Bull Hooper. Now, he expected to find a corpse or two. He donned pants, hurried to his place for a shower and quick shave, and was in route to the DuPree place in a half hour.

Daylight was nearly complete as he pulled into the shrub packed, rear circular drive. Hooper, several uniformed officers, the low rent wife...whatsie, uh, Eula Jo, and her husband, clad in his yellow rubberized outfit, stood talking over the hood of a small yellow Dodge that Hooper had driven to the scene. Kobok noticed Homer Wayne's face was flash burned red like sunburn. However, a man who worked nights was easy to sunburn. His over the knee rubber boots were largely burned off to about ankle height.

Hooper, following the strange southern police custom, shook Kobok's hand, then said, "Kobok, you recall Homer

Wayne and Eula Jo DuPree from the other night?"

Kobok shook Homer Wayne's calloused hand but declined when Eula Jo did not extend hers. Her expression was less like a deer in headlights and more like the animal's expression just after falling off a bridge. He wondered if she'd ever get it screwed back straight. Both Homer Wayne and Eula Jo had a tall boy in one hand and a cigarette in the other.

Eula Jo's appearance, bearing, and tone of conversation signaled clearly, she was no normal socialite. She wore enough perfume to ward off influenza, warts, and most people. The compounded makeup coated her face to a depth of one eighth inch. It was not possible to look at her without thinking prostitute. It radiated off her like sunlight. Her background was painted on her cheeks and chin. The muggy, rising heat did little to enhance her wholesomeness.

"What happened here?" Kobok asked in the abstract.

"That damned old gas heater Homer Wayne keeps in the back porch blew up, that's what," Eula Jo blurted.

Homer blustered, "This warn't no accident. You damned people can't seem to figure out, somebody's been harassing my Eula Jo. Bastards been callin' her all hours makin' threats. Now they tried to kill her and damned near got me. You boys oughta be out findin' who the hell done this."

Kobok eyed Homer Wayne. "We intend to do just that, Mr. DuPree."

"How many threats did you have last night, Mrs. DuPree?" Kobok asked.

"Uh…two…no three."

Hooper said, "Sexual threats?

"Some and they was awful."

Kobok saw the answer was purely histrionic.

"What did you do?" Kobok asked.

"Turned out the lights…hid in a closet. Called Homer and then went out and hid in my Corvette. Heard the 'splosion then drove to a payphone to call the cops."

Hooper rolled his cigar stub. "Just talked to the dispatcher on the way out. She says you called to report your husband killed with a bomb."

"Well, I thought…"

Homer shook his head at her. He saw the conversation was going sideways.

Hooper asked "Hid in a Corvette? Why didn't you call the police?"

"Damn cops don't care," Homer Wayne supplied an answer.

Kobok and Hooper told Homer Wayne and Eula Jo to remain outside while they looked at the rear porch. "It's my damned house," Homer Wayne growled. He remained by the pool. As they entered, a crime scene search van pulled into the back yard. Hooper motioned the two techs inside.

The rear glass door was hanging open. It was unlocked. A key would have been needed to open it from outside. Kobok and Hooper exchanged glances.

They found the remnant of string stretched from the refrigerator door to the baseboard where a small wad of burned material, obviously a book of paper matches had ignited. Hooper quietly told the lab techs to bag and tag everything they could which appeared of evidentiary value.

Kobok found and tested the front and a side patio door. Both were locked with a key with no inside turn-bolt. Hooper and Kobok walked back to poolside.

"Why were you using the heater, Mr. DuPree? The weather has turned hot."

"Uh," Homer Wayne stammered. "Wasn't, and the tank was near empty."

Kobok said, "You're definitely correct, Mr. DuPree, this was no accident."

Homer's expression of anger held fast. Eula Jo's expression looked as if she might run for it. Kobok and Hooper recognized her fear instantly. She had just tried to kill her husband, probably with somebody's help. Something was rotten in North Dallas. Kobok thought of his earlier comment to Homer Wayne about catching the perpetrator. They had just done exactly that. Proving guilt was a whole other ballgame.

Homer stood on his back patio, the yard jammed with stranger's vehicles, appearing totally flummoxed. Kobok saw he was work-hard husky, going slightly to paunchy, and fit enough to pick up the rear of a pickup truck. Time would prove just how tough the old man was.

Hooper motioned Homer Wayne and Eula Jo inside the glassed porch. The blast had cracked a couple of window panes and blown the baseboard out slightly where gas had accumulated heaviest behind the heater. The outside glass and bedroom wall were blackened about a foot above the floor, and the indoor-outdoor carpet on the floor fried well done. Further damage was limited to Homer's boots.

Homer mounted the steps. Eula Jo remained leaning against Hooper's car, puffing frantically on a filter tip.

Kobok showed Homer Wayne the makeshift explosive device and the unlocked porch door. "Mr. DuPree, to get in or out of this porch, somebody had to have a key. Was the door unlocked when you came in this morning?"

"No, I used my key. But we've had workmen around here. Yardboy and the like. I'll get a list of them." He inspected the lock. "Wouldn't take much to yank this door open if it had been locked."

Hooper said, "You just said it was locked when you came home."

Kobok asked, "These threatening calls your wife has been receiving. Did you ever actually hear any of them?"

"Well, hell no. They knew not to call when I was here."

Kobok tore a page from his notebook, jotted a number and handed it to Homer Wayne. "This is Southwestern Bell Security. Call and tell them you've had threats. They can set up a trap to see who's calling."

"You ain't puttin' no damned wiretap on my phone."

"Not a wiretap, just a record of who called. Then we could go pay a visit to the callers."

Homer Wayne was having none of it.

Kobok blurted, "Did it ever occur to you that your wife may have unlocked the door to whoever jiggered your propane line…set up that string and match contraption?"

"Jesus H. Christ. Some maniac is after Eula Jo and you accuse her of a crime."

Hooper said, "Mr. DuPree, after we were out last week

when your wife reported an intruder, we ran record checks on you and her. You have an old conviction where you paid a fine for assault thirty years back."

"Barroom fight. I was little more than a kid."

"Your wife has a lengthy record of arrest for prostitution, shoplifting, resisting arrest."

"Happened when she was a kid." He'd already been thoroughly warned of her background by his family when they tried to head off his marriage to Eula Jo.

Hooper said, "Her last arrest for prostitution was three months before y'all were married."

"Damned police harassment. Y'all can get the hell off my property before I throw you off."

Homer Wayne was tough, but not that tough. Hooper and Kobok both smiled.

Hooper said, his bald head glistening, "First of all Homer Wayne, it's a crime scene and as a matter of fact, I'm going to have a uniformed officer escort you off until we're done looking at it. But, old timer, if you want to have a go at tossing us off, stop standing there running your mouth and get started tossing."

Homer Wayne, a fool with love, was not a total lunatic. He backed down, spent fifteen minutes explaining his activities of the night before, added he had no enemies that he knew of who would attack his home, and agreed to wait at curbside until the crime scene had been thoroughly examined.

Hooper wanted to ask him who the hell was dumb enough to hide from terrorists in a Corvette sitting in plain view, but Kobok shushed him. They already showed too much of their hand. Time to wait and watch Eula Jo to perhaps see who was helping her attempt to murder her naïve husband.

Kobok and Hooper drove off in separate cars, followed closely by the crime scene van and the last patrol car. The blast had not disabled the electricity, leaving the interior with AC. Although a slightly burnt rubber odor remained, the place was cool enough for Homer Wayne to be snoring like a beached sperm whale on his lumpy bed six feet from the explosion in ten minutes.

Eula Jo sat in the rising heat on the patio. She downed three more tall boys and went through a full pack of Winstons. Them damned cops—that gorilla looking, bald headed old city cop and that fed—they damned well knew she had tried to rid the world of that useless plug, Homer Wayne. Feds? She'd heard from the girls on the street, them damned federals tapped telephones and had secret recording stuff. It wasn't fair, dammit. Homer Wayne needed killing. Just plain needed it.

My God, it was only Monday. Surely, he'd call her before the week was out. If there was a God, her Prince would simply know to reach out in her time of distress. Where the hell was he? My God, if he called would them damned feds be listening. She cried all afternoon and through the night.

Then, the following evening, like rays of Spring sunshine, he called. Again, Homer had just walked out. Breathlessly, she blurted her rough treatment at the hands of the law, stressing she had told them nothing. He ordered her to the rendezvous immediately. When she arrived, he informed her he had to have the Corvette for several hours. She drove back to the mansion, handed over the keys, and was heartbroken when he peeled out onto the quiet street.

She was dozing in a poolside chaise, mellowed by four tallboys, and three lines when he rolled around the corner of the house at somewhere past 2 A.M. Damn that telling time thing again. As she stripped for her dose of abuse, she noticed he was highly agitated again, bathed in sweat and visibly shaky. His abuse was harsh that night, leaving injuries which would scar over and be permanent. He summarily announced he wanted to go back to Northwest Highway. He stepped out just as dawn lit the Eastern sky and walked away without comment. In pain both physical and mental, she sobbed all the way back to the mansion.

CHAPTER 12: POKING A SLEEPING GIANT

Kobok's previous week had been what's called in the cop-trade as a "hummer". He'd taken several swings and hit nothing but air. Two days had been blown on the Rosie Beckman firebombing. Then wasted more time with Hooper trying to convince that idiot Homer Wayne what the hell ever his name was, that his wife was bad news and would eventually murder his stupid ass. Over the weekend, he'd received no calls. With Anne and Tad, he visited a nearby waterpark on Sunday.

He'd spent the following Monday scouring records trying to equate Jerry Kincaid to Gilbert Rincon and Rosie Beckman. He got nowhere. He'd sneaked home early and endured the marathon game of catch with Tad in the courtyard.

He'd enjoyed an evening of being wiped out by Tad in Monopoly on a stomach loaded up with spaghetti, and then paid for dinner with a rather tepid performance in the bedroom. At 2:47 A.M., with a touch of indigestion, he was dozing beside Anne, dreaming of fishing in Lake Texoma. When her phone shrieked, he vowed never to do his sworn duty by telling the answering service where he was hiding out.

"Kobok, how ya' been, dude?" inquired the on-duty clerk. Of course, he had no clue to her identity.

"On my deathbed. It's Hoof and Mouth Disease."

"Funny. I need to come back over and straighten you out."

"What's up, kid," he stretched what memory he had trying to recall the kid's name.

"Detective Hooper says they need you at the Green Bull on Northwest Highway. Bomb detonated in the men's restroom. He says two dead, four transported to Parkland. The address is…"

"Don't need it," he said, his sixth beer, middle of the night funk stifling his ability to figure out who, exactly had called him from the switchboard.

"Call me, stud," she said as he closed the circuit.

Sultry night air smothered Kobok like a wool blanket as he pulled on the previous day's clothes and strolled out to the Plymouth. No need to doll up to go to a bombing.

The Green Bull on Northwest Highway east of Harry Hines boulevard was frequented, particularly post-midnight, by the usual selection of drunks, tourists, perverts, and errant husbands. Kobok had interviewed Stephanie "Sparky" Manner, a dancer there a few days before regarding Gilberto Rincon, the suspect in Rosie Beckman's Cutlass firebombing. *Connected?* The thought crossed his mind. But there were plenty of topless dives in Dallas. Chances of a connection were slim to none, but he'd keep the thought in mind.

Kobok had only dealt with the day manager, Freddie Maroney when he'd interviewed Sparky. But he knew the owner, Anthony David Calbacci, who would damned well know more details than he'd admit to the cops.

Calbacci, a Sicilian with suspected connections to organized crime families in New Orleans, Kansas City, and New York, had developed a reputation among the Dallas underside, as a guy to avoid. Next to his photograph on the wall of the organized crime strike force, along with many others whose names ended in vowels, was the notation he was known inside the organization as "Tony Bones." A native of the Kansas City area where his family had traditionally been in the retail clothing business, he had seen greener pastures in the sunny Southwest and moved his operations to Dallas several years earlier.

Although Kobok had not dealt with Bones when he'd interviewed Sparky, he knew Bones. The Big Italian had "cooperated" when Kobok had arrested a fugitive from Detroit the year before. That meant in cop-speak, Bones was not below trying to bank an "attaboy" by snitching to the feds for leverage next time he got caught dirty. He'd fingered the fugitive, trying to gain goodwill. Kobok didn't really care for the man or his cooperation but being civil was part of the process.

Kobok found the Green Bull surrounded by emergency

vehicles, three TV news vans, and a gaggle of half, to fully drunk spectators, held at bay by yellow, plastic barricade tape. He parked on a sidewalk outside the barricade tape, pulled on rubber boots from the trunk, and badged past the uniforms manning the perimeter.

The seat of the blast, evidenced by a gaping hole in the concrete block front wall, had been on the front of the building. The Green Bull was housed in a single-story, flat-roofed building common to the area with an asphalt parking lot. The lot was occupied now only by three vehicles damaged so badly by the blast they couldn't be driven away and several emergency vehicles. Kobok recalled the parking lot was usually well occupied with cars and pickup trucks of customers drawn to the noise and bare flesh inside. Tony Bones was going to be plenty pissed at somebody.

"Kobok, I'm mad as hell," Bones rasped from just inside the front door which was still intact within feet of a sizeable blast. The voice predicted big trouble for somebody if chips fell just right. An inch or so under six feet, Calbacci weighed upwards of 250 with a long Italian nose and about twelve pounds of jet-black hair which he kept neatly parted down the middle. Bathed in sweat in his white shirt, and coated in gray dust, he appeared ghostly in the dim light. He was flanked by a white man the size of a front door. Bones retained at least two "associates", one or more of whom never left his side.

"Hey, Carlo", Kobok smiled up at the big bodyguard. Kobok was just over six feet and moderately husky. He estimated Carlo outweighed him by at least two to one.

"How's it hangin', Kobok?" Despite the size difference, the paid bodyguard involuntarily edged backward from any arm of the law.

"You all right, dude?"

"Yeah, I was on the front door, but the blast blew the front wall out onto the parking lot and for some reason, not sideways, or I woulda bought the farm." Kobok could hear from the twang in the big man's speech he was Texas bred and not an import from Kansas City.

As standard procedure, Dallas Fire had killed the electrical current at the pole across the street, but the interior was dimly illuminated by flickering light from several small generators chugging away on the parking lot.

"Who'd you piss off, Tony?" Kobok allowed his eyes to adjust to the interior.

"Good question," Sicilian eyes flashed death. Tony Calbacci was an extremely poor selection of man to rub the wrong way.

"Kobok!" Bull Hooper's stocky figure emerged from the gloom inside. He motioned Kobok to follow him to the shattered doorway of the men's restroom. Even in shirtsleeves, Hooper was sweat-soaked, the top of his hairless head coated with damp dust.

The men's room was a two-holer. By flashlight examination, it was obvious the bomb, probably relatively small, had been detonated at or near the base of the commode. Only a sewer hole remained to confirm the prior residency of the plumbing fixture. Fragments of the commode, which had been directly against the outside front-wall, were blown along with other debris, halfway across the parking lot.

Fragments of shattered white porcelain were strewn across the men's room floor. A thousand more were imbedded in what remained of walls and the ceiling. A pool of blood in the "ready" position where the urinal had stood told a gory story. The partition formally assigned to wall off the commode from the urinal was flat on the floor beneath the recognizable remnants of the standup urinal. The inside destruction reflected damage Kobok had seen from outside. Despite tearing up the john, overall damage was fixable.

Kobok studied the black residue coating the interior three walls which were still standing. "Looks like black powder and amateurish as hell," He remarked. "Lemme take a closer look before we make up our minds."

"Gotta be a patron." Hooper observed. "I've never seen a beer joint bombing go down while the place was open for business.

"I'll bet some jerkoff was pissed at one of these dancers or at Bones…or both."

Kobok said, "Our answering service said two dead, four transported."

Hooper pulled out his notebook. "Uh, one dead here," he pointed to the pool of blood, "One DOA was in the doorway and uh, four transported, one not expected to survive. All victims male, not surprisingly. The right hand of the guy standing in front of the urinal was imbedded in the ceiling."

"Losing a hand musta killed him of shock," Kobok speculated.

"Had his dick in it," Hooper said solemnly. "Guess he was standin' over the facility takin' a leak." He centered his flashlight beam on the spot where a urinal had been. "Bled slam-ass to death." He jiggled the light around the floor. Kobok realized he was standing in semi-dried blood which had been blown beyond the pool closer to the urinal.

"We know Bones is supposed to be mobbed up," Kobok began again, "but I've never known the mob to do a deal the way this went down. This looks amateurish as hell. If they wanted some of Tony, he'd already be history. And if they wanted to take this place down, they sure woulda done a better job than this half-assed attempt with the place full of witnesses...or murder victims. They woulda waited until 4:00A.M. and we'd be looking for parts three blocks away."

"I agree, Dr. Kobok," Hooper grinned, wiping sweat from his brow on the back of his already saturated sleeve. "I'm no mob expert, but that sounds correct."

While Hooper attempted to isolate what witnesses remained at the scene, Kobok spent the next hour in the sticky hot air, gathering debris into the standard unused paint cans from his car trunk. Tony Bones passed the shattered restroom frequently, creating increasingly complex profanity combinations each trip.

Kobok quickly confirmed the bomb had indeed been loaded with black gunpowder, wrapped in paper, probably detonated with a firecracker fuse. The ingredient in fireworks, black powder, which can be purchased over the counter in sporting goods stores will explode at the slightest spark. The method was extremely dangerous. Easier to buy than dynamite, black powder is a poor product to use in a bomb because of its tendency to "low order." Despite being dangerously easy to explode, some powder, instead of exploding, tends to scatter, unexploded.

Even if the bomber used two feet of firecracker fuse in the cramped Green Bull restroom, his escape time was a minute at most. But two dead and another extremely critical was a gory toll for a so-called amateur. Kobok concluded the perp had probably stashed the device in a cardboard box or sack on the floor between the commode and urinal and walked away. The dead guy who got his hand and business blown off should have seen it—unless he was too drunk.

Although bomb debris evidence would normally be sent to the ATF laboratory in D.C., Kobok decided the crude, unsophisticated debris gathered here would be examined by the Dallas Crime Lab in the Southwest Institute.

CHAPTER 13: AND BEHIND DOOR TWO...

Tony Bones sat in the back seat of Kobok's Plymouth, the A/C blowing wide open. Hooper sat in the rear beside him. Kobok, behind the wheel, twisted sideways to allow him to see into the rear.

The bulky bodyguard leaned against the trunk of the car. The glut of onlookers had largely drifted away. Although the yellow barricade tape was intact, the uniformed police perimeter had cleared the scene and the fire department had gone back to their station-house beds.

"Had any threats, Tony?" Kobok began. Both he and Hooper knew full well the line of those who would like to see Tony Bones in the ground would stretch down the block, but the question was relevant.

"Not really...at least nothing unusual," the Mediterranean features reflected sincerity.

"Let me clarify the question," Kobok continued. "Everyone knows you're supposed to have friends in New York, New Orleans, and so on. We all also know if this was anything to do with that part of your life, then you're screwed, because they'll be back and they won't miss. But if it is them, their technique is going to Hell in a hand basket."

Bones sighed, "Kobok, this ain't no mob deal. From what I seen in the movies, they ain't never done no dicked-up mess like this. Besides, I never had nothing' to do with those guys anyway," he grinned through the overhead dome light. Kobok wondered if that kind of lie counted in Hell against Mafioso guys. He envisioned Bones sliding a horse's head into a movie guy's bed.

Hooper said, "Tony, we dug a body outta your dumpster

last year. A guy from Kansas City. Would that have been some kinda message from the mob?"

"Crap, Hooper," Bones snorted. "I'm all the time killin' people and dumpin' 'em in the dammed dumpster behind my joint. And from what I seen in the *Godfather*, they didn't screw around dumpin' people in dumpsters."

Kobok and Hooper already agreed with the no-mob theory, but they weren't about to tell Tony Bones that, or anything else. "Tony?" Kobok said. "You're the only one who's gonna know about that kind of action. Me and ol' Hooper aren't invited to meetings. But don't tell us and you might wake up dead."

"Y'all ain't gonna give me no crap about protecting me, are you guys?" He glanced sidelong toward his "arm", still leaning on Kobok's Plymouth.

"It's been done…a bunch, Tony," Kobok peered through the glass at the big man. Bodyguard be damned, if the mob wanted Bones, he was history.

"No way, Kobok. Like I already said, this ain't no mob deal, period. It's gonna be one of them punks come in the club. They got two bucks in their jeans and screw around with these goofy, doped up bimbos we got jumpin' around on the tables. We have trouble every so often. Hafta throw out two, three, four every week when they start fightin' or other rough crap with some of these chicks."

"Who'd you throw out lately?" Hooper asked.

"Some clown night before last as a matter of fact. Carlo put one dude on his ass right there outside the back door," he pointed. "That crap don't normally happen, 'cuz these mopes are scared of Carlo. This one was a real dork."

"Can you describe him, please?" Kobok asked.

"Yeah, Mexican dude. He'd been sweet on one of the dancers. I guess you'd say, dating. He come in here last night, maybe ten o'clock and slapped her right in the mouth square in the middle of my joint. Tell the truth, we probably saved his life by chuckin' his ass out, 'cause the place was full of macho-drunks who mighta lynched his ass. You know…for hittin' the chick."

Kobok knew the scenario exactly. Naked women elicit

strange responses from all men, especially crumb-bums—and Kobok too.

"Can we talk with this girl?" Kobok asked.

"Yeah, she's sittin' on the fender of my BMW right over there."

Kobok glanced in the direction bones pointed. Several girls were standing around a black BMW.

"What's her name, Tony?"

"Uh, Stephanie somethun'. They call her Sparky."

Kobok told Bones they'd get back to him and hurried to catch Sparky before she disappeared into the gathering dawn.

She plopped in beside Hooper, wearing a t-shirt pulled over a G-string and fogging a filter tip. Hooper, seeing the signal to lightup, flamed a foot long cigar. Kobok, a non-smoker thought he might suffocate.

"Sparky," he began. "Remember me?"

"Yeah, the fed."

"Tell me the Hispanic guy who smacked you in the mouth is not Gilberto Rincon?"

"Sorry, but he promised to pay me back for stealin' my Cutlass. He's a handsome dude and most of the time, nice."

Nice?" Hooper interjected.

"Yeah, he's sorta like inclined to smack me during sex, but not very often."

Kobok asked, "How the hell did you get hooked up with him again?"

"Aw, he come around like last week. Said the cops...feds actually, had rousted him over a bum rap. Needed a place to crash...and he promised he pay me back for the Cutlass. Christ, I really liked the dude and we jes' sorta got together."

Hooper growled, "Less than a week and he's slappin' you in the mouth? Why did he...?"

"Wanted money and I tol' him I didn't have none."

"He have a car?" Hooper asked.

"Naw, not that I know of."

"Is he at your apartment, now?"

"No. Dunno where he's staying right now. He spent a couple of nights at my place, then moved on until he come in the Bull night before last and started some shit. Ol' Carlo settled his hash."

"We're gonna give you a lift home," Kobok declared.

"Awesome, man. Do I gotta give y'all head to pay for the ride?"

Hooper and Kobok laughed in unison. "Not necessary," Kobock chuckled. "Taxi service on the house."

A quick search of Sparky's place on Webb Chapel Extension disclosed no Rincon. Sparky invited both back for action as needed, stripped and hopped into the shower, and they left. Kobok left the front door unlocked. "Never know who she may need to entertain," he grinned. "Don't wanna restrict free trade."

They picked up Hooper's car from the deserted parking lot of the Green Bull. In the early daylight, Carlo was supervising three men who were boarding up shattered outdoor openings to the building. Kobok wondered where they'd found plywood so early in the morning. "Whadya bet," Hooper said. "Bones has the place open tonight. He said he would."

Kobok studied the work in progress. "Bull, what are chances the perp, Rincon being the best suspect, doesn't have enough sense to get the hell out of the area?

"I agree. I think he'll turn up…like rotten meat."

They found a greasy spoon on Harry Hines. While they stuffed on grease and eggs, Kobok went over the Beckman firebombing and his encounter with Rincon. He glossed over contact with the vivacious Marilyn Crawford.

"Rincon has gotta be a prime suspect in the Green Bull bombing," Kobok said through a mouthful of biscuits and gravy. "I'll stop by the autopsy and also leave the bomb evidence while I'm there. Then, I'd like to see what makes Jerry Kincaid tick. Not sure just exactly how to do that at this point, but somehow, he's dirty. He's a small-time doper but my gut says he knows a hell of a lot more about Rincon than he's admitted."

Hooper agreed, but begged off on the morgue, citing the need to submit an initial report on the Green Bull bombing to a fussy lieutenant.

Hooper merged into morning traffic. Kobok headed to

the morgue, convinced Rincon would never show back up at the Green Bull, whether or not he'd planted the bomb. But experience had proven one sure way not to catch him in the vicinity was to not look.

CHAPTER 14: THE HOUSE WHERE DREAMS END

The Southwest Institute was just opening for the day when Kobok wheeled the Plymouth behind a dumpster beneath a "No Parking" sign. He elevatored to the third floor to drop off the Green Bull bombing evidence. He explained to the explosives tech that he already knew the nature and construction of the bomb. It was the possibility of fingerprints from the masking tape that were important. The tech promised to expedite analysis.

The elevator did not go to the basement morgue. Entrance there was handled by a larger car capable of handling cadavers on gurneys. As he started down the stairs from the main floor, the fragrance of lavender enveloped him.

"Hey, Kobok," a sexy female voice hailed him from behind. It was Kelly, Dr. O'Hara's administrative assistant. She looked as good as she smelled and sounded. In spike heels and a skirt which stopped well above the knees, topped with a sweater which showed interesting cleavage to somewhere just above her navel.

"Hello, uh, Kelly. How's tricks?"

"Couldn't be better, dude." She stopped, leaned close, jotted a telephone number on a post-it note, and stuck it on his shirt.

"Try that number to see how tricks really are." She smiled and clacked down the hall.

Kobok walked one flight down to the worst place in Dallas County, perhaps the whole world.

Homicide investigation and conviction in Texas was enhanced considerably by the presence of at least one officer as witness to the autopsy. Being dead wasn't enough. Prosecution had to prove the dead guy was dead. The alternative was for a relative to take the stand and identify the remains in autopsy and/or crime photos as their loved one. History had shown some dire results under those circumstances.

On a scale of things Kobok didn't want to do, attend an autopsy was a principal contender for top billing. Although homicide wasn't a federal offense, jurisdictional lines were often intermingled. The murder here was actually the jurisdiction of Hooper and the DPD, but the bombing was the purview of ATF. The abundance of crime demanded interagency cooperation. The two jurisdictions got along very well, despite TV cop show depictions to the contrary.

The Southwest Institute of Forensic Sciences, commonly called the morgue was wedged behind Parkland Hospital which sprawled several blocks along Harry Hines Boulevard. The location was handy for unsuccessful patients from the hospital as well as for students from the Southwestern Medical Center. Southwestern was a branch of the University of Texas Medical School housed at the north end of the Parkland complex. Parking at the morgue was no problem because there wasn't any.

He punched in the door combination and stepped from lavender to the nearly unbreathable stench of dead tissue.

Three teams of pathologists/dieners hovered over wheeled, Teflon tables, doing their grisly task. In morgue-speak, the pathologist was in charge, but the assistant, called a "diener" actually handled the bulk of knife work. The diener dissected and removed, while the pathologist examined the removed or partially removed parts, adding a cut or two for clarification.

"Kobok, over here," Dr. Lynn O'Hara hailed from the far side of the vast room. Kobok walked over to see her diener and she bent over a battered and burned corpse. Fictional TV images of a morgue invariably show the deceased slid into a stainless-steel cabinet and drawered out, covered by sheets. Dallas County, in line with several other facilities Kobok had seen, handled corpses naked on movable gurneys. Being deceased, the modesty of a sheet was unnecessary. Sheets simply added another laundry bill. The tables had grooved gutters around the perimeter to prevent fluids spilling onto the floor. Richard was prying out body parts of a battered mess which had to be one of the Green Bull victims.

O'Hara's diener, Richard Garner, a quick to smile black man of fifty or so, offered Kobok the mandatory jelly donut from a box on a sink board. Kobok figured they kept the pastry around to gross out visitors, i.e. the cops. A journeyman of the morbidity-wars, Kobok chewed his red, gooey donut after he'd fetched a cup of morgue coffee.

"What's up, cowboy?" O'Hara asked, holding up a handful of gore Kobok thought to be the victim's liver. When a speck of gore flipped onto Kobok's snack, he finger-ticked it away and devoured the last bite. He figured a solid show of barbarity would keep the morgue crew at bay for a while. He leaned forward and by the victim's crotch wound, he confirmed the deceased had been the poor soul at the urinal.

"Doc, this guy lost a critical piece of his anatomy...blown off while he was taking a leak. It would be fitting to bury all of him."

"Damn, Kobok, my name is Lynn. And we already got all the missing parts." She reached into an oval "spare parts" bowl at the head of the gurney and pulled out a severed right hand and a ragged piece of flesh. "Didn't have much to lose," she quipped in morgue-speak as she tossed his manhood back into the receptacle.

Richard pried out a glob, handed it to O'Hara, and said, "Heart." The anatomy lesson was for Kobok's benefit.

O'Hara sliced the body part vertically like fresh bread, laying back the divisions with a knife half as long as her arm. "Christ, look at that arterial blockage," she declared into the microphone hanging at head level. She plopped the heart into the round spare parts bowl, then killed the microphone, "Too many damned hamburgers. Getting blown away saved this fat boy from a coronary. You're next," she eyed Kobok. "Gotta watch that diet." The twinge in his heart corresponded to her unofficial, but probably accurate medical opinion.

The second victim's body bore signs of burns, severe trauma from flying commode parts, plus bandages and the greasy salve Parkland had spread on his burns during the brief period he had lived after the blast. He had apparently only been almost DOA and Parkland had tried to treat his injuries. The result was an odor like burned roast and menthol-rub.

Kobok retreated while Richard sawed off the top of the head with a small power saw with an extend arm which operated a small circular blade at the end. Gore on the ceiling revealed previous operations. He pried out the brain, stripped off the dura-matter, a clear, extremely tough membrane which encases a brain and handed the organ to O'Hara. She turned it in rubber-gloved hands for several seconds as if choosing a cabbage at the corner grocery, carved the organ several times, declared it "unremarkable," and tossed it into the tableside pot. The new autopsy dictated a fresh spare parts bowl to avoid Richard stuffing parts into the wrong body when the butchery was complete.

Death wounds included a dime-sized hole in the victim's skull about an inch deep, from which emergency room surgeons had removed porcelain shrapnel. Several similar injuries on the front of the body, all appeared potentially fatal. He had apparently been in line at the urinal in the "ready" position behind the victim whose hand and other part were imbedded in the ceiling when visited by eternity. After twenty-five minutes of knife work, she determined the man, Caucasian age 22, was dead as hell of traumatic shock and multiple fragmentation injuries resulting from close exposure to an explosion, to wit: a bomb.

While Richard "replaced" organs in the two bodies and stitched up the "Y" incision with a large needle, O'Hara motioned Kobok into a small, corner office.

"You should call. We can do lunch," Lynn O'Hara sipped a cup of the morgue's stale coffee. She neglected to include one of those three-day old jelly donuts with her caffeine boost. Kobok considered the "sauce for the goose" line but didn't speak of it. Lunch was a long shot. They hadn't done lunch, only each other, including once in Kobok's Plymouth behind the dumpster under cover of early winter evening.

Several visits to her apartment had ended in wild scenes on her den sofa. He concluded they'd destroyed it. Kobok felt she had her way with him and tossed him aside like yesterday's bath towel. The things a man must endure for the betterment of mankind. He hadn't been as close with Anne and Tad in those days.

"I'll do that, Doc...I mean Lynn." He lied, debating internally if that sort of lie, intended to maintain domestic tranquility, really counted in hell.

He caught the elevator back up to street level, passing Dr. O'Hara's office. Kelly, O'Hara's assistant sat inside the open doorway, typing at warp speed. "Call me," she mouthed the words as they made eye contact. Her eyes beautiful blue, and the low-cut, "no secrets here" sweater told Kobok he'd better evacuate the area, quick. He nodded furtively and ducked out the front door. If he got caught with Kelly, survival might not be possible. Lynn O'Hara had too many sharp instruments.

As he walked back to the Plymouth, he was confronted by an angry City of Dallas uniformed security guard, ramped up over the car parked behind the dumpster. Kobok ignored the pseudo-policeman through several invectives beginning with "dumb." But when he opened the driver's side door and the guard actually placed a hand on his holstered revolver, Kobok had heard enough. Pulling back his coat to reveal both pistol and federal badge snapped on his belt, he said, John Wayne style, "Pull that out dipshit and I'm gonna run it up your ass and pull the trigger." He stared evenly at the man who instantly grew smaller. The hand separated from the holster as if cobra bitten and the stalwart security man faded out of view behind the dumpster.

CHAPTER 15: RICH LADIES HAVE NEEDS, TOO

With a pair of autopsies under his belt, traffic was late lunch lethargic as he threaded the Plymouth downtown to the Earl Cabell Federal Building. He found a spot in the GSA parking structure and walked the block north to the cooled caverns of the building. He'd often wondered who Mr. Cabell was or had been but had never taken time to inquire.

Nearly every desk in the squad room was occupied. He checked his mailbox adjacent to Tootie, the group clerk's desk.

"Howdy's on the rag," she whispered. She was black, smarter than any agent in the place, and very resourceful. H.D. "Howdy Doody" James, the Arson and Bomb Squad Supervisor, a total idiot in the eyes of any normal human being, was terrified of tangling with her. All others, however, were fair game.

"Kobok, a minute," Howdy said as Kobok walked by his glass cage.

Kobok detoured inside and remained standing. "Yes?"

"Why the hell didn't you leave a message on my telephone. You responded to a major bombing and D.C. don't know crap about it."

"Would they know much more if I sent them photos, James? Got the call after 2:00 A.M., busted my ass all night, made the autopsy, and I'm here at just past midday. Next time, I'll call you outta bed and you can call D.C. from the scene. Now I need to knock out a preliminary report and go see a key witness." He turned to leave.

"Evidence?" Howdy asked.

"Black powder bomb wrapped in paper. Strictly amateur. I left the samples with the Dallas crime lab at the Southwest Institute. They can come up with anything D.C. can because the device was so crude and simple."

"Protocol demands we send stuff to D.C."

"Next time, James. You c'mon out and bundle up evidence however you want it." *First, you'd have to learn what evidence is,* he thought. But talking with this clown was similar to trying to convince a fireplug to sing.

He walked over to his desk, roughed out a report and tossed it on Tootie's desk. As he was leaving to drive to Denton to have another talk with Jerry Kincaid, high society interrupted. Tootie answered her telephone, covered the receiver and said, "A Marilyn Crawford says she has important information."

Kobok walked back to his desk. "Kobok."

The voice was husky and sexy. Practiced, Kobok thought. "Mrs. Beckman's maid is over there this morning, Kobok. Don't know how long she'll be there. If you need to talk with her, better come now."

"On the way, ma'am."

Traffic had slacked. Kobok herded the still unwashed Plymouth down the tree shrouded, immaculately maintained neighborhood.

After two or three minutes at the Beckman door with no response, Kobok wondered if the maid had left for the day. Then, Marilyn Crawford glided across the lawn, again gorgeous in tennis shorts which this time were pale blue. The weather had warmed, preparing for the giant leap to hotter than hell later in the day. He subconsciously appraised her anatomy, hoping the lust didn't show beyond his imagination.

"She's probably afraid to answer the door because she doesn't know you, Mr. Kobok," she said easily. "When she sees me out here on the porch, I'm sure she'll open the door."

Her prediction proved correct as the door instantly opened to a clone of the lady he had confronted at the front door of the Crawford residence days earlier. Kobok learned in sixty seconds the maid had no earthly idea how to contact Mrs. Beckman in Europe. In fact, she wasn't sure where Europe exactly might be, except somewhere out beyond the railroad tracks. She did, however, state that she had been paid regularly by Harless Androvski, Mrs. Beckman's lawyer.

He jotted down the info and turned to Mrs. Crawford.

"Do we have any idea when Mrs. Beckman might return, Mrs. Crawford."

"Marilyn?"

"Is her name Marilyn, too?"

"No, but mine is."

She interjected an interesting comment. "Do you have time for coffee, Kobok? I just made a fresh pot."

"Coffee sounds like a capital idea, Mrs. Crawford," he replied stupidly. Obediently following the blue shorts back to the Crawford residence, he pondered if they kept track in Hell that he was pondering what exactly might come up with Mrs. Crawford, so to speak. He glanced at his Plymouth which he'd parked at curbside. He hoped that by being on a public street instead of the Beckman circle drive, the Beckman maid wouldn't have it towed.

"You should call me Marilyn, Kobok," she threw over a shoulder.

"Uh, yes ma'am... uh, Marilyn", Kobok stammered as he entered the Crawford layout. "Where's the maid?" he looked about innocently. He rationalized that the carnal thoughts tickling the corners of his mind were normal and harmless.

"She's off today," she smiled sidelong, her countenance sending some sort of signal. But of what, he wasn't sure.

"Mrs...uh, Marilyn, how is Rosie doing?"

She stared at him intently. "What do you mean?"

"Well, somebody firebombed her Cutlass. Is she stranded?"

"Oh, no, she has a BMW. She's fine."

"I forgot to ask what she did. Does she work?"

"Oh no, she's a pre-law student at Southern Baptist. Why do you ask?"

"Car firebombing. Do you know a car dealer named Jerry Kincaid?"

"Uh, no." He saw the lie in her comment instantly. What the hell was that about?

She served coffee on a silver tray in the comfortably furnished library off the front entry hall. He took a seat on the brown, leather sofa. The décor was darkly finished oak with the million books shelved which he'd noticed before. "Do you and your husband collect books?" he asked lamely.

"I guess you could say so, sort of," she laughed, pouring two cups. "When he's here." As she had during his earlier visit, she slid close against him, a bare, tanned leg brushing his trouser leg. Up close, she smelled of an intoxicating fragrance, which he couldn't identify.

"Does he travel?" Kobok asked hoping to mask any display of his evil thoughts which were picking up steam rapidly.

"Yes. Matter of fact, he's out of town now in South America. He's in oil exploration. He's basically a wimp and an asshole." Her tone was as if she'd just ordered a pizza. A delicate little finger waved above her coffee cup as she sipped.

From the looks of the resplendent furnishing in his massive home, Kobok guessed that the wimpy asshole had found some of that oil, an abundance of it.

"You have a lovely home Mrs. er... Marilyn." Peripherally, he was unable to ignore her interesting bustline.

"There's more to life than expensive possessions," she moved closer against him on the sofa.

"How did you get that scar on your face?" she reached over to run a polished nail over his cheek, causing an electric sensation to find root in his spine.

"Fell down at a boy scout meeting." He knew she would never believe the true origin of the scar, the sharp end of a beer can opener. Her perfume was overpowering, but nicely so. If he didn't get up and get the hell out of there, animal lust might consume him.

"You have a certain rugged appearance that appeals to me, Kobok. You're all beat to hell up, but sexy, I guess," she studied his face. "You look like you could wrestle a bear."

Kobok hoped he didn't faint.

She added, "You're too scruffy to look like a federal agent... maybe a clerk in a goodwill store," she giggled. "But you look pretty tough. You wouldn't be too rough with me, would you?"

"No," he managed, thoughts of forbidden desires were boiling his blood. But Marilyn Crawford solved his dilemma.

She was out of the tennis outfit, quicker, Kobok thought,

than Superman could jump over what the hell ever it was. She fell upon him on the sofa, tearing at his clothes. He helped her as much as he could. Scruffy stuff can be tricky.

"Mrs… er, Marilyn, shouldn't we at least close the door?"

Nude and ravishing, she glided to the double oak door, pulled the opening shut, and turned the bolt lock. She then came back to the sofa with an urgency that caused him to wonder if her husband had been in South America since a year ago last Easter. He felt so used, but sometimes a man must do what's necessary to uphold the law.

After a marathon on the sofa, she dumped the now cold coffee in a flower pot and poured two more cups, still nude. Then, the unmistakable squeal of halting car brakes drifted in from the street. Kobok stepped to the front window and parted the drapes slightly. A gray haired, distinguished man of about sixty was paying a cabdriver at curbside. He appeared very much like he belonged in the Crawford house. The cabbie looked like he belonged in jail.

"Is this your husband?" His adrenaline rush would have earned him a 200-yard NFL rushing day.

She came to the drape. "No," she said casually, "it's my husband's lawyer. You slip into the bathroom," she pointed to a small room off the library. "Get dressed while I entertain him." She brushed a kiss across his cheek. "When we go up the stairs, just let yourself quietly out the front door. Slam the door and Harless will have heart failure." She seemed amused by the whole scenario, but Kobok's pulse rate was rapidly closing on apoplexy.

He clawed on his clothing in the cramped bathroom at the speed of light and was back in the library in time to hear the sound of footsteps going up the stairs just outside the library door. He waited another two minutes and cracked the library door slightly to allow a view of the hallway, hoping the lawyer couldn't hear his heart pounding. The coast was clear, not a lawyer in sight. He walked back to the sofa to make certain he hadn't left anything. Suddenly it struck him Marilyn Crawford's tennis clothing was still on the floor in front of the sofa. She had met the visitor at the door in the buff. Small wonder he had been easily persuaded to mount the stairs. Possibly a case of one mounting following another was in progress. Ms. Crawford and the lawyer apparently were old acquaintances. He figured somehow it didn't count against rich people in Hell.

He slipped out the front door, walked across the manicured grass to the Plymouth in front of the Beckman mansion. Suddenly, he realized why the visitor had come in a taxi. The cab eliminated the need for a telltale car to be parked in the Crawford driveway while the lawyer was conducting business, or whatever. Hell of a deal, he thought.

He waded through traffic, deep in thought, trying to figure out just what the hell game Marilyn Crawford was playing. How could a lady who owned a trillion books and lots of oil in faraway places, know a low rent flack like Jerry Kincaid? Her lifestyle required that she be a skillful liar. Why flunk the test over Kincaid? He wished he'd asked her if she knew Gilberto Rincon. He'd save that question, and others, for another visit and possible interview on the library sofa. Hey, maybe she was just horny.

CHAPTER 16: NAW, BAD PENNIES NEVER COME BACK

He felt the need to drive to Denton and lean on Kincaid. But to do so with no more leverage than a rich chick from North Dallas batting an eye at the mention of his name would be wasted effort. Somehow, Gilberto Rincon, Rosie Beckman, and Kincaid were more closely entwined than met the eye. Rincon was first up for the Green Bull bombing. He decided to hold the Beckman firebombing open, or at least not stuff it into the back of a drawer.

Having been out and about nearly 14 hours, he opted to go home. He made his apartment by 4:15. By 4:30, he was dozing on his sofa. By 5:30, he had gotten up for a quick shower. Then, he called the answering service.

"Oh, Mr. Kobok, A lady called. Said you knew her as Sparky and it was urgent."

He dialed the number. "Green Bull," a female voice answered. Earsplitting music spewed out of the receiver.

"Kobok, here," he shouted. "Federal Officer. Need to talk to Sparky right away."

After several seconds delay he recognized the dancer's voice above the din as she answered. The music suddenly dropped to about ten percent volume. Sparky had picked up the extension in Tony Bones's office.

"Kobok, Beto jes' called here. Said he's comin' by tonight to kill Carlo. Said he broke into my apartment and is gonna kill me, too. Shit, I ain't done nothin' to the dude."

"He's in your apartment now?"

"No, but he said he was callin' me here from my phone. You know he ain't gonna be there now."

"He give you any idea what time he's gonna show up at the Green Bull?"

"No, but he never came 'round until past eleven or so."

"We'll come by there, Sparky. He calls again, try to get him to meet you somewhere, like maybe that convenience store on the corner between the Bull and your apartment."

"Kobok, I'm scared to meet him."

"We'll meet him, kid. You wouldn't need to show up."

Kobok hung up and called Hooper at home. When he explained Sparky's call, Hooper immediately made his case for why he should come to the Green Bull. Kobok knew DPD officers had a hard time getting paid for overtime. Feds were paid for a fifty-hour week to make allowances for overtime. It rarely covered the time, but the system beat getting nothing.

"Bull, if Rincon really called her, which I doubt, the chances of the little twerp showing up are just below zero. He's a sneaking little weasel, but he's got no *cajones*. I'll drop by there later for a beer and if I need you, I'll call. You have another beer and stay home."

Hooper said he'd phone the Northwest Division substation and ask the district sergeant to alert patrol officers in the area of the possible problem.

Kobok had just found clean underwear when the small knock announced company. "Doors open, Tad."

The tow head appeared. Kobok wondered why the kid still knocked on the door before entering.

"Mister Kobok, mama says you can come over for dinner if you want," the voice was innocent. Regret that he had to grow up crossed Kobok's mind.

"Oh boy, pardner, I gotta work tonight."

"I'll tell mom." Kobok was moved that someone actually wanted his company for positive reasons.

"Wait. Tell mama I'll be over as soon as I get dressed." He handed the kid a fudge bar from his scantily furnished freezer. The boy was gone as quietly as he'd arrived.

He pulled on fresher gear including running shoes, stuck the pistol inside his shirt and walked the two hundred feet to Anne's apartment. She answered the door barefoot in short shorts and halter-top; a powerful temptation to forget working that evening.

"Tad says you gotta work again tonight." She smiled in mock petulance. "Tell me it's some secret, but safe, little deal," the smile drifting to concern.

He picked up on her adoption of the universal police term classifying any police activity automatically as a "deal."

"It's just another nothing situation," he lied, having no idea of what the evening might bring. The lie-in-hell phobia he carried in his hip pocket at all times stirred but remained at rest.

They lingered for over two hours over dinner and a three handed game of Monopoly. Tad won. Kobok felt genuine regret when at ten, he had to end another session of the closest thing to a family gathering he'd known in years. He'd had dinner and spent time with Anne and Tad before, but this evening had been very refreshing. Incredibly, his inexcusable incident with Marilyn Crawford made him appreciate Anne.

"Can you stop by later?" she extended a proposition difficult to sidestep, particularly behind her soft smile.

"How late is too late?"

"Got any parameters?"

"It could be in the mid A.M.," he concluded.

"All right, the welcome mat comes in at midnight," she laughed easily. "By the way, genius, you gave Tad a fudge bar just before dinnertime."

"Oh hell, sorry."

"He's had worse." She stepped out of the still open doorway into the late afternoon heat, reached up, and smothered him with a lingering kiss. Up close, she smelled of sweet honey. Retreating back into the doorway, she looked him up and down appraisingly. "You gotta know, big boy. You prowling around among lunatics...I mean, if one of them finally blows off your head, the greatest impact on those stupid bureaucrats in Washington would be a sprained ankle they got jockeying for position where it wasn't their fault. And you should have ironed that damned shirt." The face reflected concern.

"No iron." He said lamely. He knew she was right, but again was unable to see beyond the brick wall of failing to see what else he could do. He found the Plymouth and started for the Green Bull.

In the mid evening traffic, Kobok could confess many personal shortcomings. He liked her...and the kid. She...they were more than he deserved. He envisioned the halter top. She was shinier by two light years than Marilyn Crawford and pleasantly less expensive. But how the hell could he explain incoming contact with topless dancers, mafia guys, and general human backwash, all upcoming on the radar. In cop-wife-life, a husband worth a nickel should come home smelling the same way he left.

The hours of measured violence had cost him his first wife, a high school sweetheart. She was remarried to a lawyer in Kansas City, an unsuccessful one, Kobok faintly hoped. Fortunately, there had been no kids. Anne could easily bag a lawyer who actually made a living. Commitment and permanent could be hard terms to embrace in Kobok's sideways world.

Perhaps he should rethink his relationship with Anne. He'd only known her a few months and had always figured the deal was temporary—a pair of souls passing in the city. There had been no promises, no commitment. He'd always figured that someday a keeper like her would find a better offer and move on. Perhaps he could maintain some contact with Tad. The word, "perhaps" was a tone of uncertainty that drew way too much water in his world.

He swung the Plymouth into a crowded Green Bull parking lot. As he'd vowed, Tony Bones had managed to reopen in less than 24 hours. Plywood nailed across the blast hole marked the scar. Someone standing outside the patch could easily look through the cracks, if anyone was interested in peeking into the men's john. If the cracks were into the women's area, a riot would have been more likely. The cool interior of the bar offered smoky but cooler welcome shelter from the Dallas outdoors.

Atop a table near the front door, amidst a circle of men in varying stages of intoxication, Sparky wigwagged, wearing only a tiny G string and red spike heels. In the smoky noise and flickering strobe lights, she looked winsome and sexy. Kobok, having seen her in bright light, knew otherwise. Two other girls in similar lack of costume danced on separate tables across the room. It crossed his mind that the first obstacle to being a table-top dancer was to avoid falling off.

An overweight, bleach-blond female bartender with sad, tired eyes showed him through the haze to Bones's office. He didn't see the need to tell her he'd talked to her on the telephone earlier. A large black man unknown to Kobok sat on a spindly chair outside Bones's doorway. He eyed him wordlessly as he entered. Bones had warned his new sentry of authorized incoming company.

"Hey, Kobok," Bones greeted through a crooked smile, standing up from behind a battered desk. His yellow, pullover *Ralph Lauren*, a size or two too small, strained at the midsection to cover his considerable stomach. He looked mean as Hell, because he was.

"Ya wanna beer or somthin'?"

"Okay by me." Kobok, still stumbling with the inability to get his mind around his love life, felt in need of the alcohol.

Bones, his dark eyes flaming, already knew of Rincon's call to Sparky. When Kobock told him he intended to sit "out back" for a while, Bones offered to sit in the car and help. Kobok declined the assistance.

Before walking to his car, Kobok visited the men's room. A plumber, hopefully not at gunpoint of one of Bones' stooges, had installed a commode and a urinal.

Kobok maneuvered the Plymouth to a spot near the rear of the parking lot where he could see both driveway entrances and the only door left open during business hours. Carlo's big frame stood ominously in the door. He figured Carlo was carrying a piece, which was illegal. In view of the circumstances, he looked the other way. Maybe Carlo could blow Rincon's head off. If so, Kobok would put him up for a medal.

He backed in, facing a slightly elevated railroad track that ran behind the property two hundred feet on the opposite of where he sat. The steep banks of loose cinder and heavy rock would make access to the parking lot difficult, from that side, or so it appeared.

He left the engine running to use the air conditioner against the stifling heat and humidity. Even at a distance, music from the Green Bull was so loud, anyone walking close to the Plymouth would have to actually touch the car to realize the engine was running.

CHAPTER 17: A Shot in the Dark

Surveillances have a peculiar similarity. Interest wanes in direct proportion to the longer they last, compounded when the time passes into the wee hours of the morning. By midnight, Kobok was already working at convincing himself the chances of Rincon making an appearance were slim. By 12:30, it seemed that if he was going to show up, he would already have done so.

When, at 12:41 A.M., two staccato claps, unmistakable to Kobok's experienced ear as pistol shots were audible over the music, his reluctance exploded to pure adrenalin flow.

From the single door to the Bull, a small, wiry figure burst on a dead run. Carlo lumbered out behind him waving, not to Kobok's surprise a large revolver. The small figure turned and snapped two shots at the big bouncer at a distance of thirty feet. Carlo went down and the little man broke away from Kobok toward the railroad tracks which Kobok had thought to be impenetrable.

Kobok grabbed his flashlight and bailed out in pursuit. As he passed the doorway, Carlo had regained his feet. Tony Bones, also waving a revolver, stood just outside the door.

"Dial 911!", Kobok shouted as he ran by. Ahead, the fleeing man scrambled up the right- of-way and disappeared into the darkness. Kobok followed, finding poor footing in the loose rocks.

The tracks ran at an angle. The fugitive clambered down the opposite side and was visible a half block ahead stumbling through tall weeds which flanked the tracks. Kobok knew that about a block ahead, the tracks crossed a side street which allowed access via the railroad overpass to nearby Webb Chapel Extension.

Suddenly, the running man tore his way through the weeds to an adjacent sidewalk. In the limited light, Kobok could see the underpass to Webb Chapel ahead where the tracks crossed oveerhead. Kobock stayed up on the tracks, finding smoother running on the railroad ties.

On Kobok's right, he saw the man cut left under the tracks. Kobok, intending to cut him off, scrambled down the left side of the tracks. After he passed under the trestle, he stumbled and slid down the grade, losing his flashlight, but not his pistol.

As he struggled, the fleeing man appeared from the semi-dark beneath the bridge and fired two shots at him. He missed, but flying cinder and rock caught Kobok in both eyes. Temporarily blinded, Kobok aimed at the sound and fired one round. The man grunted in pain. Kobok could hear him fleeing, but in the seconds it took to clear his vision, the man was gone.

He decided against further pursuit in the dark and out of breath. The area ahead was a maze of apartment complexes and alleys. The chance of the shooter "laying in the gap" to use his pistol again, outweighed the possibility that Kobok would manage to find him.

A marked squad car whizzed up, emergency lights flashing, then another. Kobok gave both officers what limited description he had, a description that fit a majority of men in the area. He hitched a ride back to the Green Bull with another uniformed officer. Soon the Bull parking lot was crowded with squad cars.

Aside from heavily injured pride and a skinned knee and elbow, Kobock was uninjured. After a quick beer, he borrowed Tony Bones's telephone to fill Howdy in on the situation. Howdy, who should have followed protocol and hurried to the scene did not. Kobok assumed he'd never find the place. Howdy could call the duty officer in D.C. and go back to bed.

He was dialing Hooper's number when Bull pulled into the lot in his pickup.

He looked at the torn knees of Kobok's trousers. "You need an E.M.T.?"

"Only if they can treat my ruffled feathers."

"Damnation, fool. I shoulda been here."

Kobok said, "Don't even say that or that you knew I was

gonna be. Some dip in Internal Affairs will try to trump up a dereliction of duty case. I was in the neighborhood and parked on the lot after one of the dancers said an old boyfriend called her."

"Was it Rincon?"

"It was him that called. Probably him I just traded shots with. I don't see how the hell he made the only outside door without me or Carlo seeing him."

"He missed Carlo, too. The toad needs to take target practice."

Hooper lit a foot-long stogie. "Can't believe he missed you at ten feet or so."

"Or that I missed him. I heard him grunt, but he got away."

A uniformed sergeant walked in and motioned Kobok and Hooper outside, out of the noise and smoke. "You hit him, Kobok. Crime scene is working below that underpass. Blood splatter. Don't seem bad, but you put a hole in him. Looks like you got him in an arm or somewhere he could clap a hand on to disguise blood flow. He might show up at a hospital."

Hooper exhaled poison. "I'll see that all hospitals are covered. Problem is, we get so damned many gunshot vic's show up at hospitals, we'll have trouble finding the right screwup."

Tony Bones' walked up, Carlo close behind.

"Who's guarding the door," Kobok looked around Carlo.

The giant grinned. "Bartender. She's tougher than me anyway. Glad that sumbitch cain't shoot straight, Kobok."

Kobok returned the grin. "Two of us."

Bones echoed, "Me too, Kobok. Glad he missed. I catch that turd, he'll wish he'd stayed clear of us."

Kobok said, rather fruitlessly he figured, "Tony, you get a line on who the hell ever did this, you gotta let us handle it."

Bones's smile was right out of *The Godfather*. "Sure thing, Kobok. Sure thing."

Kobok and Hooper exchanged glances. Both knew Tony Bones had very good connections and sources and was not limited by little inconveniences like constitutional rights. Rincon caught was Rincon in the Trinity River. And Bones had the juice to reach far into the system for information.

The sergeant approached again. "Uniforms say no trace of the suspect. Lotta guys around here who fit the description."

Kobok gave details to an attractive young blond uniformed patrol officer who scratched out a field report. She thanked him and walked back to her patrol car.

Bones, an expert purveyor of T&A, gave her backside a professional once over. "Damn, we put her on the stage inside, wearing one of them cop caps and a gun belt and she'd triple her salary."

The sergeant, still within earshot said, "Make her an offer Calbacci. I believe she might shoot your ass."

Bones laughed. "Jes' kiddin', sarge. Jes' kiddin'. She couldn't work in this joint anyway. She can read and write."

Kobok picked up a six pack at the convenience store a few doors away for sustenance on the way to Spring Valley Road. A silver Corvette swung slowly through the store parking lot, then peeled rubber South on Webb Chapel Extension. He didn't catch sight of the driver.

Although the door mat was theoretically retracted, he banged on Anne's door. He saw movement at the peephole before the door swung back. Anne, in the nude, stood smiling. "You can't tell time for crap, dummy." She reached around and shut the door behind him. "How'd your deal go?"

"Piece of cake."

She stepped back. "What happened to the knees of your pants?"

"They self-destructed, waiting for you to help pull them off."

CHAPTER 18: THE PLAN, Revised

Eula Jo was petrified with fear at the thought of telling the Prince his elaborate propane and matches invention had failed; not only failed but didn't even hurt the old bastard. She vowed never to tell him the police had interrogated her, asking pointed questions with eyes that reflected they didn't believe her answers. Throughout all day Tuesday she continually experienced a surge of horror each time she recalled the expressions of them damned cops when they asked Homer about the locked sun porch door. The thought made her sick to her stomach.

Finally, the Prince did call her late, after midnight. She was flooded with a gush of emotion and relief, nearly causing her to lose control on the telephone. Before she had the chance to deliver the bad news, she heard the urgency in his voice. Come to the regular convenience store meeting place and come now. He added that since the feds were involved, they might try to follow her, and she should take an alternate route. When she asked what alternate meant, he cursed and told her to come a different way.

When she left the mansion that night, she roared away, making several quick turns immediately before speeding away toward Harry Hines. She didn't see any pursuing police vehicles behind her.

As she initially pulled through the store parking lot, she noticed many flashing emergency lights at some sort of nightclub a block down. She circled and made a second pass, turning South on Webb Chapel Extension before he stepped out of the bushes and waved her down.

When she haltingly told him that Homer Wayne had not

only easily survived the blast, but was uninjured, she braced for a ration of his venom—even a slap in the mouth. Instead, he seemed unperturbed, even amused.

When they got back inside the mansion that night, she vented her overwhelming need to have sex with him by engaging in her best dog-and-pony show. He used her that night while he was fully clothed, a first. No matter, Eula Jo would have been in eroticism's heaven if he'd chewed off her left arm.

The Prince, who regularly tended toward rough handling of her during the normal heat of passion unloaded a particularly harsh and cruel attack. He forced her hands behind her and tied them with the belt of another one of Homer's bathrobes from the closet. Despite her pleas that she would remain still for whatever he wished, he tossed her onto Homer's wide bed. He removed his wide leather macho belt—wider even than Homer's belt he'd used to scar her back before. He lashed at her for several minutes. She relished the abuse but was too intimidated to tell him that Homer Wayne would see the welts from the belt sure as hell.

Homer had always insisted on keeping his original bed from twenty years hence—a worn mattress which lay on top of an old, open, bed-spring. There was no box-spring and little stability. The arrangement allowed the old mattress to yaw to side or center toward the greatest weight. Eula Jo, hands tied painfully, was trapped in the center valley of the mattress, each side elevated several inches by her center weight on the bed.

Then suddenly, he fell upon her, violently penetrating. As he sensed his climax approaching, he stopped to reach bedside and light a cigarette. He resumed his rape, using the lighted cigarette to touch her left nipple several times. Eula Jo lay helpless, but willing to endure the unendurable of her love in silence. At the end, he told her he loved her; words that he had never uttered in her presence before. The words flooded her with joy, but she was sure he really meant them. She would have to hide the bruises of the belt and the trauma to her left breast from Homer. She was so enraptured from the evening's session that she would fantasize about it constantly in the coming days.

After he'd sated his lust, he did two lines on a bedside table and downed nearly a quart of the cheap wine she kept in the kitchen fridge, while leaving her nude, bound, and in painful agony on the bed.

Then, he untied her and reopened the subject of eliminating Homer Wayne. He professed to her that he had knowledge of bombs and such, most of which passed over her head after the first few words. But, bomb it would be. She would have nodded assent if he'd suggested sending in the tooth fairy to assassinate the old fool with a rolling pin. The very sight of him talking violence charged her motor for hours.

This time they would make certain that he wasn't warned off by some stupid odor of gas. They would construct a bomb, a device powerful enough to put Homer, or at least parts of him, in the next county. A bomb would kill the old bastard easily. This time, he would be an easy kill for sure. The Prince gave her a list of components to buy. It wasn't very elaborate, batteries, ten pounds of black powder (she wondered what the Hell that was), a roll of masking tape, a small battery powered alarm clock, and a lawnmower battery. He told her he already had something called a "blasting cap", causing her to again wonder the purpose of the item.

Eula Jo went bomb-shopping the very next day while Homer slept from his night's labor. She proudly displayed her horde that night when she picked him up on Northwest Highway. She didn't tell him she'd had to ask at several home improvement stores for black powder before she was routed to a firearms dealer on Central Expressway.

He sat at her kitchen table, working into the small hours with wires, tape, black powder, and some gadgets he had brought with him. He removed the cover of the cute little alarm clock she had bought at Target and taped the little plastic wires to something or the other. He left the ten pounds of black powder in the cardboard boxes in which it had been bought, wrapping the bundle in yards of masking tape. She marveled at his handsome face and his ingenuity as she watched in silence.

A window of the Homer Wayne's downstairs bedroom faced the side yard, about eighty feet from the house next door. Homer Wayne, always the country boy, had installed a window air conditioner unit in the side window years earlier. The single unit allowed quick cooling of the room when the central unit wasn't moving enough air to quite satisfy the sweaty hulk of a laboring garbage man who slept during the hot Dallas daytime. The noise also provided a buffer against sounds outside the house. Homer Wayne's side of the old, rolling bed was directly against the side window, where he could reap full benefit of the small air conditioner when day-sleeping. In fact, the window ledge was within a foot of the pillow where Homer would rest his head the very next morning. This device would not fail. Homer Wayne DuPree was a dead man, the old bastard. An easy kill.

When the Prince had finished, he carefully carried the bomb around the outside of the house. He wedged the masking tape bound black powder between the side of the window and the air-conditioning unit. He stuffed the little clock in atop the black powder package and set the lawnmower battery on the ground beneath the window sill. Reaming out a hole in the black powder with the handle of the pliers, he inserted the little cylindrical thingy he called a blasting cap into the hole. He wrapped one wire around the short hand of the clock and the other around the long hand. Eula was limited in that she could only tell time on a digital clock.

The Prince bent the long hand outward where it appeared to Eula Jo it would connect with the short hand if they came together. Then, he taped one long wire to the long hand of the clock, a second long wire to the short hand, and extended one long wire each to the red post on the lawnmower battery and one to the black post.

The first half of his treachery complete, he announced that the clock, although not turned on, would detonate the bomb in 59 minutes from the time the "on" button was punched. She was to take him home, wait until she heard Homer Wayne's pickup pull into the drive, then step out to the window ledge and punch the "on" button. She would have nearly an hour to escape. After he showed her three times how to switch on the clock, she was still nearly immobile with fear.

"What do I tell him about being outside?"

"Jesus, yer a dumb bitch. Wait til he takes a leak or something."

After the instrument of death was left balanced precariously in the window, he led her back inside. He told her Homer Wayne would come home as usual at 6:30 or so. She was to go to the window and turn on the clock. Homer Wayne would probably down at least one beer from the kitchen refrigerator—the sun porch fridge had been burned out of service when the propane ignited—and be in the bed by 7:00.

She was to watch the digital clock on the wall and be gone by the time an hour passed. As soon as the old loser was dead, she would be heir to a fortune. She was relieved that death would invade from outside the house, the sure way of cutting off those smart-assed cops' questions about locked doors. Nobody thought to consider that she could wait until Homer Wayne was asleep, turn on the bomb, and get the hell away.

Then he tore at her clothes, an action totally unnecessary, causing her the terror tinged thrust of ecstasy she had felt the first nights he misused her. She begged not to be tied, promising to be hurt in any position he wanted. Her plea appeared to only drive him harder. Out came the bathrobe belt-handcuffs and then the leather belt. Passion was amplified tremendously by the nearness of death by explosion inches away. The imminent death of that old fool Homer compounded her ecstasy.

Before he finished, she was near to fainting. But at the end, she experienced a climax greater than any ten she had known combined. He had to cut the tie on her wrists locked behind her because the cloth had knotted too tightly to loosen.

Then he told her he loved her, caressing the burned nipples with lips that once again expressed tenderness she had never seen in him. Neither conspirator noticed that as they lay in the valley in the center of the big bed, the sides formed upward a full foot in a "V" pattern. Neither could have seen the window air conditioner from the low spot in the center. But it didn't matter, as they weren't using the cooler at that exact moment.

She sped evasively back to Northwest Highway. As she neared the mansion, daybreak was showing in the eastern sky.

The pain in her nipples strangely filled her with a lingering passion beyond anything she had ever known. God, she loved him.

Homer Wayne hurled her into a state of horrified panic when he didn't arrive home on time that morning. The bedroom clock rolled past 6:30 A.M., moving resolutely to 6:40, then 6:42. In panic, she ran outside and turned on the clock of death. The creeping clock hand quietly became an eternity of agony. She was near hyperventilation when the old pickup pulled into the backyard at 6:45. Hellfire, her arithmetic skills were too limited to tell when an hour passed, digital damned clock or not.

"Got caught by a train," was his only explanation as he slid into bed with her. She struggled to regain her breath. She could have killed him for being late. Of course, she was about to do just that.

Her loathing was unbearable when he began fondling her. Eula was capable of faking a sex act with two goats and a one-eyed mule if need arose, but this particular morning, she had no time for that action. Eternity was ticking on her window ledge. Besides, she was too sore and marked to bear examination or handling by this old bastard. The loving-whore explained to him that she'd been ill the entire night, having thrown up more times than she could recall. She gagged once or twice for effect.

He re-ignited her panic when he sprang from the bed and offered to drive right down to the drugstore for whatever medicine was necessary. She swallowed the urge to vomit at his offer and coaxed him back into bed, promising to get well as he slept that day and to give him a special treat when he awoke. That did it for Homer Wayne. By 7:12 A.M., he was snoring loudly and buck naked on his side of the bed, his head resting within a foot of eternity. Great God, how much time had elapsed since she'd tripped the death-switch at…what the hell time had it been?

At 7:15 A.M., she was up and into her slick, newly-purchased, yellow jogging suit. She already owned an old warm up suit, but this one was solely to celebrate the riddance of Homer's sorry old ass. It seemed a good morning to jog; about six blocks from the bedroom window ought to do it.

As she cleared the bedroom, Homer, more or less involuntarily, rolled toward the center of the bed in his sleep. Then, he rolled even slightly more to her vacant side, compensating for the change in the balance brought on by her exit from the mattress. The mattress obliged his shift in position and weight by elevating even more on the vacant side. The old mattress was now totally shielding Homer Wayne from the flow of the air from his window air conditioner. It didn't matter because he hadn't turned it on when he went to bed. Later, he would need to wake up and turn the little machine on, but at 7:30 A.M., enough night air remained to make the temperature tolerably comfortable.

The bomb worked about as well as black powder devices ever work. As with the Green Bull bombing, different explosive materials explode at different rates. Explosion is basically a matter of rapid burning of highly unstable combustibles which in turn cause rapid expansion of air and anything else adjacent to the blast.

Black powder, used primarily by sports enthusiasts to load and fire muzzle loading firearms, was at one point in history the only game in town. It's the stuff of movie fame being poured down the barrel of that funny looking long rifle in Davy Crockett's hands. It worked but was inefficient because of its tendency to "low order" and not fully burn, fouling the guns.

Eula Jo's Princely assassin had wrapped the cardboard boxes in several layers of masking tape, building in padding. A handful of nails would have increased the kill zone considerably. But ten pounds of black powder was still enough to take out anyone around if the blast caught them just so.

At 7:41 A.M., the little clock carried home its mission and the bomb exploded on the window ledge of Homer Wayne DuPree's bedroom. Eula Jo had heard the blast five blocks away, instantly exhilarated with the knowledge that Homer Wayne had been blown all to Hell. As she ran joyfully back to the mansion amid a throng of others drawn by the noise, she began screaming.

"Call the Goddamn police. They done kilt mah husband."

Homer hadn't been blown all the way to Hell, however, only part way—about 22 feet as well as they were able to later calculate. The black powder had, predictably, "low ordered". The two separate cardboard boxes had been the first problem. One box, the one with the blasting cap, had fully blown. The second, insulated by the cardboard wall of the two boxes, had merely spewed raw black powder all over Homer's bedroom and the ground outside.

However, the blast had caused extensive damage. Every downstairs window in the DuPree house was knocked out. All windows on the near side of the house next door were shattered plus $10,000 additional damage. Parts of the little window air-conditioner were imbedded in the neighbor's house. The entire rear wall of Homer's bedroom had been blown out through and well beyond the still damaged rear sun porch. Brick and debris cluttered the back yard in and around the pool.

Homer Wayne had always believed that when a person dies, they were left in a black vacuum until some higher authority decided what to do with them in the afterlife. Laying naked beneath a mattress at poolside, he'd been lucky not to have landed in the water and been drowned while tangled with the mattress. For several minutes, he lay, motionless, on the debris littered pool cool-crete. He began to grow typically Homer Wayne impatient, waiting for some afterlife official to show up. Authority was on the way, but of an earthly origin.

One of the first officers to arrive thought she saw movement by the mattress. She lifted it and found Homer Wayne lying nude, dazed, and bleeding from minor cuts, under the devastated mattress. The mattress had acted as a cocoon, carrying its passenger safely through a solid brick wall. Incredibly, a fragment of air conditioner, clock or brick had not penetrated the mattress and torn off his head. By the time a neighbor had found one of Homer's bathrobes in the shattered closet of the bedroom and helped wrap him in it, Homer was frantically searching the house, crying aloud for Eula Jo.

The neighbor had been unable to find the cloth belt of the bathrobe. Homer continued searching for his Eula Jo. He was hindered by having to hold the robe shut against his nudity with his hands. When Eula Jo came puffing up from her jog, Homer Wayne was elated. A camera, if available, would have recorded her look of shock at the sight of him as slightly different from Homer Wayne's analysis. He read her as concerned and grateful that he was alive. The truth was that she couldn't believe that the old bastard was still upright and breathing. My God, what was the Prince going to say?

CHAPTER 19: Catch Me When You Can

Kobok had dropped off to sleep after a marathon session with Anne, intending to go to work a couple hours late after the long day before. After years of early rising, by eight, he was awake and summoning the strength to invade Anne's kitchen to make coffee. His hangover was tolerable. He figured he might live until noon. Then he saw the note on a nightstand "coffee's hot and so are you." Anne had left for work a couple hours earlier.

When her telephone sang its song of despair at just past eight, somehow, he realized Hooper had learned Anne's number. He gambled on the caller's identity. "Good morning Bull, how's things?"

"Christ, Kobok, don't tell me you've turned clairodelic?"

"Would you believe clairvoyant, Bull. I been takin' these smart pills."

"Then you shoulda known all about this one, genius. I'm on a payphone on Royal Lane. Forgot to have the alarm office call you. Major bombing at the DuPree mansion."

"Did they get him killed off this time?"

"First responders say no. Some kinda bomb planted on a window ledge outside his bedroom. Not only uninjured, Homer Wayne has so far refused to be transported to a hospital. You comin'?"

"On the way."

Kobok slipped on his torn trousers, hustled across the courtyard for a quick shower and was gone in fifteen minutes. The lateness of the hour had slimmed traffic. He plugged in his portable flashing red light, tossed it on the dash, and made Newmanshire Lane in less than a half hour.

The route took him within three blocks of Marilyn Crawford's den of iniquity. He made a mental note to call her about Rosie Beckman's mother. He rationalized that whatever else came up, so to speak, would have to be handled as circumstances dictated.

The street in front of the DuPree estate was crammed with emergency vehicles, with a glut of neighbors and news types held at bay by yellow barricade tape. He pulled on rubber boots from the trunk and strode past fresh lawns in the heat and humidity. As he ducked under the yellow tape, several newsies barked questions.

"No comment, folks, just make up a story like you always do."

"Kobok, you sorry bastard," a male voice called out. Kobok ignored the comment.

Homer Wayne was standing in the back yard along with a neighbor, Bull Hooper, and several firefighters and uniformed cops. Unable to find the belt-tie, Homer Wayne still hugged his soiled, belt-less, terrycloth robe closed by folding his arms across the chest.

At the sight of Kobok, he bellowed loud enough to be heard four blocks distant, "They're tryin' to murder us all." Kobok observed he was half correct.

"Whut the hell is the federal guv-ment gonna do something about his shit?" he bellowed as Kobok drew closer.

Hooper, fogging a long cigar, said, "Bomb went off by his head. Not hearin' so good. Guess it makes him talk louder." In the humid, rising heat, Kobok's boots were beginning to fill with sweat.

Preliminary examination readily disclosed an explosion of considerable force had detonated between the window air conditioner and the edge of the window, blowing the rear wall and the glassed-in sun porch onto the rear patio. The a/c unit lay in pieces around the window, both inside the bedroom and on the ground outside the window. A tractor sized battery, remnants of wire still wound around the posts were nearly buried against the foundation in residual black powder and debris. An old mattress—Homer Wayne's savior - lay in the debris near the pool. Bits of paper and splotches of undetonated black powder were scattered around the wrecked room. Shards of metal, unmistakably parts of a clock, indicated the perpetrator had rigged and detonated the bomb with a timer.

Although the Crime Scene Search Unit would bag and tag all debris, Kobok had seen enough bombings to recognize the damage had been caused by an electric charge from the battery, through the clock to a black powder bomb. Use of the battery told him an electric blasting cap had been used, an odd combination. Black powder could have been ignited with a firecracker fuse, as had the bomb used in the Green Bull bombing.

Three additional ATF agents, hearing the radio traffic, made their way to the scene to help as necessary. Kobok organized the three agents to assist the Crime Search people in gathering debris evidence and photographing everything in sight.

Homer gave details of his night's activity, confirming he had worked all night in the presence of witnesses, before arriving home a few minutes before 7:00 A.M. With Homer Wayne temporarily deaf, Kobok asked Eula Jo into the spacious mansion living room. It was windowless and without air-conditioning but otherwise undamaged by the blast. The explosion had knocked out the electric panel on the back porch, causing room temperature to inch quickly straight upward. This time, Homer Wayne was tricked into being occupied with Hooper. Eula Jo would have to go it alone. She slumped on a sofa. Kobok sat across from her in a stuffed chair.

"Where were you when the thing went off, Mrs. DuPree?" Kobok leaned forward as he asked.

"Jogging." She said rather unconvincingly, her soft frame hinting the only thing she had run in many years was a house of ill repute.

"Do you jog often?"

"Well, yeah, lately. I only jus' started a regular routine." Kobok studied her features closely. Ten minutes in an interview room and she'd disintegrate like a martini glass shattering on concrete. But here, on familiar turf, he could see she'd hold on long enough to outlast him.

"Had any threats lately?"

"Yeah…yeah, two last night," She stammered unconvincingly. Kobok thought her next comment might involve the dog eating her old jumpsuit, because he noticed the one she was wearing was spanking new. Eula was a liar up the whazoo. She had an accomplice and he had no idea who to look for or where to look for him.

"Look, Eula Jo, I…we know damned well you've tried twice to murder your husband. I figure you'll eventually get the job done. We know you got some hard-dick maggot helping you. Keep it up and we'll have both your useless asses. You gotta know if you managed to kill him, it's the three-needle cocktail."

"Whut?" Her eyes reflected terror. "The three whut?"

"The death penalty, Eula Jo. They strap you on a gurney like on a cross, then pump poison into your veins while me and a bunch of other people applaud. You can just feel that old icy poison working up your arm headed for your heart. Then, Boom, your eyeballs pop out, one down each cheek." Eyeball ejection was a fabrication, but it had it's effect.

She sprang to her feet and burst out the front door in tears.

"Guess it's time for another jogging session," Kobok muttered. He calculated that Eula Jo would not repeat his rough interrogation to Homer Wayne.

He walked out through the devastated back door and porch to join Hooper and Homer Wayne on the patio. He and Hooper cornered Homer Wayne and tried to gently explain Eula Jo's possible involvement, which caused Homer Wayne to erupt in angry indignation. When they again showed him her lengthy record of previous arrests and convictions, he absolutely refused to believe his Eula Jo was the same person in police records. If it was, he shouted over his deafness, it was kid stuff and he loved her anyway.

Homer Wayne again became belligerent and ordered them off the premises. Hooper again told Homer Wayne the place was a crime scene and they'd leave when the evidence crew had finished. "As a matter of fact, Mr. DuPree," Hooper exhaled a cloud of smoke. "The E.M.T.'s are gonna have to transport you to Parkland for examination. It's a necessary part of a bombing investigation."

Homer, calming slightly, said he would need to get dressed and accept a ride to Parkland.

Kobok and Hooper lingered at the scene, looking for anything of value, then met for coffee at Denny's on Royal Lane.

Kobok said, "Bull, we're gonna have to set up on that damned Corvette and try to see where Eula Jo goes."

Hooper chewed his cigar stub while sipping coffee, an interesting combination, Kobok thought.

"What if her boyfriend has his own wheels?"

"Maybe if we watch her, she'll lead us to him, whether he has a ride or not."

That afternoon, Kobok drove out to the DuPree neighborhood and in ten minutes learned from a neighbor that Homer Wayne and Eula Jo had moved temporarily to furnished guest quarters on the fifth floor of a high rise condo unit on Northwest Highway near Preston Road.

Kobok drove to the address. On seeing that the basement garage entry required a pass card, he parked in a shopping center across Northwest Highway and walked down the ramp. Homer's battered old pickup and the silver Corvette were parked in a pair of slots marked 512. The dysfunctional lovebirds were found.

That night at nine, they formed a perimeter with four cars, including Kobok in his Plymouth, Hooper and another homicide officer in separate cars, plus another ATF agent in a separate vehicle. At just past eleven, the Corvette peeled out onto heavy Northwest Highway traffic westbound, turned north into a residential neighborhood, made several sharp turns and lost them in less than three minutes.

They re-established their surveillance positions, noting that the Corvette returned before midnight and disappeared down the parking ramp with what appeared to be a male in the passenger seat. Kobok left his car and ran down the ramp to see the elevator door closing. He was unable to identify either of the two people as the door slid shut.

The next night, Thursday, they added one additional DPD car and an extra ATF car, plus arranging for a DPD helicopter to idle on a nearby school parking lot. They arranged with the condo management to park a surveillance van near the basement elevator. By five A.M. the following morning, they concluded the Corvette had not and was not going to leave the garage.

On Friday night, Kobok alone, parked his Plymouth across Northwest Highway. The Corvette burst up the ramp at just past midnight and lost him in traffic in minutes. He waited until 2:00 A.M. The Corvette did not return. He had no way of knowing the Prince had "borrowed" the Corvette and had dropped Eula Jo on Northwest Highway. She'd taken a taxi back and let herself in the rear door of the high rise.

Hooper and Kobok discussed a long-established truism regarding surveillance: "You can't follow anyone who thinks they're being followed." Surveillance was discontinued.

The next day, Saturday, Kobok attempted to sleep in in Anne's bed. Tad derailed the plan by creeping in just past daybreak. Tad, Anne, and Kobok drove to Six Flags in Anne's Honda and spent the day, plus a day's pay. Kobok suffered until nearly 6:00 P.M. before he had his first beer of the day.

On Sunday, Kobok made two passes around the rented condo, parking nearby each time and scouting the parking garage on foot. The Corvette was not in its normal parking spot, nor could he spot it anywhere in the neighborhood. Several days would pass before he would learn the fate the Corvette had met several miles from Northwest Highway.

On his second trip down the ramp, he barely avoided being spotted when Homer Wayne, and Eula Jo exited the elevator. They loaded into Homer Wayne's pickup and drove away. Kobok, a detail-oriented man inclined to pursue the slimmest of leads, hid behind a column as the pickup puffed up and out onto Northwest Highway. He assumed they were going out for Sunday afternoon chow. And again the "Assume" monster had reared its head. For the second time in recent days, he had failed to follow up on a lead that would have been golden if he'd done his job.

Failure to follow the pair would be a mistake that would weigh a ton and a half.

CHAPTER 20: CORVETTES: EASY COME, EASY GO

When the window bombing failed to get rid of the old fool, Eula Jo was heart-broken and trapped in the lowest prison cell of despair. The cops had all left the mansion, but they knew she was involved. They knew! She could see suspicion and blame in their eyes. Dirty Bastards, they knew! That fed asshole had scared the hell out of her with the death penalty threat. That bald, gorilla looking city cop was a monster. That crap wouldn't stop her Prince. She would have to double her efforts to mislead her Prince by insisting the police knew nothing.

After stupidly clutching his beltless bathrobe around his fat gut he found some clothes. The old skinheaded cop had insisted and Homer Wayne had been whisked away in an ambulance. Maybe he'd friggin' die on the way. Later in the day, he'd run his dumb mouth that Parkland Hospital had declared him uninjured and, despite ringing ears, was released.

What neither she nor he knew was that the paramedics, on orders of superiors, had hung around Homer Wayne to report back the exact time when he would die from his injuries. A man who had taken that sort of violent contact, had to have internal bleeding or something fatal.

On the way back to the mansion, Homer talked the E.M.T.'s into stopping at Pizza Pete's all you can eat where he pulled out a wad of cash four inches in diameter, bought for the house, and promptly ate the young paramedics under the table. Later in the afternoon he rented a condo on Northwest Highway and by early evening had the place almost completely furnished with rented furniture and Wal Mart kitchen and bathroom doodads. Homer Wayne's rugged construction should have been a subtle warning to Eula Jo, but she wrote off his survival to dumb luck instead.

Eula Jo was furious. His first dumb act when he showed her the new condo, was to order her to strip. He fondled her on the bed, which surely was made of cement, through an agonizing eternity consoling and holding her and in particular fondling her breasts. Her nipples were so sore, had she a pistol, the drama would have ended there. She put him off by swearing she was too upset for sex, which was true in regard to him, and shortly he was snoring soundly on that damned concrete bed. She doubted he would have gotten it up anyway.

Eula Jo was in a hell of a fix. The bomb had knocked out all the utilities in the house, including the telephone. She had no contingency plan to make contact with her Prince. Old dummy Homer Wayne snorted awake in an hour or so and drove her back to the mansion. God must have loved her she concluded, because the telephone company truck was parked in the drive, with a redneck repairman bent over the outside telephone inlet box.

Homer Wayne announced he needed to drive back to the new condo to let the telephone company in and run a couple of errands. He invited her along, but she declined. She lured the telephone guy upstairs, gave him the Eula Jo "fix the goddamned telephone" special and shortly she had a dial tone. What she didn't have was a call from the Prince. And he sure as hell had no way to call her at that ugly condo. She'd camp out somehow at the mansion.

Presently, Homer Wayne drifted back to the mansion. She solved her absence from the condo easily, insisting she needed to be present at the damaged house to supervise reconstruction and prevent damage to her "things." She pointed at the nearly exhausted, freshly used telephone guy as an example of workmen who might need supervision. Homer Wayne would believe nearly anything she told him. He found some work clothes in the mangled Mansion and left for work early.

But still the Prince didn't call. She spent the stifling late afternoon in a lawn chair out by the pool, seeking what shade and comfort a pool umbrella, six warm tallboys, and two lines could provide from the killing June sun. The telephone guy returned in the afternoon, telling her he was there to check her dial tone. She enticed him upstairs again, this time bedded him for the Saturday Night Special, using up the last of whatever dial tone libido he had left. She asked him when he could restore the electricity, so the A/C could save her from certain death.

But alas, she should have sought out and seduced the electric utility guy, because the dumb red-neck telephone repairman could no more restore electricity than she and the Prince could manage to murder her husband. Late that evening, she drove to the new Condo. Tuesday night would come and go in heartbreaking failure to communicate. Christ, the meeting place on Northwest Highway was only fifteen minutes away from that stupid condo. Darling, please call.

The next day, Wednesday, she resumed her wretched vigil while Homer Wayne slept like a wounded warthog over at the condo. She was a goner in the heat sure as sundown. She must have sweated off ten pounds. Then in the late afternoon, just as she prepared to breathe her last, the heavens opened. The telephone in the pool house jingled relief, blessed relief. Now she could give him the condo telephone number. She lied and told him Homer Wayne had been seriously injured but wasn't going to die from the blast. He again surprised her by seeming unperturbed.

He ordered her to pick him up on Northwest Highway that very evening. When she left to pick him up, she rammed the Corvette through a residential neighborhood although she did not see the parade of cops trying to follow. They returned and spent the night in the rented condo on the hard bed. He ordered her to strip and lay flat on her back, spread-eagled on the bed, telling her if she flinched or cried out, she would be tied in a closet for the rest of the night.

She endured the abuse for hours. Homer's robe would never be necessary again. Her Prince need only to wish and she would obey. His commands would become steel handcuffs on her wrists. In the end, he burned her with a cigarette butt as she lay pinioned in mental confinement, far worse than ever before. The cigarette would leave permanent scars on her breasts to augment the belt scars from previous beatings. When finished, he repeated his love for her, only this time adding a kicker. If she wanted him, Homer had to go next time, period. At that, she would have chewed Homer's throat out, swallowing the parts and relishing the taste.

Then he let her up, downed a quart of the cheap wine, did a line, and told her this time his plan to off the old numb nuts was foolproof. He'd bought a book at the Dallas Gun Show which explained how to make a bomb with a mousetrap trigger. She wondered how he'd gotten to the Dallas Gun Show but didn't want to risk a beating by asking. He said he had another blasting cap, but he needed twenty pounds of black powder this time, plus a large rat trap and another roll of masking tape. He cautioned her to go to two different gun stores to buy the black powder to avoid suspicion.

The next night, Thursday, he didn't call, and she died the usual endless deaths of abandoned, tortured souls. The agony was too intense to categorize. Great God, he had to be spending nights someplace. It had to be that bitch from the match cover.

The next night, Friday, he called, and she picked him up. He told her he had to have the Corvette overnight. Christ, what could she tell Homer? Not his problem he replied. Tell him to get screwed. She taxied back to the condo, again in the depths of depression and despair. When he had not returned in three hours, then four, she sank deeper into sickening revulsion of the thought he was in the arms of another woman, with by God her Corvette.

Homer came home, stinking and on time on Saturday morning. Again, the old idiot had failed to be killed in a garbage truck accident overnight. She waited for him to say something about the Corvette that was not parked next to his slot in the basement. Did he know? God, no, Homer Wayne DuPree was just too dumb to miss the absent car. She gave Homer her best that morning, cooing that she loved him and eventually inducing a form of sex. He was snoring on that God-awful concrete bed in an hour.

The Prince's political enemies of the corrupt FBI had gotten him. They wouldn't be able to find her from the Corvette license plate because she wasn't at the mansion. But them cops, that big bully Hooper or the fed, what's his name would eventually run her down. Oh Jesus, what was an earnest, decent woman like herself to do?

Then, well after noon, the telephone shocked her back to reality and some initial happiness. It was him, but the news was bad. He had wrecked the Corvette. No, he wasn't hurt. No, he wasn't in custody. He had fled the accident on foot, abandoning her Corvette. He ordered her to find a taxi and pick him up immediately, which she did without question, ecstatic that she was needed. Thank God she hadn't yet gone murder shopping for gunpowder and the fixin's. The ingredients would have been stashed in the Corvette.

She—actually the cabbie—finally found him by the telephone booth at the Belt Line Road exit on Interstate 35 on the far north side. Exhausted, he had a bump on his forehead. He ordered the cabbie to stop at a WalMart. Eula Jo handed over a handful of cash and he came out of the big store with a pair of polo shirts in a plastic bag. He then ordered the cab through a McDonald's drive through where he devoured a Big Mac. When he changed into one of the new shirts, she noticed for the first time the scratch on his side, just above the belt line. No longer than her finger, it was straight and not deep. Although it appeared partially healed, she assumed it had been a result of wrecking the Corvette.

He whispered instructions for the police and her stupid husband. Obviously, he'd thought out the story. When the cops asked about the keys, tell them she must have left them in the car. If that canceled the insurance, then old dipshit Homer could buy more. Then, he dug into his pocket, glanced furtively at the cabbie, and handed her a pistol. It was small and black and terrifying. Did he mean for her to kill Homer Wayne?

No, he said, just get rid of the gun. She nodded tentatively but would do her Sunday best to obey his orders. Homer Wayne be damned. He was a dead man anyway.

He whispered Homer would be dead in less than a week. He could handle it. Macho man could handle anything. He was a plenty bad hombre while riding the high of sexual abuse—doubly mean as hell. She handed him a wad of cash as he stepped out at the convenience store on Northwest Highway.

He did not offer a thank you.

She taxied back to the condo. Christ, she had no idea what to do with the pistol. She stuffed it into a box of underwear, something she seldom had need of. She woke Homer and told him the Corvette had been stolen right out of the basement. He swore it was parked next to him earlier that morning.

Homer Wayne paid cash for a brand new one, also silver on a sunny Saturday afternoon. She hoped upon hope that the Prince would call that night. Homer was dumb enough, with half the money in Dallas, to continue working on Saturday nights on that nasty garbage truck. Maybe the Prince would call her that night. It didn't happen, and she was again unavoidably circling the drain.

Just before Homer Wayne left for work that evening, a Denton Police officer arrived to tell them her Corvette had been totaled following a car chase on I 35 in that city. The officer explained that when they received no answer on the DuPree home telephone, he had been ordered to drive to Dallas and find the owner. A telephone repairman working at the mansion had given the officer the condo address.

No matter, love, Homer advised her. They'd drive to Denton the next day, Sunday, and see the damage. She could keep her new Corvette. They'd leave the other for the Denton cops and his insurance company to dispose of.

CHAPTER 21: A Suspect in Hand—Sort Of

Kobok had failed to follow Homer Wayne and Eula Jo in his pickup on a bright Sunday. He'd learn later they drove out to inspect her wrecked Corvette. He drove back out to Spring Valley Road, played catch with Tad in the rising heat, consumed several beers, and had dinner with Anne and Tad. At 7:30, the answering service found him.

"Gotcha, dude," the clerk chirped. "Called your apartment, but we have this number on file, also." He made a mental note to keep better records of answering service ladies he'd known. "Call Sparky...is that right, Sparky?" When he didn't answer, she gave him a number which he dialed immediately.

"Uh...hello," a young female voice answered. It was not Stephanie "Sparky" Manners.

"Sparky asked me to call her at this number. It's Kobok calling."

Sparky's voice came on the line. "It's Gilberto Rincon."

"Rincon? You sound like Sparky." His humor was lost in transit.

"No, he came by here a while ago. We saw him through the peephole but didn't answer the door. He shouted he was gonna come back and kill me 'n Melinda both."

"When?"

"This afternoon."

"He's coming back this afternoon?"

"Oh, tonight."

Kobok called Hooper. He knew the DPD officer would have to pull his lieutenant's teeth to get overtime. "Bull, It's probably a false alarm. I'll go down and sit on these chicks' sofa for a bit. Betcha this Rincon never shows."

Hooper insisted that he go, too. Driving his personal pickup, he met Kobok on Northwest highway and caught a ride at the government's expense. They drove to the apartment on Webb Chapel Extension north of Northwest highway.

Kobok parked the Plymouth near the rear stairs and with Hooper, knocked at the second story apartment. Neither was surprised at the screeching music which struck them like hot wind when Sparky opened the door, nor that she was wearing only a G string. The "hot" and "cold" tattoos were prominent on her chest.

Also not surprising was a second young woman appearing from a hallway in a transparent robe. In a mini strategy session, they agreed Kobok would wait inside and Hooper would wait in Kobok's Plymouth in the parking lot. If a suspect approached, Hooper would lay on the Plymouth's horn.

Kobok said to the girls, "The pair of you get some clothes on." Both girls seemed disappointed. Both cops were well aware that sex with either would not only be illegal but could result in a combination of deadly diseases, none treatable by antibiotics and some unidentifiable.

Sparky led Kobock into a small kitchen and shouted over the din that she'd get dressed and turn down her music. The apartment was inundated with boxes, beer bottles, assorted fast food wrappers, and related junk. Kobok was certain he could get high from the heavy aroma of marijuana smoke on the air.

Suddenly, access to the only path around the small table was blocked by the biggest Doberman Kobok had ever seen. The monster's yellow eyes, formed narrow slits of carnivorous determination, seizing Kobok in an eye-ball death grip. If he wasn't going to have Kobok for supper, he appeared willing to maim him a bit for invading his turf.

"Whoa, Sparky," Kobok shouted over the noise. A mere .357 magnum round would only make the beast sick for a short while and probably in no way stifle his appetite for invader-flesh. He considered running for it, but the beast would have him by the ass before he made the kitchen door.

"Oh, man, that's just Bozo. He's only a pussy cat."

Bozo appeared likely to have consumed pussycats in lots of

five with possibly a crocodile or bear thrown in when available. The yellow eyes followed Kobok with a look mirroring Bella what's his name as Dracula when his victim was a trapped, dead-bang cinch. Kobok remained frozen in the kitchen doorway, stymied. If Rincon actually did show up, he'd be Bozo's pre-supper snack.

Sparky brushed by the dog in the narrow passageway around the table. "C'mon," she remarked back, then, "Dammit Bozo, sit!" Unbelievably, the animal sat.

Kobok mustered the grit to ease between the black menace and a pile of dirty laundry. The dog bared a mouthful of 100 plus teeth, eyes following Kobok peripherally without turning its head.

Bozo passed at crotch height at a distance of eighteen inches. It was apparent he could bide his time before grabbing a whole scrotum-load the first instant his silly mistress dropped her guard.

As he edged his way into the kitchen, Bozo formed up a barricade across the door to prevent any exit, better to cut and slash when the mark couldn't escape.

She giggled again, and then suddenly disappeared down the hall toward a bathroom visible at the end. As Bozo stood, drooling in anticipation, the screech of acid rock from several speakers around the apartment continued with enough volume to terminate the hearing of anyone within a hundred feet. The sound would muffle any screams when Bozo chewed off Kobok's genital area.

Kobok stood, unmoving against a combination sink-stove built into a cabinet, glued in Bozo's death stare. The dog began inching closer, confident of a sure bite deal, while shooting an occasional furtive glance at the door Sparky had exited. The coast was clear. Kobok pondered drawing his pistol, blowing off the dog's head, dashing down the stairs, and shooting the first small, dark-skinned man he encountered.

Then Bozo crept forward at a half crotch-crouch.

However, God sometimes watches over fools. Atop the stove was a large, iron skillet, which remarkably, in view of everything else visible in the place, was clean and free of debris. Apparently no one on the premises cooked. He inched a hand onto the skillet handle careful a sudden move would bring on instant death. When Bozo slithered to arm's length, he foolishly shot a final look back at the doorway before attacking.

At the instant the beast looked back, Kobok delivered an iron skillet, overhead smash which would have made the professional tennis crowd proud. The bonk of dog-head was imperceptible above the acid rock. Bozo never made a sound. He bellied up, dead center in the narrow pathway, urinating upward in a small stream that fell pitifully back on his hairy belly. He rolled accommodatingly onto one side, sort of under the kitchen table, spasmodically twitching a leg for several half strokes. Then he lay still, very still.

Kobok regretted the incident. He was actually very fond of dogs. Bozo was only stunned. He'd recover, but temporarily, he was on injured reserve.

Returning the skillet to the stovetop, he noticed a small indentation barely visible in the bottom.

Sparky pranced into the room wearing a see-through, butt-length nightgown.

"Oooh, Bozo," she laughed giddily, "You're supposed to sleep by the front door to keep out burglars."

"Yeah, ol' Bozo just crawled under there and went to sleep," although his comment was sort of true, he felt it was skillet or be de-emasculated.

At that instant, Hooper provided an escape from Bozo's terror, loud music, and half naked women. The Plymouth car horn was barely audible over the loud music.

Kobok looked through the door peephole. A small, slender man was standing on the landing of the stairs.

Carefully opening the door, he stepped around the piles of junk and assorted crap. He fumbled open the deadbolt, thankful Bozo wasn't close behind to eat choice parts, and started down the stairs as fast as years of sin and degeneracy would allow. After nearly bagging Rincon a few days earlier behind the Green Bull, he didn't intend to fail again.

As Kobok opened the apartment door, the man on the stairs suddenly realized the Plymouth horn was announcing his presence.

He jumped the stair railing, dropped ten feet, and ran directly back beneath the stairway, out of Kobok's sight. Kobok quickstepped down the stairs. The fugitive was heading for the street. Kobok shouted at Hooper to follow in the Plymouth as he chased the man through the complex then southbound on Webb Chapel Extension. Behind him, he heard the Plymouth roar into life. Hooper would have to swing the car around the complex before he could join the chase.

"Rincon, stop while you can!" Kobok shouted.

The runner continued in headlong haste, a half block ahead of Kobok. He stumbled and fell over a curb, then bounced up and continued South. The fall allowed Kobok to close to twenty feet. The man narrowly avoided being killed as he crossed the six lanes of Northwest Highway. Kobok near-missed a grip on long black hair as the man skidded into the 24 hour convenience store on the corner near Webb Chapel Extension. He could hear screeching traffic as Hooper busted the light in the Plymouth, crossing Northwest Highway.

Three customers and a clerk were inside: Two hookers waiting for their pimp to give them a ride home and a fat white kid of about nineteen, reading dirty books in violation of management policy. Kobok would later quip the kid was Howdy's illegitimate son. The clerk on duty was an illegal alien who spoke the mandatory fifty words or so of English necessary to find employment in similar stores across the metroplex. They later learned the ladies of the night, who had futilely hit on the penniless fat white boy for sex, money, or a cigarette, were leaving. The fleeing man stumbled through the door near exhaustion from the chase by a disheveled man waving a revolver. Fortunately, the two hookers jumped back inside the door.

Kobok probably should have determined something was amiss when the little man began screaming, "Heelllp, sonbitch," as he raced madly up and down the small aisles, knocking merchandise asunder. With another "heelllp, sonbitch, murder," down went a potato chip rack, bags flying.

"Hold it right there Rincon," Kobok ordered in cop-talk, pointing but fortunately not pulling the trigger of the revolver.

The man was on his third lap around the display shelves, hysterically out of control. So much for this tough guy Rincon, Kobok thought.

At that point, Hooper, screeching up in the unfamiliar car, misjudged the braking action and crashed the front third of the Plymouth through the doorway. Bursting glass and store parts exploded in an arc ahead of the car. Hooper, cigar stub in place, climbed bald head first out of the driver's side window of the battered Plymouth to join the chase.

"Heelllp, sonbitch, murder." Shrieked the fugitive, now on his fifth or sixth pass around the convenience store racetrack. Shorter laps were now necessary because the Plymouth blocked the first aisle, canceling any chance of escape via the door.

"Heelllp, sheeiit," screamed one of the hookers before fainting headlong in the debris.

"Heeey, man, you gonna get me fired off my chob, man. Get that dude outta here," ordered the clerk, trapped behind his checkout counter by the Plymouth grill.

"Screw me," declared the fat white boy from the dirty book rack.

"Forty bucks," called out the whore still standing.

"Everything's under control. Everybody's safe," Kobok added idiotically to the melee, knocking over another snack rack. "We're Federal officers," he waved his badge, the impact much like throwing a pebble at a charging bull elephant.

The man apparently didn't quite fully grasp the safety part. "Heellp, sonbitch," he continued to shout at volume audible two blocks away.

Kobok and Hooper managed to circle in opposite directions, cornering the man in the frozen food section. Cowering, he was trapped. Then, in the way of a man on the cusp of eternity, he lunged partially past Hooper. The three went down in a struggling heap on the tiled floor.

"Heellp, sonbitch," he was wearing out a line. He was on the bottom, face down. Hooper pulled out handcuffs and grappled for a wrist. The little man urinated all over the floor and Kobok's leg, rolling his head backward in a final plea with his murderers. The movement allowed full view of his facial features.

"Oh, hell," Kobok declared.

"Oh, hell," Hooper echoed. "Kobok, Rincon looks Vietnamese as hell to me."

He was definitely Asian, one of many in that area. He was also a poor candidate to be named Rincon.

"What's your name," Kobok holstered the revolver.

"Heelllp, sonbitch."

"Listen, sir, we're Federal officers. Rest assured, you're safe with us," When Hooper removed his knee from the center of the little man's back, the left sleeve of prisoner's shirt had been torn off. Blood trickled from his nose.

"Heellp," he wasn't yet convinced. They assisted him back to the devastation, formerly a checkout counter, where one whore, one clerk, and one fat white boy, dirty book dropping from his grip, stood locked in place by astonishment and unable to exit because a Plymouth was stuffed in the front door.

The whore on the floor remained flat on her back, a position indigenous to her profession.

"Officer, you gotta a cigarette." She groaned from the floor.

Hooper surveyed the smashed storefront and the wounded Plymouth. "Kobok, you need a brake job," he said matter of fact.

"Maybe we oughta sue the owners for building this store too close to the parking lot." Kobok could visualize the mounds of paperwork necessary to explain the slight misstep, as well as documents transferring him to a place where there was no electricity.

"Sue, man. No way. You ain't getting' my chob, man," retorted the store clerk from behind the lop-sided counter.

Sirens were audible in the distance—many sirens.

They spent the next hour making field statements to the swarm of DPD Officers who responded. Harper uncuffed the devastated prisoner from the door handle of the Plymouth just before a wrecker dragged it away. With the definitely-not-Rincon in tow, they began the impossible quest to bring order from chaos.

They had captured the man, but his name remained a fugitive from proper translation. The best phonetic spelling of his name they could manage was "No Fun."

"No Fun," a Chinese immigrant produced identification showing he was a resident of the apartment building next door to Sparky and Melinda. He admitted in broken English, he was a habitual peeping tom. The night before the chase, he had stood on the stairway watching Sparky and Melinda with not two but three male friends do their thing.

He had gone out for a walk at midnight. Seeing a light where he'd scored previously, he climbed the stairs to the mutual landing shared by the two apartments, hoping for Act II. Then madmen had begun chasing him. At first, he was trying for his apartment. Then he was fleeing for his life. Now, he was captured alive and was prepared for the gory execution that these pursuing devils would inflict.

They took a Polaroid after ascertaining date of birth, next of kin, and other vitals before sending him on his way with their best fabrication of how lucky he was they weren't deporting him or clapping him in a dungeon for being a peeping tom, for resisting arrest, and for causing Hooper to knock down a convenience store.

"Think he'll sue?" Kobok asked as the man scurried away.

"No, he thinks he's lucky to be alive." Hooper lit a cigar. "But some lawyer might."

Kobok directed the responding wrecker service to tow the damaged Plymouth to the ATF contract auto repair shop. Hooper dropped him at his apartment at 4:45 A.M. He dozed fitfully, dreaming of chasing small, black haired men.

CHAPTER 22: DEAL WENT SOUTH?

MANAGEMENT COULD HAVE DONE IT BETTER

Anne banged on Kobok's door at 7:15 A.M. "We hadn't heard from you champ," she looked genuinely concerned. "You look like you've been up all night."

Feeling and looking like death at dawn, he mumbled a short version of last night's deal. She said something about being late for work, pecked him on the cheek, and was gone. He shaved, showered, and found presentable clothes while wondering if he'd finally managed to drive her away.

Hooper called. "You up?"

"Yeah, getting no sleep always lights my fire. You don't suppose last night's caper could possibly be fatal for Howdy, do you?"

"Only if he contracts latent ear irritation infection syndrome from calling all his buddies trying to deflect blame." Kobok recalled Anne's admonishment about sprained ankles in Washington in event of trouble.

He hit the office at just past 9:00 A.M. and spent the next hour rough-typing about twelve pounds of reports explaining dents in official government equipment, particularly when said equipment had been driven through the front of a convenience store. If they hadn't "bent" the car and store he probably wouldn't have reported the little misdirection of chasing and subduing the wrong man. In fact, if accused of chasing somebody named "No Fun" up and down the streets of Dallas, Hooper and he would have disavowed any knowledge. However, the Dallas Police Department had their names, so vitals and explanation were in order.

At just past ten, Tootie strolled over waving the first gleaming axe. "The body shop just called and left an estimate to repair your Plymouth, Kobok. I never figured that old junker was worth that much."

"Oh my," he managed.

"$4757.95". She tossed the message slip atop the paper mountain already on his desk. "Howdy's gonna have a stroke," she smiled at the possible good news.

Kobok looked up, befuddled. "It isn't worth half that." He quickly considered the car repair estimate at the rate of exchange on the African Continent where he might just end up shortly.

Tootie walked back to her desk and 60 seconds later, buzzed him with an incoming call. "The contractor hired by the store to clean up your leavings is on the line with the estimate." He listened and hung up. Howdy, lurking nearby, waddled over. "Well?" he looked at Kobok.

"The good news is, the whole store won't have to come down. The repair estimate, however, is $174,500." Kobok studied the figures he had jotted down. "Maybe me and you and Hooper can go out there Saturday and fix the place." He grinned. Howdy did not.

Howdy strutted across the squad room to call an ally in D.C. If only Howdy had been standing in the convenience store doorway at 12:32 A.M. Suddenly, he reappeared at Kobok's desk.

"Did the whore really faint?" he smirked. "Y'all shoulda gotta Poloroid of her layin' in the middle of the wreckage. I woulda hung it on the wall over there."

"Dropped like a shot rhino," Kobok said, causing Howdy to cackle. He would have used the photo to try to convince someone he'd been involved in something besides reading dirty books.

"Okay, here's where we are," Howdy said. "Internal Affairs will fly down from D.C in a day or two. Have the facts straight. They'll need to talk to Hooper, too. I'll call his lieutenant."

"Brakes failed on worn out equipment," Kobok remarked dryly. "Maybe I'll sue the management. I coulda been scratched or something. I gotta have another vehicle. If it still runs, I can make do with that old Chevrolet pickup over in the pool."

Howdy shrugged indifference. As long as no one got their grubby hands on his brand new, low mileage Crown Victoria, he didn't mind if Kobok used the spare junker. "Get the reports done," he tossed over a shoulder as he walked away.

"Tootie has them all, Guv," Kobok called out. He turned back a third time with new ammunition. "IAD is scheduled to look into the gunfight at the OK Strip Club," he gestured. "They might wanna throw in an investigation about the old car in the convenience store screw-up while they're here. I don't need to tell you this will put you way up on the shitlist in Headquarters. You could land in South Florida on the dope and crocodile squad." He stifled a smile.

"Alligators." Kobok said softly.

"Huh?"

"Florida has alligators. Crocodiles come from Africa." Kobok eyed him evenly.

"Well...Y'all shoulda gotta picture of the whore," Howdy snorted and walked away, delighted someone was in trouble. Kobok was more than aware he could easily be stationed where crocodiles were used as pets.

Kobok had just stood up to walk down to the snack bar for a cardboard sandwich when Tootie pushed a call to his desk.

"Hello," greeted Marilyn Crawford.

"Hello, Mrs. Crawford."

"It's still Marilyn, Kobok," she purred. "I saw lights at the Beckman place. Nobody answers the door and I haven't seen the maid. Unless it's burglars, somebody's over there... or was." She giggled like a third martini. Kobok was wary but needed whatever investigative help he could get. Find Rincon and avoid Miami...or Mexico City...or the Sub Sahara.

"I'm uncomfortable about door traffic at your place," he said uneasily. "I'd like this to be strictly a business trip." He wondered if she had a taxi substation in the back yard.

"Well, boy, wait for dark and we can get naked and lay out in the backyard under a tree." He envisioned her doing just exactly that, probably with the good lawyer what's his name. But he also could not ignore her lead.

"Be right out," he hung up.

He walked to the motor pool and was surprised that the Chevrolet pickup started without a jump and also had gas in the tank. More surprising was that the A/C blew cold—sort of. He pulled into the Beckman driveway at 12:20 P.M. Banging on both front and rear Beckman doors, roused no occupants, including burglars.

Marilyn Crawford glided majestically across the immaculate lawn, wearing an expensive looking robe. When she got close enough, he observed that it must not have been too pricy, because it was semi-transparent, requiring very little cloth in its manufacture. The yard was full daylight in the midday sun. Perhaps the neighbors were elderly and couldn't see the semi-nude sideshow.

"Kobok, I may be able to shed some light on the destruction of Rosie's car." She turned back to her place, any thought of burglars apparently out of mind—if they'd ever existed. Standing mid-yard uncertainly, he snap-decided to follow the silk robe when a passing driver, in double, then triple take of Marilyn, nearly drove into a street-side tree.

Trading protect and serve for malice aforethought, then outright lust required only a few short steps across the manicured lawn, close behind an equally manicured backside.

"Cops are supposed to use the back door, fool," she turned in the doorway, her finer points showing prominently in the flimsy robe.

"I have trouble with direction." He squeezed past her through the massive front door into the refrigerated caverns of the big house.

"Drink, Kobok?"

"Far too often. Beer please, if you have it." He supposed if he was going to Hell anyway, more beer on duty wouldn't hurt.

"Yes, I keep it for my yard boy." She disappeared into the back of the house. Kobok wondered if the yard boy drank his beer in the library where he was sitting. Presently she appeared with not one, but two beers in one hand with her martini in the other. She then overpowered the seriously fatigued public servant and dispensed with the cumbersome, see-through robe quicker than the cat could go over a fence. She was having her way with poor Kobok before he could get two pulls on his first beer.

Later, when she was finished with her carnal use of him, she sat back on the leather sofa, still nude, and nursed her martini. "Is your husband still in Africa?" he asked lamely.

"No, as a matter of fact, he's down at the athletic club. He should be home any minute now." Her reply was incredibly even.

Kobok's adrenaline level exploded to a deadly level. He began frantically groping at scruffy clothes, expecting husband, assassin, lawyer and five or six guys from Internal Affairs to break the frame of the door simultaneously. Hell, they'd probably bring two news photographers and twenty or thirty senile neighbors, all aristocratically prepared to tell what ever story IAD ordered. Oh damn, what a score for Hell.

"You needn't worry my dear. He probably won't come into the library. He'll be too drunk to read, and besides he'll have Roger with him."

"Who the hell is Roger?" He desperately pulled on one boot. Great God, it was on the wrong foot. He struggled to switch it to the other.

"You've got your pants on backwards, darling," she observed casually.

Kobok figured if he could just find that dammed pistol, he might could shoot his way out the back door, or the side door if he could find one. The front door was probably blocked with a taxi load of lawyers.

"Roger is my husband's lover. They've been together many years. They share the master bedroom upstairs. My husband only keeps me around for appearances."

"Mother of...?" The sound of a key turning in the front brought instant, sharp pain to his chest, causing his heart to miss two, maybe six beats. He stood, fully intending to dive headlong through the library window, pants on backwards be damned.

"Sit down, Kobok, you haven't finished your beer," her tone as if she was ordering a hotdog at Cowboy Stadium.

He was frozen in room-center, trouser fly open because it

was in the back, holding a boot in one hand when the library door swung open. Contrary to her prediction of not entering the library, a tanned, graying man of fifty-five or so dressed in a yellow warm up outfit entered like he owned the place. Kobok assumed he did. He was fit, smiling, and only slightly drunk. A younger, larger version of the man, wearing a matching yellow outfit, was visible behind him in the entry hall.

The younger man didn't enter the room but stood smirking over his owner's shoulder at Kobok. He had to be Roger, the lover, Kobok concluded. If flight was necessary, he was going through and then over ol' Roger.

"Marilyn," the graying man greeted amicably, as if he was arriving at the Spring Rose festival.

Kobok realized in stark technicolor the silky robe was still lying on the floor.

She rose majestically, wearing only her martini. "Harold, this is Mister Kobok, a friend of mine."

Kobok had already concluded Harold would get the gist that they were acquainted because of her outfit. The yellow suit stepped confidently across the library with a diamond adorned hand extended, cultured nails visible.

"Kobok." He reached to Kobok's side and grasped the unextended hand. "It's nice to meet Marilyn's friends. We must get together for golf soon." He looked down at Kobok's trousers in reverse. "Got your pants on backward, dude."

"Good God," Kobok managed.

"Good, then, it's a date," he spun and walked athletically out the door, his wife standing in sculptured nudity beside the sofa. Roger was still smirking when Harold pulled the door closed.

"Uh, Ms. Crawford, we still need to know if Mrs. Beckman came home," he said in absolute idiocy.

"Well, I suppose I was mistaken. She must not be back. If she was, she'd have your old pickup towed by now. She glided over and locked the library door—a trifle late, Kobok thought. She turned back, lust glistening in untroubled, beautiful eyes. Hellfire, he thought, Harold and he were practically a golf twosome. Maybe Roger would caddie. He needed to turn the scruffy pants around anyway. Marilyn helped.

When he pulled out of the Beckman drive at midafternoon, he was no closer to bagging Rincon or to developing any additional real leads on the Green Bull bombing than just before he began chasing "No Fun" down Webb Chapel Extension.

CHAPTER 23: THE PLAN, PART III

On Monday, Eula Jo was stuck with Homer Wayne, who had slept the night because Sunday was his night off. Infuriatingly, he was up and about during the Monday daylight hours. The Prince had told her to go bomb shopping nearly a week earlier. Failure to comply with his every wish would be bad news for her. She gave Homer a spurious excuse and set out murder-purchasing in the brand-new Corvette the old fool had bought for her.

She managed to buy gunpowder at two locations as the Prince had ordered. The other parts were easier to find. She stowed the four heavy boxes marked "Danger—gunpowder—explosive" next to her on the seat while she chain smoked filter tips. When she parked in the condo basement late in the day, she shoved the powder in the little catchall behind the seat while balancing her cigarette between her painted lips. One spark, and her death march would have taken another turn completely.

Eula Jo did not have to endure the usual torture of gaps and irregularity in the Prince's calls. Her phone at the Condo jingled just after Homer left on Monday evening. "Bitch, did you get the stuff?" was his first question. She was delighted to say she had.

She picked him up at the usual convenience store at Northwest Highway and Webb Chapel Extension. He was standing in the darken corner of the parking lot. The place was shut down and the front boarded up with plywood. Some damned fool must have driven a car through the front door.

After they had openly ridden up the condo elevator, he brought up the new, foolproof plan. Attacks on the mansion were too chancy. It was only a matter of time before the police began suspecting her. They'd leave a little surprise beneath one of his garbage cans, like a great big bomb. She shuddered at how she'd deceived him when he smirked at how the cops had been so stupid thus far in not accusing her of trying to do in Homer. They had suggested, she just hadn't told the Prince about it.

Before they made the bomb, they'd need to slow trail the idiot to see just where to leave this new instrument of violent death. On the way to the offices of DuPree Corporation, where all of Homer's trucks would be stored, he made her stop at a drugstore and buy him a cheap pair of binoculars. They were rewarded with near-immediate success when the Prince saw Homer through the binoculars driving off the lot in Garbage Truck Number 14. A heavy-set black man was riding shotgun. For three hours while the Prince nursed a quart of his favorite cheap wine, they followed the bulky rig. Homer steered it skillfully up against what seemed to be a thousand metal trash dumpsters, the great truck hoisting the one-ton metal boxes like cardboard. At length, he drunkenly ridiculed any man stupid enough to work like a dog.

When Homer Wayne and his partner drove into a residential pickup area in the Oak Cliff District, where residents leave their garbage in the alley behind their houses in metal cans, the Prince came to life. By God, one of those would serve to end Homer's miserable existence. They saw they were in the right place. Rather, the Prince saw the proper place. What the Hell did she know?

The alley behind the residences made a gradual, sweeping curve around a long block, making view of the middle area of the alley impossible from either end. The metal can was lodged up against a frame, two car garage. From down the block, they would watch the alley and see the flash of explosion as the old fool disintegrated. They were beside themselves with glee. She drove them back to the condo where she proudly showed him the stash of death behind the Corvette seat. The next night would be the old bastard's last.

At the kitchen table, she watched him perform magic. He was so sexy taping and wiring. This time there was no clock, but the device had wires, tape, and batteries, and the rat trap.

A rat trap to blow a sorry old rat to Hell, he told her. Plenty of firepower this time. She sat and admired in passionate, perverted ignorance, that at minor misconnection would vaporize them at the kitchen table.

The mousetrap would be placed under the can with the spring drawn back. The weight of the can would hold the spring down. He then showed her that he would run leg wires up the back side of the can to twenty pounds of powder which he would leave inside the can. When the can was lifted, the rat trap would snap shut closing the little metal circuit he had just assembled, the current from the batteries would detonate the electrical blasting cap which would, in turn detonate the bomb.

Pieces of Homer Wayne, the old bastard, would be floating back to earth for two days. With a little luck, the blast would kill that fat black guy riding in the truck with him. No witnesses would be hunky dory. Again, she had no idea what a blasting cap was and dared not show her ignorance by asking. He was a genius. She also didn't know that black powder, even twenty pounds was still a low grade, amateur's set up.

The next night, he made her follow him on foot down the darkened alley, he gingerly holding the handful of death and she holding the flashlight from the Corvette. He tested the mousetrap two or three times in the dim light, satisfying himself that the can would hold the spring down and consequently not blow as they tried to walk away. He attached the wires to the trap, removed the can lid to disclose a load of unspeakable garbage, and laid the bomb carefully on top of the squishy mess. The open can unleashed horrible odors in the night air. She watched as his trembling fingers then inserted the little metal blasting cap with wires that trailed down from the can to the rat trap with a battery taped to it.

They parked three blocks away, eager to hear the end of Homer. Within thirty minutes, they saw the ponderous sight of Truck Number 14 lumber down the alley next to their trap. She could sense his urgency born of the violence as the minutes ticked off. She began massaging his crotch in the darkened car.

Down the alley by the booby-trapped garbage can, another player in the continuing saga of Eula Jo, Homer Wayne, and the

Crown Prince of Draconia had entered the scene. His name was Tom. Tom had been born out of wedlock in a car behind Mrs. Wheeler's garage and had lived as a homeless drifter in the area most of his life. His mother, Bridget, had no idea who Tom's father was and didn't care.

As Tom grew to adulthood, he became a giant with a mean temper to match. He had sisters and brothers, but he never learned their whereabouts. Having never done a productive act in his life, he spent most of his day sleeping and much of his nights prowling. When he couldn't beg food, he would resort to eating from garbage cans. Wherever Tom went, others quickly learned to move from his path, other males that is. It happened that Tom was a bigger lady's man than could seem possible. When he wasn't stealing or brawling, he was seducing. By this night, Tom had sired more illegitimate offspring than could be counted. His many street fights had left his ears mostly chewed off, his nose a mass of scar tissue, and his left eye permanently damaged. But, he was a stud and in the dark the ladies flocked to him.

Tom was waiting by the metal garbage can that night, standing by for a rendezvous with a lady of Asian extraction who would happen by at any moment. He hadn't eaten that evening and the smell of the metal garbage can, offensive to Eula Jo, was not nearly so unpalatable to one who hadn't eaten all day. He sat on the can, pondering if sex was more important than eating.

He hadn't decided when Truck Number 14 turned down the alley from the far end, the curve of the alley keeping the headlights from showing directly upon Tom atop the can. Tom was not one to lose heart and run at any small danger. He sat there, defiant, the oncoming truck lights tinting his sharp, piercing eyes to brilliant yellow.

Truck Number 14 was ten houses away, roaring. Then seven houses, then two, then the headlights caught Tom full in their glare. But, the best of those of the night have only so much courage before discretion seizes the better part of valor. Tom sprang from the can sharply, tipping the can away from his flight as he went.

An explosion scattered pieces of shattered garbage can, pieces of exploded garbage, and pieces of a giant, homeless alley cat known as Tom over a wide area of the neighborhood.

The explosion smashed the front windshield of Number 14, fifty feet away, but the shatter-resistant glass kept injury to Homer and his rider limited to a few scratches.

The blast nearly got Cleopatra, Mrs. Wheeler's Siamese cat, who, in season, was beating a path to Tom's garbage can when the tragedy occurred. There was another near-casualty three blocks away. Eula Jo nearly bit off the Prince's penis at the instant of the very, very loud thunderclap of the dynamite bomb. The lurch of teeth caused only minor teeth marks, but in an area of indescribable delicacy, any abrasion was multiplied by ten thousand.

Anne's bedside clock read 3:56 A.M when the telephone rang. Guessing it was for him, Kobok swung upright and answered it. "Tell me you're not the answering service?"

"Well hell no," Hooper gruffed. "Alarm office just called. Another bomb in the Homer Wayne DuPree parade to oblivion."

"Dead?"

"Him or the attempt? It's no and yes. This time looks like they booby trapped a garbage can out in Oak Cliff. Premature explosion. Someway, the dumb bastards missed again."

"Other injuries?"

"None I know of. I gotta go by the station and check out a car. Then, I'll meet you there."

Kobok beat Hooper to the scene to find Homer Wayne standing in the alley, flanked by a half dozen uniformed officers, a Dallas Fire Department engine crew, several reporters, and many curious neighbors. A blast hole approximately a foot deep was next to the remains of a garage, which itself had been blown largely into the back yard of the frame house to which it belonged. Remnants of a yellow tabby cat were strewn amid garage parts, garbage, and other debris.

"Kobok, some sumbitch is tryin' to kill me and Eula Jo." Homer Wayne remarked blandly.

"Looks like they got the cat instead, Homer," Kobok touched severed cat tail with the toe of his boot. A gray Siamese cat sat on a nearby garage roof, wailing into the night. Hooper walked up, carrying two lidded coffees in a cardboard holder from the Red Cross truck parked at the end of the alley.

Homer Wayne said, "Yeah, I saw the cat. Big yellow sucker jumped off the garbage can in the truck headlights, which ain't nothin' new. The can tipped, it was silver, then boom. Damnation boom!" He was wide eyed and had a cut on his nose, but to Kobok's eye appeared sturdy enough to drag the truck back to his parking lot by hand, if necessary.

But the need would not exist. Homer drove his garbage truck back to the company yard that morning, only after completing his night's run with a shattered windshield.

Before he resumed his route, Hooper and Kobok pulled him aside. "Goddamit, DuPree, when are you gonna get your head around the fact your wife is trying to kill your ass?" Hooper asked roughly.

Homer Wayne irately re-mounted his garbage carriage and with his helper, drove away.

Hooper, mad as hell, declared, "Kobok, if they don't get him killed soon, I'm gonna do it for them."

At 5:00 A.M. the humid morning air was thick with heat. At 5:25 A.M. daylight gave its first offering in the eastern sky. By 6:30 A.M. two additional ATF Agents, hearing radio traffic, showed up to help the Dallas P.D. Crime Scene Search Unit. Remnants of an electric blasting cap dug from the bottom of the blast hole and the presence of considerable unexploded black powder signaled the murder attempt was the work of the suspect in the previous bombing. Enough of the blasting cap had survived to determine the manufacturer, which would narrow the search down to about 10,000 people who could have legally purchased or stolen it.

By day-light-thirty, they had collected several metal paint cans of debris and photographed everything except the Siamese cat who'd gone home to breakfast before the camera guy got around to her.

Kobok and Hooper separated to canvass the neighborhood for several blocks in all directions, learning what they'd expected: Nobody saw anything. A lady three blocks away, halfway to the

Crawford mansion, awakened by the blast, reported hearing, then seeing a light-colored sports car, possibly silver, roar away recklessly immediately after the blast. They would never know for certain, but based on what they'd learn later, a bitten tallywacker is ample incentive for a rapid, reckless getaway. The bomber had been injured about as badly as the victim, painful evidence the plan had misfired in more than one way.

By nine A.M., the temperature had passed ninety degrees. Kobok and Hooper cleared the scene, leaving the bomb site abandoned to public inspection. Kobok dropped the evidence at the crime lab in the Southwest Institute and drove to the Cabell building to type a preliminary report.

Later in the day, two rats from Internal Affairs gave him a going over about his pursuit of the Green Bull suspect with shots fired. They also punched up how it came about that an innocent Asian suspect and his assigned Plymouth had ended up inside a convenience store on Northwest Highway. Their case had no legs and both they and Kobok knew it.

Around 3 P.M. his day was already approaching 12 hours. He locked his desk and called Hooper, hoping to meet at Adair's for one or three beers.

Hooper answered like an angry grizzley. "Have ATF's version of IAD been down to see you yet?" Kobok knew he would have to submit to interview with the DPD equivalent of the rat squad in the next day or two.

"Here, now. I was just fixin' to call you."

"Try to speed them up and I'll buy."

"Won't take long here, but we got another issue."

"Yeah?"

"You know that Kincaid guy you drove up to Denton to see?"

"Yep."

Just saw on the bulletin, Denton Police Department found his daughter's nude body in the center median of Interstate 35 on the southern edge of Denton. Truck driver spotted it in the tall grass...probably discovered about the time we were screwing around with Homer Wayne. I guess it's bad."

"Good Christ," Kobok spat. "You already know a very good suspect. Did he really dump her right next to the freeway?"

"Yessir."

"I'll stop by the morgue and handle the witness thing in case we get involved. Matter of fact, I'm already involved. I'll call you at home tonight,"

"Ten-four, Ace."

In sinking horror, Kobok sat back down and thumbed his Rolodex for the Department of Motor Vehicles in Austin, as he should have done two weeks earlier. The first inkling of guilt that had he followed thorough procedure after the Rosie Beckman firebombing, he probably would have figured out that whatever Kincaid told him was a lie.

He explained to the DMV clerk that the request was urgent and she agreed to do an immediate hand search of the title history of Rosie Beckman's long dead Cutlass.

In five minutes, she droned into the receiver information which began as routine and immediately burst into flames. "The car was originally sold new nine years ago by DuJohn Motors of Dallas to Thomas Medberry of Dallas. It was traded to Smith Motors of Dallas a year and a half ago, then purchased by Stephanie Manner, address on Webb Chapel Extension, Dallas. Next it was transferred to…the name's Hispanic, Mr. Kobok, I'll spell it for you: R-I-N-C-O-N, Gilberto Ibarra Rincon. Rincon transferred title to the last owner of record: Jerry W. Kincaid of Denton. Last week, the car was scrapped to a Dallas junkyard and the title surrendered to us. We got it yesterday."

Kobok, scribbling furiously, thanked the lady and hung up. The Cutlass had ended up in a junk yard. He figured that Rosie Beckman's apartment complex had ordered the car towed and that no insurance company had been involved.

He studied the notes. For openers, Rincon had not stolen the car from dancer Stephanie "Sparky" Manners. She'd sold it to him, probably for drugs. Rincon, the probable car fire bomber had somehow been in contact with Jerry Kincaid, whose daughter had just been abducted and murdered. Rosie Beckman had sworn she bought the car from Kincaid after answering a newspaper ad. How did the Cutlass get from Rincon to Kincaid in his own name and not through his dealer's license, to Rosie's apartment? Needless to say, there was a flat tire in used car land.

CHAPTER 24: THE CONSTABLE ERRS
AND THE CRIMINAL GOES FREE

Kobok threaded the old pickup up Harry Hines Boulevard to the morgue. In view of the dilapidated condition of the vehicle, he tossed an "ATF Official business" placard on the dash. In shock over the news he'd just received, he wasn't up for conversation with the overeager security guard.

Lynn O'Hara, her day of carving up humans completed, was in her first-floor office, scribbling in a folder. Kelly, her winsome assistant, from behind the receptionist's desk, gave Kobok an up and down as he passed through her invisible field of lilac fragrance and temptation. In red spike heels and a very short skirt, her expression signaled party time. Totally out of character, he didn't break stride as he entered O'Hara's office.

"Hey, Turkey," O'Hara looked over her half glasses. She was attractive even though she still wore her green smock which looked like she'd spent the day cutting up chickens. He supposed her duties weren't much removed from just exactly that. "You need to call me, buddy," she whispered.

He nodded. "Doc…er, Lynn, I want to see about the little girl that came in today from Denton… Sherry Kincaid."

Her eyes switched from flirt mode to all business. "That involve the feds?"

"She's… actually her father, is involved in a firebombing and probably something much worse."

"We haven't had a firebombing case in here in a month…?"

"No fatalities…until the kid showed up in the weeds."

"Uh, I remember the case. You want the file or, we still have the body downstairs." She tapped her pen on her desk.

"A Denton funeral home has already called for a time they can pick her up."

"Kelly's probably got that file typed and ready for storage. She'll help you. I have a full plate."

Kelly's bright blue eyes lit like a loaded Christmas tree when he asked her. "I just sent it up to the third floor. I don't like to go up there alone. Follow me and I'll find it for you." She sprang to her feet and out the door into a hallway. Kobok found following her was more pleasurable than he'd expected.

She punched buttons to allow access into the gloomy room of storage racks and the definite odor of morgue decay. Although no soft tissue ever made it to this place, the odor of the basement did. The smell did not, however, override Kelly's perfume.

She found the freshly filed folder immediately. While he looked at it on a small table, she slid behind him, reached around, and fumbled at his belt.

Agitated from the shock of learning Sherry Kincaid was dead, for one of the few times in his life, he said, "Sorry, kid, but I gotta take a raincheck." He wondered if he'd lost his mind.

O'Hara's report read: "Cause of death, gunshot, left center forehead. Nude body displays various burns consistent with lit cigarette. Wrists show evidence of restraint. Traces of semen found on victim's face" He studied the death photos. The burns, bruises, and abuse nearly caused him to vomit. The camera had been rotated to show Sherry's left ear still held a small, star shaped earring through a pierced earlobe. The right ear did not. He dug around in the storage box and found a small plastic envelope containing the single star from her left ear. The killer had either taken it as a souvenir or *it was still at the murder scene.* He removed an extra copy of the death photos and the envelope containing the earring, gave Kelly a peck on the cheek, and started out the door.

"Don't forget that raincheck," Kelly said softly behind him.

When he slid into the pickup, the uniformed security guard was standing a safe distance away. Apparently, he could read well enough to have heeded the placard on the dash. Considering Kobok's mindset, caution probably saved his life.

Kobok parked a block down from the Crawford residence.

Having made better time than expected on the North Tollway, he arrived at 4:15 P.M. He approached the Crawford house from the opposite side from Beckman's, thus being out of sight of lawyers or anyone else on sentry duty over there. Attempting some measure of stealth, he walked to the Crawford back door which was also out of view of the Beckman address. The kitchen door was open and his way was only barred by a screen door.

The screen door was unlocked. He stepped into the gleaming kitchen with the intention of calling Marilyn rather than wandering around the house and chance being kissed by Mr. Crawford's boyfriend. He was, all things considered, early and thought about stepping back outside. From down a hall he heard muffled voices. "Marilyn?" he said softly.

He moved toward the voices and found himself in the hallway outside the familiar library door. Not surprisingly, the door was slightly ajar, leaving a narrow peep-crack. Being deservedly snake-bit about other guests he'd met in the Crawford Library he peered through the opening to identify the guest of honor. What he saw was another episode in the continuing quest by Marilyn Crawford to be the sex model for all occasions.

Marilyn, not to his surprise, was nude and horizontal. She was laying full length, atop an equally nude, dark haired sex partner, both busily engaged in lovemaking of an unusual sort. He was retreating to leave by the same route he'd entered when slight movement of Marilyn to one side revealed the facial features of the partner she was smothering on the sofa. It was the stuff porn films were made of.

The sight of Rosie Beckman flushed and entranced in what she was doing nearly caused Kobok an involuntary "Oh hell." He leaned closer to confirm he was really seeing Rosie Beckman, when a footfall on the stairs behind him semi- stopped his heart. He whirled, expecting God only knows who to show up at that library door. But it was nobody of any significance; only Marilyn's husband, dressed for golf. He had half expected a full baseball team arriving to help with Marilyn's needs. Crawford waggled a finger in front of his lips. "Naughty, naughty," he whispered and without further comment or breaking stride, walked out the front door. Kobok heard an expensive car roar to life and slip away down the side driveway. Unable to resist, he peeped back through the door slit. The Marilyn and Rosie show hadn't missed a beat.

Angry and frustrated by the Sherry Beckman situation, he stepped in and loudly cleared his throat. Both occupants of the sofa bounded up and pulled on robes. Facetiously, he said, "Sorry, if you're into something, Marilyn, I can come back."

Marilyn said calmly, "Damn man, you could have knocked."

"Yep." He half expected her to decoy him by doing cartwheels, then try to steer him upstairs, a la lawyer Androvski, while Rosie beat it the hell out the front door. Rosie, struggling to put on the robe, stepped into the corner restroom.

Instead Marilyn invited him to sit. "I really do have information you might be interested in." She scooped up her martini from an end table. "Rosie is in the bathroom freshening up," she smiled. Another drink, apparently untouched, rested on the end table. "Can I get you a beer, Kobok?" she walked out of the room without waiting for a reply. That she had bothered to put on any clothes actually surprised him.

Rosie Beckman came meekly out of the bathroom, flushed, holding the robe around her. "Hello, Mr. Kobok," she greeted. "Where's Marilyn… I mean Mrs. Crawford," she reversed the name preference Marilyn had pressed on him.

"I'm here, dear," answered the see-through robe matriarch appearing in the doorway with a beer.

"Kobok," she continued, "Rosie and I have been acquainted since she was a child. Our relationship may not quite be what you think," she eyed him closely. He'd already pretty much figured out the "not quite what you think" part.

"Rosie came to me and admitted she hadn't told you all the facts about the car. The one that burned," she held his gaze, apparently seeking understanding.

"I understand, go on." He understood very little.

"Tell him, Rosie. Please be as frank as you were with me," there was demand in her expression.

"God, I don't know where to start." Rosie slumped in a leather chair. Kobok and Marilyn took seats on opposite ends of the sofa, about eight feet further apart than during original visits.

Kobok started on the beer. He refrained from saying, "From the beginning," and instead asked, "Something doesn't square, Rosie and now Jerry Kincaid's daughter has been abducted and murdered. I think it's closer to home with you than you've admitted...or maybe even know."

"Daughter...dead. Oh my God," Rosie began to cry.

"How and when did you meet Jerry Kincaid?"

"At a club on Greenville Avenue around Christmas."

"How and when did you meet Gilberto Rincon?"

"Through Jerry... Jerry Kincaid. About a month later. Maybe January of this year."

"Do you know how Kincaid managed to own the Cutlass?"

"Yes, he got it from Gilberto Rincon, but he didn't buy it. Jerry took the car away from him because Beto... Gilberto owned him money. Beto signed over the title. As well as I knew, Jerry had made him sign the title before he gave him the dope. Beto couldn't pay and Jerry kept the car."

"Did that piss Rincon off?"

"Oh yeah. His macho was kicked in the butt. He was plenty mad."

"Any idea why Kincaid titled the car to himself instead of kicking it through his car lot?"

"I don't know for certain, but I think it was gonna be his wife's car." At "wife" she shot a glance at Marilyn.

"You told me that first day you'd dated Rincon. Was that true?"

She again looked to Marilyn who sat solemnly sipping her martini. "Yeah, some."

"Did you date Kincaid?"

"Yeah, some," the glance at Marilyn reflected more than slight apprehension. "But listen, I couldn't stand Betto's arrogance. It didn't last long."

"Were you... intimate with one or both?" She'd said she'd made it with Rincon the first day he'd talked to her a couple of weeks earlier.

"I can't discuss... I mean that's too embarrassing to talk

about in front of Marilyn…er Mrs. Crawford."

"Oh, for Christ's sake, Rosie," snapped Marilyn Crawford in an uncharacteristic loss of cool.

"Tell him you were screwing half of north Dallas, or three fourths. And that doesn't count the women you've laid up with." She turned on the sofa to stare disgustedly out the library window.

A suggestion of more tears appeared in Rosie's dark eyes. "Yes, both."

"Kincaid and Rincon?" Kobok asked.

She nodded in agreement.

"Tell him the rest, Rosie," Marilyn interjected maternally. "The business about the night of the fire. While you were in there screwing Kincaid." Her countenance had expanded to extreme hostility.

The emotional eruption, Kobok thought, was not surprising in light of the sofa love scene he witnessed moments earlier. These two ladies were pretty chummy.

"Okay. Jerry was at my apartment that night. Beto had threatened to burn me out. Partly because I'd cut him off… I mean I'd stopped dating him and like I said, I stiffed him on a marijuana deal. He was plenty pissed at me and Jerry both. Jerry spent a lot of time at my apartment." She looked apprehensively at Marilyn, who continued her interest in matters outside the window.

"Beto was a wimp you see. He was scared of Jerry. Jerry is a tough guy. We both knew it was Beto that burned the Cutlass. Jerry told me to tell the cops I bought the Cutlass from him, then tell the cops Beto burned the car. Maybe, you know, they… y'all would screw with Beto."

Kobok bought the story except the Jerry as a tough guy part. The deal sounded dumb as dirt to him. They'd overestimated the give a damm factor of the law about routine firebombings.

"So you never actually bought the car from Kincaid?"

"No."

Realization suddenly struck Kobok like a clawhammer behind the ear. "Kincaid was visiting your apartment. He'd driven the Cutlass. There was no intention of leaving it with you. When Rincon firebombed it, he…and maybe you, fabricated the story of him selling the car to you to cover his ass for being at your place?"

She nodded, sobbing.

"And when you and I were chatting in your living room, that mope was hiding in the bedroom, listening?"

She nodded. "You got there that morning before his ride came to pick him up."

"Have you seen Rincon since the firebombing?"

"No, Jerry neither."

"Anything else?" he looked from lady to lady.

"I don't' think so Mr. Kobok." More tears flooded down.

"There is one more thing you little bitch," hissed Marilyn standing over the cowering Rosie.

"Kobok is going to use you before he leaves. Start stripping, you little harlot."

Rosie looked up, terrified. This was definitely not a simple relationship.

"Strip bitch," ordered Marilyn, trembling visibly.

"Marilyn you made me do it to that lawyer, Androvski while you watched. Please, not again." she fumbled with the belt of her robe.

Kobok thought Marilyn was certainly intolerant of her lover's sexual outlets in view of her own transgressions, a touch hypocritical.

"Gotta go ladies," he rose to leave. No one asked him to stay or even appeared to notice he was leaving.

As he cleared the library door, he overheard Marilyn say, "Rosie please, I'm sorry. You know you're everything to me." He didn't catch the conclusion as the great door closed behind him. He set his empty beer can on the stairs. Maybe Roger would trip over it and break his neck. He eased out the front door and walked down the circle drive.

As he reached the sidewalk, a taxi whizzed to a stop. Harless Androvski stepped out, handed the cabbie a twenty, and turned to Kobok.

Angrily he leaned close to Kobok on the quiet residential street. "Are you that goddamned fed who's been harassing my clients?"

Kobok bit his tongue and took a step backward. "Damn, counselor, you should try breath mints. And yeah, I'm the man of whom you speak."

"You're to make no contact with any member of the Beckman or Crawford families without my express consent."

"You know, Harless, all those stories you hear about federal agents and cameras and wiretaps, and crap?"

"I certainly do. Gestapo tactics."

Then it's ok to tell you that we have a camera mounted at the top of that utility pole two doors down. We have an outstanding shot of Marilyn Crawford meeting you in the doorway buck naked. Her husband doesn't give a damn, but does the Dallas Bar Association, your wife, and the news media know you're hosing both Marilyn Crawford and Rosie Beckman?"

"Uhhhh…"

"Then I guess I'll interview who the hell ever I please. Have a nice day, sir." Kobok walked away.

CHAPTER 25: Professionals, Almost to the End

As he pulled away from the Crawford house, he wouldn't have been surprised to see the president of the Drover's and Merchant's Bank of Amarillo riding up the driveway on a three-legged zebra. He pondered Eula Jo DuPree and Marilyn Crawford, practically neighbors, socially a thousand miles apart, but 9morally, both dead even with the floor.

He drove the pickup to a payphone, called Kincaid Motors in Denton, received no answer and headed home. Tomorrow, he'd have a come to Jesus meeting with Jerry Kincaid, tough guy. Kincaid wasn't going to like it worth a damn.

He spent the night at Anne's and called Hooper, explaining he could make the trip to Denton alone. He would only learn of the plight and subsequent flight of the two stalwart IAD rats later. Had he known Act II of Ringling Brothers South was occurring while he played Scrabble with Tad, the kid would have whupped on him worse that he actually did.

He'd never see the report, but the IAD investigation had gone somewhat as follows:

The pair of Howdy's former comrades had proceeded via a rent car directly to the Green Bull, arriving at about the time Kobok had used Anne's shower. Tony Bones had greeted them into his office. Then on learning that their inquiry into the shooting incident of the two nights previous, could reflect poorly on Kobok he considered making sure neither man would live to see another sunrise. Fortunately, Bones thought better of erasing two Washington bureaucrats.

Tony and his big bouncer, Carlo, both verified that the involvement of Kobok had been completely defensive. Both insisted that only a miracle had prevented Kobok from stopping a bullet from an unprovoked attack by the assailant beneath the railroad trestle a block away. When Bones declared with cold-eyed finality that the enemy of Kobok and Hooper was also his enemy, the air undoubtedly grew Antarctica-cold. At that point, know it or not, the office-oriented IAD types were beaten, and would have done well to catch the next flight back to Disneyland East, cop speak for D.C. Tony Calbacci then informed them that Sparky had not reported for work that evening.

The IAD men then navigated by map in the strange city to the address on Webb Chapel Extension reported by Kobok. They intended to find him in the wrong for at least a minor infraction or two. By chance, they tried the Asian's door first. It was on the same common stair with Sparky's place. No Fun understandably refused to answer the door so the two then knocked at Sparky's apartment.

She appeared at her door in her transparent nightgown and being no virgin, promptly offered to engage either or both men in a sex act or multiple acts of their choosing for the small sum of only fifty dollars, slightly more for certain exotic variations. Her roommate must have been out searching for an off-duty company of firefighters to bring home, so the bedroom was apparently empty.

Both stalwarts of the Internal Affairs Division eventually declined only after a lengthy discussion. They were probably from the school of agents who seldom had wandered far enough from the office to learn that such carnal opportunities existed in the more sordid parts of the world. Learning that the two somber appearing men were, in fact, sent more or less from the same office as Kobok, Sparky dropped the invitation of sensual pleasure and ushered both men into the cluttered apartment.

The afore-described fugitive, No Fun, now convinced that he was the target of a horde of violent, giant lunatics sent to chase, beat, threaten, torment, and eventually end his miserable life, saw the two IAD men on the patio. He had cringed inside the apartment, praying to the great spirit of his ancestors for the two monsters to leave. With a speck of luck, he could hitchhike to Houston and perhaps quietly slip aboard a merchant ship bound for Russia. When, through a crack in the drape, he saw

Sparky allow the two IAD guys inside, he seized the opportunity to bolt for the stairs in a desperate dash for the Houston Ship Channel. However, destiny being what it was, he wasn't going to make it.

Bozo figured heavily into the next part of the story. Yes, poor old bopped-on-the-head-with-an-iron-skillet Bozo. Who would have figured that being brained with an iron skillet would create a certain sense of caution in the big critter?

Bozo, near to but not quite across the finish line to mandatory retirement, having lain under the kitchen table of the messy apartment for many hours, began to revive at about daybreak. By noon, he had dragged himself into the hallway near the front door of the apartment. Since Sparky and her roomie weren't the types to pay much attention to detail of any sort, they hadn't noticed that Bozo had resided on the floor in a state of semi-consciousness longer than normal. They probably assumed he was sleeping. Well, actually he was, sort of. He was about to fully recover, however, much like a NASA moonshot blastoff.

When the IAD men had appeared at the apartment door, Bozo was in the distant twilight of recovery. When they stepped into the apartment, Bozo had achieved a sort of intermediate state of dog-amnesia. His last real recollection was the night before when he had been lining up for a bite or six of some damn fool who had been foolish enough to enter "his" kitchen and lean against the cabinet to be eaten at his leisure.

The sudden entry of the two IA men suddenly snapped closed the gap into Bozo's recollection. The yellow-eyed monster sprang back to life, roared to his clawed feet, and took one large, bloody bite out of the left ass-cheek of the younger, fatter man, while fantasizing he was eating where he left off the night before.

The IA man responded with a series of agonized screams which could be heard three blocks away at the convenience store where workmen were laboring overtime to repair the devastated front of the store. Desperately, the pudgy IAD man, Bozo with a firm bite on his fat butt, cleared the door immediately behind the fugitive, No Fun, who was fleeing down the same stairs.

The first move of the tall fellow, who had been one of New

York's finest before becoming a Fed, was to draw his issue .357 magnum revolver and shoot what he thought to be dead center between Bozo's yellow eyes. He missed. The man's second move was to follow his partner down the stairs uncertain of this strange den of disaster, fourth in line behind No fun, the fat IAD guy, and Bozo holding a mouthful of IAD flab. For all the hell he knew, Sparky had in reserve a dozen more of these man-eating beasts set to devour all the IAD men Washington could offer.

Sparky's first move was to lose her bladder at the explosion of the magnum revolver at close quarters. She then followed the first two out the door, not for any reason exactly. Runnin' is runnin'. She simply decided the thing to do was to run after everyone else who was running down the stairs.

No fun, seeing his fate doomed by pursuit of another posse of armed madmen, this time accompanied by a semi-naked woman, again jumped from the stair-landing. Only this time, he tripped and went over head first, landing head down on the concrete sidewalk below. The result was a concussion.

When the Dallas Police began arriving in large numbers, they quickly learned that for the second night in a row, ATF was responsible, and the victim was the same Asian. The night before, they'd only softened him up some, this time they'd damn near killed him.

Dallas Fire Department ambulances eventually transported all four to Parkland Hospital; No Fun for a concussion, the taller man for chest pains, Sparky for nervous anxiety brought on by the untimely runaway of some guy named "Bozo" for whom she kept screaming, and the shorter, fat IA guy for being bitten in the ass.

No Fun, still unconscious, had been taken under the protection of the Chinese-American Association, who would allow no further interviews in the absence of legal counsel. The IAD men had already declared that Kobok and Hooper were blameless in both events of the preceding evening hoping to get back to the safety of a secure office in Washington. Kobok and Hooper were free men, again. IAD agreed that Kobok's shooting incident was justified, that the previous night's pursuit of No

Fun was acceptable procedure, and that no further inquiry was necessary.

When he eventually learned of the second No Fun escapade, Kobok felt much better. An IAD rat bit in the ass is worth two in the bush.

CHAPTER 26: Who Ever Heard of No Damned Hit Woman?

As Eula Jo drove the Prince back to Northwest Highway that Wednesday morning, they had no way of knowing Tom got his on the garbage can and that damned Homer had not. They assumed the bomb had finally canceled Homer. She had bitten the Prince's man-part severely. He'd rewarded her with a slap in the face which raised a blemish enough to require an elaborate story as to its origin. No story at all would probably have been enough. Her face was so street-worn and swollen from the Prince's sadism, an extra lump or two would have been difficult to detect.

Thank God, the Prince's anatomy would recover. She was sure the police would show up to tell her that bastard Homer was finally dead.

She was disconsolate to the point of suicide that morning when Homer came chugging up in his old pickup at the regular time. But screw suicide, Homer was supposed to die, not her. The rotten, low life loser. Why wouldn't he just damned die and let her get on with her life? When he told her of the bombing, she froze in the kitchen in terror that he could read knowledge in her face like those damned cops. He described the last, fatal leap of the big, yellow cat and the following blast. Holy Hell cursed by a stupid cat.

She was speechless, enraged, then outraged, because he used her that morning. Apparently pitched off keel by the night's events, he was more forceful and virile than he'd ever been. He took her to bed on the new mattress, having his crude way with her. Always before, she had been able to con and control, but this morning he used her roughly, although with a certain loving tenderness. She hated him with a loathing beyond description.

Her breasts and private parts were inflamed and tender from the Prince's brutality. She bore Homer's touch with an agony in a distant world from the mistreatment of the Prince. She struggled to avoid vomiting as he sated his lust. Later, when he snored beside her in the new bed, she contemplated slipping into the kitchen, finding the biggest knife in the house, and slitting his filthy throat as he slept, the horrible monster. But she couldn't summon the courage.

As Homer snored on the cement bed, she died her usual thousand deaths waiting in agony, to tell the Prince they had failed again. When the telephone jingled its joyous tune, she pulled the bedroom door closed. She rushed toward the instrument in the den at a run, pre-blessed in the pleasure of talking to him.

But it wasn't him. Instead, it was a voice from the past. A voice seeking a handout, loan, stake or any leg up on a little cash. It was a voice inadvertently sent to provide the final solution to the Homer Wayne DuPree nuisance. The call was obviously divinely dispatched, although she didn't snap on it immediately.

"Hello."

"Eula Jo?"

"Yeah." Realizing it wasn't him, she began sinking like a burst balloon. Probably one of her hayseed relatives wanting a handout. She had guessed the financial motive correctly, but the identity was a shocker.

"This is Ida. Ida Sue Price, remember?"

"Yeah, sure Ida… How ya' doin'?"

"Oh, okay, Eula Jo… I guess. Heard you struck gold, kid."

Ida Sue Bolinski had been born 37 years earlier in rural Ellis County, south of Dallas, not far from the old haunts of Eula Jo. Although Ida Sue was several years older than Eula Jo, they'd been acquainted for years. During Eula Jo's formulative years in breaking into the prostitution world, Ida Sue had been a sort of mentor. Later, when both had gotten hooked up with Dallas pimp LeBradford "Quick" Lafayette, they had done threesomes with tricks who were willing to pay for multi-girl sex.

Eula Jo, a more adventurous type than Ida Sue, had soon

dropped Quick, spending the next several years as a "solo". The pimp/hooker relationship is hard for the straight world to understand. Whores, with few exceptions, genuinely loved their pimps. Eula Jo, who'd never loved anyone or anything except herself before she met the Prince had no problem with the separation. Since Quick chose not to murder her for blatant disloyalty, she moved on. She maintained a loose relationship with Ida Sue for the next couple of years, even joining in a group sex show with her old friend occasionally.

Ida Sue, however, had stayed put with Quick. Then, eight or so years earlier the inevitable march of age, compounded by harsh life on the streets, had edged Ida Sue past the expiration date. Quick beat her with a coat hanger and tossed her out on the street.

Ida Sue walked down to a pawn shop on Cedar Springs Road and with her last $27.00, bought an RG Rohm .38 caliber revolver and six bullets. She walked back to the apartment and gave Quick all six rounds, rendering him deader than hell. She waited there for the police and entered a guilty plea in Dallas County. The judge gave her a rather harsh sentence for a pimp killing because she had previous felony convictions: twenty years in the Texas joint.

Now, at a million miles of road age thirty-seven, she was paroled back to Dallas with little hope for assimilation into society. She spent a few nights at a homeless shelter and two nights in an abandoned car with three guys. The night's rental there was one blowjob apiece. After prowling her old haunts for several days, she was actually reduced to begging passersby for coins. She learned from another whore, Eula Jo had hit the jackpot. It took some doing, but in two days, she had telephoned Eula at the Condo.

"Eula Jo, I guess ya' know I been in the joint."

"Yeah, for doin' Quick, It's okay, Honey. That asshole needed killin'."

"God I'm glad ya' feel that way. I was afraid ya' was gonna be pissed."

"No, Ida Sue, hell no. When did ya' get out?"

"Last week."

"Whatcha gonna do now?"

"I dunno. I gotta find somethin'. Got no money. I'm really on my ass."

Ida Sue gave her the address of a convenience store on Cedar Springs and in an hour, they were in a passionate embrace at a motel on Harry Hines that specialized in rooms by the hour. Eula Jo had paid cash for two hours. She'd be home before stupid Homer woke up that afternoon.

"Eula Jo, I gotta get aholt of some money somehow." She noticed the bruises and welts on Eula Jo's body but declined to ask.

As Eula Jo pulled on her pantyhose, she said, "Well, hon, all I got on me is two hunnert." She was "short" of cash because the Prince had demanded more and more lately.

Ida Sue took the money, loaded Eula Jo up with a lingering kiss, and said, "Christ almighty, Eula Jo. Two hunnert dollars. Can I wash your car or somethin'. For that kinda cash, hon, I'd do anything…any damned thing atall."

The blast of opportunity struck Eula Jo in the chest like a stone. "Ida, you jus' got out for murder."

"Yeah, Eula Jo. Christ, you already know all about that." The worn face showed confusion. Was Eula Jo going to renege on the two hundred?

"Ida Sue, I trust you never to repeat this. Swear to me now you won't."

"I swear to God," Ida Sue committed blasphemy while telling the first lie of her part of the conspiracy. Eula Jo could not have reasoned that across the world, prisons are loaded with inmates who had received sworn assurances from conspirators that words would never be repeated.

"I…I mean, we… want ya' to shoot my old man, Homer Wayne DuPree. I can pay you to do it. Is a thousand enough?"

"We?"

"Yeah, I got this sexy, handsome dude…he's from a royal family."

"I still get the two hunnert now?"

Eula Jo nodded. "Absolutely, hon. The Grand comes after you off the old puke."

For a thousand bucks, Ida Sue would have immediately agreed to parachute from the Diamond Shamrock Building blindfolded holding a roman candle in each hand. Completing that jump, however, would require some further thought when she reached the precipice. "When?," she asked.

"Tonight, if I can lure the old prick to the right place. Like Quick, the old bully turd needs killing."

Ida Sue, fumbling on shoes, was astonished. "I ain't got no gun, but hell yeah baby, I'll do it," she held out a hand as Eula Jo handed over a wad of twenties.

To Eula Jo's brain, which grew increasingly weak north of her ears, a murderer was a murderer. If you'd done it once, why not again? It never occurred to Eula Jo that Ida Sue had shot and killed her pimp in a fit of passion partially brought on by heavy narcotics dependency and partially for the bizarre romantic attachment of thwarted whore to pimp. She was no more capable of correctly completing a contract killing than Eula Jo, or Bambi, or Santa Claus.

Eula Jo drove them to a nearby burger joint where she was mildly surprised to see Ida Sue devour her meal like a hungry dog. Then, feeling proud of her self-initiative, she found a gun store on Cedar Springs. She bought a cheap, silver plated, six shot, .32 caliber revolver. Using her Texas driver's license as identification, she signed the yellow federal form swearing she was not a convicted felon nor a mental defective. The form contained no restriction on shooting her husband.

When she ordered six rounds of ammunition, the salesman advised store policy required ammunition be sold in boxes of fifty rounds only. She paid for the fifty, asked the man to load the gun, and told him to keep the remaining rounds. The following week, the salesman would not only vividly recall the two painted ladies, the partial box of cartridges would still be on the shelf behind him. What went unsaid, was that a .32 caliber cartridge, when fired, was one of the slowest velocity rounds available. A .32 was a very poor choice to attempt to use for murder of another human being.

Eula Jo left Ida Sue on Cedar Springs with instructions to call the condo at eight sharp that evening. If a man answered, which was unlikely, hang up and call back in ten minutes. Ida Sue Bolinski Price stepped out onto the sidewalk, drifting on a cloud of prosperity. Good God, a thousand dollars, just after she'd been considering foraging for lunch in the nearest dumpster. Surely when the time came, she could close her eyes and bust six caps. If only one hit some feeble old man, it oughta kill his ass. Seemed like an easy kill.

Ida Sue had called twice that evening before the Prince called. Giddily, she explained her version of the plan to rid the world of Homer Wayne.

"Never heard of no damned hit woman, bitch," he declared before ordering her to pick him up at the usual spot. She called Ida Sue who had been standing by at a payphone outside a tavern on Cedar Springs for two hours. She'd fetch the Prince, then Ida Sue. Then they'd work up the final approach to ending the life of a useless old reprobate.

On route back to the condo, the Prince drove, with both women sharing a very tight space in the passenger seat. They sat around the kitchen table, drank cheap wine and shared several lines. Eula Jo was near to bursting with nervous anticipation. The Prince raised a valid point. Shoot the old fool the very next morning after the trash can bomb screw up would give the life-insurance company grounds to deny the claim. Worse, the stupid cops had no clue as to Eula Jo's possible involvement now. Murder so soon after the last attempt might even be a clue to them. Eula Joe sat in silent dread. If he knew the damned cops had actually accused her of being involved, he might chuck her out the window.

Instead, he declared, they wait another day until Thursday night. Eula Jo would call the stupid Dallas cops and report threatening calls, creating a record of her danger. Then when dummy Homer Wayne wandered in she'd unload her fear to him. That way, they could lure him to a remote location by having her call him and say the terrorists had kidnapped her. Homer would rush to the rescue, and bang, bang, Ida Sue would let the air out of him. Easy kill. A specialist in sucking up the fruits of others, the Prince offered nothing favorable about Eula Jo's plan to off Homer.

That night, he bedded them both. Although rough with Eula Jo during the session, he was easy with Ida Sue. He couldn't quite grasp his reservation for treating her more gently. What he unconsciously sensed was that she'd been locked up with a prison full of women for years. Ida Sue was a bigger, physically tougher specimen than Eula Jo. In the widely practiced same sex life in her prison unit, she'd become more pitcher than catcher. Although still capable of sex with a man, or with a donkey if the money was right, if this little wimp dished out too much rough stuff, she'd climb off the cement bed and kick his ass.

Eula Jo left Ida Sue at the Condo while she took him back to Northwest Highway. When she returned, Ida Sue hit on her to stay the night. Since she laid the previous two nights in an abandoned car, she would have slept in a closet. Eula Jo offered her use of a shower and a spare bedroom. When idiot Homer came home, she told him Ida Sue was her cousin and needed to spend the night. Homer hugged the new addition and invited her to stay as long as she needed a bed. Ida Sue studied Homer closely. He was a hell of a lot more loving and caring than that little creep Eula Jo was hung up with. Strangely, she felt a certain grandfatherly affection. She'd definitely have to shoot him with her eyes closed.

CHAPTER 27: CLUES TO KILL FOR

Denton, the county seat of Denton County, a burgeoning city of 60,000 or so in 1984, was in full sway when Kobok herded the old pickup into a parking spot in the "police only" lot that sunny Thursday morning.

When he inquired to the smiling, graying, front desk clerk about the Sherry Kincaid murder, he elicited raised eyebrows from her as well as from a young, male uniformed officer standing nearby. The officer stepped closer. His dark hair close cropped, he wore a name tag which identified him as C. Dykes. "And you'd be?," he asked.

Kobok, his badge case already in hand, identified himself.

The officer motioned him away from the desk. "Tom Wafer, one of our homicide guys is handling that. He's back in his office. Kobok, I found that kid's body. How's ATF involved?"

"Jerry Kincaid's name was on the title of a car firebombed in Dallas a couple weeks back. We now have evidence to show he was closer to the offense than he first admitted. I was up here and talked with Gammon in narcotics at the time."

He grinned. "Narcotics is basically night work. Al won't be in before noon. Lemme introduce you to Wafer. He'll be glad to hear anything relevant."

Wafer was in his late thirties, well over six feet, husky, with close cut sandy hair. He rose from a small desk and shook Kobok's hand at Dyke's introduction. "Have a seat… Cliff, stick around," he said to Dykes.

Kobok explained the Beckman Cutlass investigation, the facts provided by the DMV, the bombing of the Green Bull, and his chase and shooting incident with a suspect he strongly believed to be Gilberto Rincon. He did not include the account given by Rosie Beckman in Marilyn Crawford's library. "Gents," he concluded, "although we... Bull Hooper from Dallas Homicide and ATF, haven't a clue to Rincon's whereabouts, I'd put Rincon near or at the front of the line as a suspect in the Sherry Kincaid murder."

Wafer said thoughtfully, "Murder is a step from a car title and a firebombing, but stranger things happen."

Kobok leaned forward. "I actually had a talk with Rincon the morning after the Cutlass firebombing. At that time, he lived... or stayed on Webb Chapel Extension off Northwest Highway. Not there now and as I said, he's in the wind."

"Well," Wafer sighed and leaned back in his chair. "We gotta hell of a mess. Kincaid says he don't know crap about nothin'."

"Rincon is the type of cowardly little arrogant wimp who would let Kincaid take his Cutlass away from him, then retaliates by firebombing the car, then murdering his daughter. He gets tossed out of a topless joint, then comes back in and plants a stupid, amateur black powder bomb in the men's john with the place full. Two dead in that deal. He's capable of three murders as long as he can plant a bomb and run or retaliate against Kincaid's daughter when he was afraid of Kincaid, himself."

Both Wafer and Dykes nodded agreement. "Any chance of getting anything in writing?" Wafer asked. "Usually the feds are pretty close with facts."

Kobok said, "Get a stenographer in here and in fifteen minutes I'll load y'all up on all we got. You're welcome to my notes, but it's gonna be hard to make head or tails..."

Wafer dialed the intercom. "Fifteen minutes. She's in with the chief."

Kobok asked, "Cliff, how'd you happen to find the body. I saw the autopsy photos. She'd been laying there a couple of days or more."

Dykes cleared his throat. "We were lookin' for evidence or anything relevant to a car chase we'd had last Saturday morning. At just past 9 A.M. we hadda call of a silver Corvette parked on the median about a half mile South of where we found Sherry's body. Squads, including me, gave chase. A couple miles and the Corvette driver tried to pass on the shoulder at around 120 miles plus. Rolled that sucker onto the service road, bailed out and we never saw him."

"Never saw him again?" Kobok asked.

"Never saw him, period. The Golden Triangle Mall is on the opposite side of I 35 there. We figure someway he got over or under the freeway and somebody gave him a ride. That Mall has plenty of empty shops. He also could have hid out somewhere in a rat hole until we gave up. Maybe somebody gave him a ride from the scene of the wreck. We dunno."

Dykes said, "Couple days later, I got to thinkin', looked further back from where the chase started, and bingo, I find the little girl's body. Hell, I was lookin' for a stash tossed out."

Wafer said, "We hauled half of Denton in here. Not a witness who saw squat ever developed. Think it's good to put out an APB on this Rincon?"

Kobok said, "Check your computer. Dallas Homicide already has. Rats in holes are hard to find. He's a Hispanic male born on Halloween, 10-31-63."

Wafer scribbled on a notepad.

"Did the Corvette provide anything?" Kobok asked.

Wafer looked up. "It's still in our pound, but we didn't give it much going over. Never connected it to the girl's murder."

"The body was found nude. Find any clothes?"

"No, they probably went bye-bye in any one of a bunch of dumpsters.

Kobok thought of Homer Wayne when he heard "dumpsters".

The stenographer, a pleasant young lady with long black hair, entered. Kobok spent twenty minutes detailing facts as he knew them. Then he called ATF Oklahoma City on Wafer's telephone. Kobok flipped it to speaker phone.

The agent responsible for the inquiry happened to be in the office. "Tilley," he answered.

Kobok knew Tilley well. "What ever became of that inquiry about Jerry Kincaid, Denton, Texas used car dealer? FBI entry several years ago."

Tilly laughed into the phone. "Clerk wrote Kincaid's ID number down wrong. Took me two weeks to sort through.

Kincaid was arrested by the Oklahoma P.D. for statutory rape. Apparently had a fling with a sixteen-year old girl. Just learned yesterday. He kept it close to home. It was his sister. Case was dismissed without prosecution. You know the deal, Kobok, little sis declined to prosecute. Nasty, but not unusual. I called your office with the info this morning."

They hung up. Kobok asked, "Any problem if I take a look at that Corvette?"

Wafer said, "It's already had the routine police pound inspection. Help yourself. By the way, it was reported stolen in Dallas on Saturday. Dunno when or if the insurance company will claim it."

"Who reported it stolen?"

"Dunno, we got the call from the insurance company."

"Got a name?"

Wafer shuffled papers on his desk. "Uh...Dixon Mason General."

"No, I mean the owner's name?"

"Uh, DuPree. I called three times, got some hateful woman and am holding fire trying to figure what to do next."

"Dupree, huh?" Kobok refused to believe without verification, that the coincidence of names with Homer Wayne was anything more than simple chance. He did not jump to the standard cop conclusion that coincidences didn't happen in murder cases.

The Denton impound lot was a contract operation, housed in a junkyard South of town. The owner looked at Kobok's credentials and pointed out the car. The Corvette was badly damaged with considerable tearing of the fiberglass body as opposed to the usual damage to cars made of metal.

In an hour's inspection, he located what he thought to be a bloodstain on a rubber mat covering the passenger floor. When he pulled the rubber mat free for closer inspection, a tiny glint along the rocker panel caught his eye. He dug it free with his pocket knife and compared it to the morgue photo. It was a star shaped earring which had been pulled free of the little clamp that went behind the ear to hold the insert against the earlobe. To the naked eye, it appeared identical to the earring in Sherry's ear in the death photo. He pondered that if the pound routine search had not found it, would another search be done? He stuffed the little piece in an envelope and then into his pocket.

Giving the Corvette a last glance, he spotted a small, wadded scrap of post-it note in the console. Scrawled loosely were the words "blk powder, tape, battery, rattrap". Using a rubber glove as a shield, Kobok stuffed the scrap in his pocket, thinking it would probably be of no significance.

He drove to Kincaid Motors in the sinking realization that somehow, if he'd followed up on the questionable Cutlass title, the Sherry Kincaid situation might have turned out differently.

Kincaid met him in the doorway. Kobok motioned him back inside. He showed the highly nervous man the star earring he'd just recovered.

"Where…?"

"From a stolen Corvette that rolled off I 35 Saturday morning. Look familiar?"

"Mother of God," he gasped. "It's like the ones Sherry has… uh had, a box full of them." He slumped in his chair. "The funeral was only yesterday."

"Kincaid, I know the true story on the Cutlass. You didn't sell it to Rosie, but you did flim flam her ex-lover Gilberto Rincon out of it. That's before you were screwing Rosie. I know you were present in Rosie's apartment the morning I was there. I'll speak to the U.S. Attorney and see about charging you under Title 18, Section 1001, U.S. Code, tomorrow."

"Whut's that mean?" he stammered.

"False Statement to a Federal Officer. You hear it mis-stated on the news as "lying to the FBI." You shouldn't have lied to me about the Cutlass's history."

"Oh for Christ's sake, man. You can't. We jes' lost Sherry." He began to cry.

"I can and will with all intention of getting into evidence that you got busted in Oklahoma City for screwing your sister. You totally ignorant bastard, if you'd shot straight with me earlier, Sherry might be alive, because Rincon would be in jail for the firebombing."

"Rincon murdered Sherry?"

"I don't know yet that Rincon murdered your daughter, but he's the best... and only suspect. Tell you what, Kincaid. I find him, I'll give you the address, so you can kill him if I don't beat you to it."

He headed the old pickup toward Dallas, leaving Kincaid in tears in the dingy little building.

He drove into downtown Dallas and trekked in the heat to his office. He spent a couple of hours typing reports which for reasons he never could fathom, were retyped by Tootie and other clerical staff.

Howdy drifted over and asked the progress on the Green Bull bombing and of the several attempts on Homer Wayne's life. He couldn't resist warning Kobok he needed a decisive case, soon, to avoid the annual Fall personnel shuffle. Kobok considered asking him if the National Debt could be reduced by curtailing pointless transfers but figured Howdy was too dumb to know what the National Debt was.

Kobok's day was interrupted by an odd caller. Tony Bones telephoned and asked the status of the bombing of the Green Bull. Kobok told him the investigation was ongoing. He felt strongly that Bones, with his network of thieves and thugs, probably had about four times the information he did. "Kobok, I hear this sumbitch murdered that little ten year old girl in Denton...the car dealer's kid?

Kobok ignored the question. "You know Kincaid, Tony."

"Naw, jes got no damned use for a punk who mistreats kids. Word is he's bragged abut killin other little girls. Needs to disappear."

"If you turn him up, Tony, don't forget, you gotta call me."

Tony chuckled and assured him that he would before he broke the connection. So Bad Tony bones had a particular problem with baby rapers. Kobok knew of worse afflictions.

He drove the pickup to Spring Valley Road, played catch with Tad until he felt his tank would hold at least five beers, then spent the rest of the day and evening with Anne and Tad after she came home from work at just past five.

CHAPTER 28: That Old Sucka Ain't Bulletproof

Eula Jo had called the DPD switchboard three times during the night to report horrible threats. On the last, a uniformed officer had come to the apartment and taken a report. A big strapping kid with a crewcut, both Eula Jo and Ida Sue offered free sex. The kid took the report and beat it to hell down the elevator. When Homer waddled home, Eula Jo was semi-hysterical with fear and grief. Playing acting her damnedest, semi was as far as she could stretch her imagination.

The Prince called at eight on the dot. Maybe he could tell time better than she'd thought. Homer's pickup was probably still at the light at Preston Road. The prince said he didn't want to spend any more time than necessary, three to a car in the Corvette. He ordered Eula Jo to leave Ida Sue, come pick him up, then they'd make plans from the condo.

In the condo, the Prince laid out the PLAN, version IV. Eula had stoked Homer and the stupid cops to a point where she was definitely a victim. Homer Wayne's days, hours actually, according to the PLAN, were numbered. And by the Prince's real plan, her days were actually limited to two after he got his hands on the insurance money. Behind a quart of cheap wine and a pair of lines, he boasted, "That old sucker damned sure ain't bulletproof."

Eula Jo nervously and reluctantly agreed. Ida Sue, now frozen into the plot, was swept along. She had not thought it would be so soon and she was terrified. She was a whore and had killed, but she was no killer. But, she had to go through with it—it meant $1000. She'd let the hammer down on the old man.

The Prince drove the Corvette into a weed infested dirt road in far South Dallas County. Eula Jo and Ida Sue were jammed into the passenger bucket seat—two ample backsides in a space totally inadequate.

By 11:30 P.M., he had selected a spot for the execution. He got both women out of the Corvette and carefully went over details. Eula Jo and he would hide in the nearby bushes. Ida Sue would wait in the passenger seat of the Corvette and shoot the shit out of Homer when he rushed to the scene.

Re-wedged into the Corvette, they drove several miles down the road where Eula Jo used a pay telephone to call Homer's dispatcher. She tearfully blurted that she had been abducted and was being subject to hideous and unspeakable abuse and torture by a group of hooded men. She ad-libbed the hideous and unspeakable part, knowing that it would spur old stupid Homer to hurry her rescue.

They then drove back to the spot on the side of the rural road. Nobody had advised the dispatcher how the hell Eula Jo had such good directions if she was stranded or how she had gotten stranded, then gotten to a telephone, and then gotten stranded again. Also, nobody had thought what Ida was to say if a Dallas County Sheriff's car happened by. None of that ever became a factor.

Homer Wayne was immediately notified of Eula Jo's plight by his dispatcher via two-way radio.

"Good God, they've got my Eula Jo!" He cried out and struck out for South Dallas County in a fully loaded garbage truck, dropping his helper at a DART bus stop. On the way, the dispatcher was able to repeat the directions which the abductee had carefully given him. Homer never thought to inquire about the precise detail of the instructions or to dial "911."

He roared up the dark, rural road until the lights of the garbage truck picked up the silver Corvette parked at roadside. He screeched to a garbage-loaded, semi-liquid halt and dashed to the side of the Corvette. Eula and the Prince, hiding nearby, had been nearly eaten alive by insects while waiting. But, they could see the whole road show.

Homer yanked open the passenger side door to confront a shaking, terrified woman he thought he might have seen before slumped in the passenger seat.

"Where's my Eula Jo, you sumbitches," he roared in the quiet, hot night air.

"Are you Homer Wayne DuPree?" asked Ida, voice trembling, having no idea if she had the right man in the dark. Christ, she thought, she'd hugged the old fart only the day before. Why hadn't she paid more attention to his face.

"Yes, I by-God sure am. Where's my Eula Jo, dammit?"

Ida Sue struggled out of the passenger side of the low-slung car and walked slowly around to where Homer was standing angrily in the middle of the road. She turned her head, pointed the gun with closed eyes, and shot Homer with five rounds in the chest and sternum area.

Homer Wayne, his stocky, powerful body made rock harder by years of hoisting garbage, took five rounds in speechless amazement.

Then, he muttered what could be called the understatement of the era. "It's me you bastards are tryin' to kill." he declared, indignantly. And at that, failing to cooperate by falling to the ground, he walked back to his garbage truck, boosted himself up into the cab, and garbage-swooshed away.

That section of Dallas County was not true farm country in the sense that residents survived by planting and harvesting crops. But it is rural and some of the residents did limited farming. Bob White, owner of a small horse ranch he called "White's Four", had gone to bed at 10:30 P.M. He was sound asleep when his German shepherd woke him with frantic barking at just past midnight. He was not totally excited when a knock came loudly to his door seconds later.

The Dallas County Sheriff's dispatcher would, however, later describe Mr. White as extremely agitated when he telephoned to advise that a gun shot wounded man, who had parked a stinking load of garbage in his driveway, was standing in his living room bleeding all over his wife's brand new, by God, rug.

Dallas County dispatched a district car right out. The deputy was close, arriving at White's Four in five minutes. Opting not to wait for an ambulance, the Deputy quickly loaded Homer Wayne into his squad car and made code three for Parkland. As they whizzed down the blacktop with red lights and siren at full tilt, they came across Eula Jo, staggering in the center of the road.

Homer, still conscious, was trying to explain to the Deputy that his Eula had been abducted and that some ol' gal driving Eula Jo's Corvette had done shot him. Lucidly he was able to tell the Deputy that the lady in road-center was his Eula Jo. She must have escaped. They took her aboard. The nasty bruise under her left eye and across the nose was consistent with an abducted, beaten woman.

Parkland Hospital emergency room would eventually diagnose that Eula Jo had been punched in the snoot and that Homer had been shot five times with a .32 caliber firearm, no bullet penetrating into his hard frame more than one-quarter inch. That's right, one-half the length of the .32 solid lead slugs.

On Homer Wayne's emergency room instructions, the Dallas County dispatcher called Kobok's number. Fortunately, the answering service had learned to find him at Anne's. Kobok called Hooper who agreed to pick up Kobok on Garland Road, then stop by the DPD motor pool and pick up a city car. Both feared Kobok's old Chevy pickup wouldn't make the trip.

The Sheriff's office, on information provided by Homer Wayne and Eula Jo, issued an all-points bulletin on the silver Corvette, warning that the occupants were armed and dangerous. Both Homer and Eula Jo would reach Parkland while the Prince was running for his existence with Ida Sue as a passenger. The emergency room personnel accustomed to smelly situations, had already recognized the situation as very smelly if not totally rotten and prudently found reasons to stall Eula Jo until the cavalry arrived.

Eula Jo and the Prince had watched, first in joyful satisfaction as the five shots rang out in rapid succession. Then, bliss faded to ultimate horror as Homer's broad form remained upright on the darkened road, walked to the garbage truck, and drove away. The Prince was furious. She must have missed! He rushed headlong to Ida Sue and struck her with his best right punch squarely in her mouth, trying to wrestle the revolver from her grip. Ida Sue, as he'd surmised, bested him.

He then turned on Eula Jo and dealt her his best punch

into the center of her puffy face. He slammed himself into the driver's seat of the Corvette and fired the engine into lunging life. Ida desperately clambered into the passenger side seat, barely managing to escape falling back out and being killed as the silver vehicle roared away. Eula Jo was left stranded and dazed in the middle of the road.

The Prince stopped twice and tried to physically force Ida Sue out of the car on rural roads, but she was too big and strong. Finally, she pushed the .32 against his head and said, "I have one left dipshit. Slow the hell down and drive back to Dallas." They were west of U.S. 175 and unable to find the freeway. Then, just as they caught sight of the Dallas skyline from the back roads, the first flash of red lights loomed in the rear-view mirror in horrible, terrifying finality. The car chase only lasted three minutes.

Had the Prince been half the macho man he thought himself to be, the Corvette would have made short work of the Sheriff's cruisers. But, they stayed close on crooked roads until the chase was joined by one of the Texas Highway Patrol's new Mustang pursuit vehicles capable of enough speed to take flight. The Prince lost it just short of the Dallas City Limit. He then skidded down two hundred feet of bar ditch, subsequently flipping twice, and relegating the Corvette to the junkyard forever. He was still in Dallas County and Homer Wayne was out the price of a second brand new Corvette.

Ida was knocked cold by the crash and had to be cut from the wreckage by firefighters. The Prince bailed out like the rodent he was and led a foot chase which lasted another half hour, eventually requiring a dozen officers. Not surprisingly it was a rookie who caught him; a young quick officer, who dragged the Prince's scrawny body off a wooden privacy fence and into the roadside weeds. The Prince begged for his life, then cried, then vomited on the officer's trousers.

Kobok and Hooper heard the car chase and subsequent foot chase on the "inner city" radio frequency as they sped to far South Dallas County.

At first, Kobok and Hooper were uncertain if the chase they were hearing on the radio was connected to the information the Dallas County dispatcher had given about the shooting of Homer Wayne. They hurried to Parkland to talk to Homer Wayne before touching base with the Dallas County dispatcher. The night technician wheeled Ida Sue back from X-Ray as they were trying to talk to Homer, who, while still conscious, was heavily sedated. Ida Sue was parked in the next emergency cubicle in full view of Homer on his back on an emergency cart. He peered over at her, bloody, foggy, but recognizable, and also partly conscious.

"Where's the driver," Hooper asked Kobok.

"Dead if there's a God," Ida Sue groaned from a gurney, half conscious.

"Damnation, that's her. She's the bitch that shot me," Homer Wayne blurted, half delirious, pointing at Ida Sue.

"She's got no ID," called out the Dallas County Deputy who had accompanied Ida Sue in the ambulance. "She wrecked out in a car chase down toward the South City Limits. She was the passenger. A Corvette... and that baby would run down the road. However, the dork driving had no balls." He grinned over at the agents.

They attempted to obtain details from a sobbing Eula Jo, one cubicle down from Ida Sue. Neither was providing any. Eula Jo was hysterical and knocked goofier than usual. Despite a swollen face and bloody nose, she didn't look any worse to Kobok and Hooper than she had before. Homer called out for her but didn't appear rational enough to realize she was ten feet away on a matching cart.

"Okay, Eula Jo your ass is grass," Kobok declared. "We're not sure what the hell happened here, but you're caught. I think you shot Homer. We got the gun, and we got Homer full of bullets from a gun. And we got who the hell ever this is?" He pointed his chin toward Ida Sue, prostrate on the next cart.

"I ain't shot nobody," Eula Jo peered out from under her icepack, sobbing. "She did," she pointed to Ida Sue. So much for the code of silence. Mascara dribbling down Eula Jo's face curved into the corners of her mouth. Ida Sue was too out of it to comprehend the accusation.

Kobok said, "Well, we can send both of you away for a

long vacation...unless Homer Wayne dies. Then, ladies, it's the needle." He turned to Ida Sue, who suddenly was hovering in partly unconscious semi-hysteria. "What is your name please?"

In response, mechanically, like a military prisoner in a foreign land, Ida Sue gave name, date of birth and confirmed she'd just gotten out of prison. They didn't bother to ask her occupation because her profession was recognizable twenty feet away. Homer Wayne had already fingered her as the shooter. Kobok realized the edge of caution for giving a Miranda warning was near, so Hooper read both their rights from his pocket card. After thirty minutes of listening to a litany of denials, sobs, and babble, they knew little more than when they'd walked in the door.

A husky young uniformed deputy stuck his head in through the curtained compartment. "We just brought in this skinny little dork who was drivn'. He's three curtains down handcuffed to a gurney. Little jerkoff calls himself the Prince of Draconia."

"Oh, my God!" Eula Jo shrieked. "Don't you bastards lay a hand on him or I'll kill every Goddamned last one of your asses."

"My, my, Eula Jo," Kobok laughed. "You need to say what you really mean and not beat around the bush like that."

Eula Jo screamed again, "He's a political fugitive. Y'all are part of the conspiracy to send him home to be beheaded."

Ida Sue, regaining partial consciousness, rose slightly on her cart in the emergency room. "Prince, you rotten piece of shit," she snarled. "I oughta break your Goddamned skinny neck. You said he'd be easy to kill, an easy kill." She slumped back on the cart. "An easy kill."

"Shut your trap, bitch," Eula Jo called out. "I dunno who that bitch is."

Kobok looked at Hooper. "By golly, Bull, I believe we finally have Eula Jo's little helper in the ongoing quest to murder Homer Wayne."

Hooper grinned through his cigar stub. "I can't wait to see this guy. I may pull off his damned head."

They moved down three cubicles and pushed through the curtain.

Two uniforms sat in metal chairs, flanking a skinny, dark, swarthy little prisoner. He had numerous insect bites on his arms and neck and his dark face was marked by scratches and small cuts from an automobile accident. He spat cusswords like a Thompson sub-machinegun.

"Leave him be, dammit!" Eula Jo shouted through the curtains.

"He confess?" Hooper asked the deputies.

One looked up. "Naw, he says royalty don't gotta talk to cops." Both deputies stepped out, laughing.

Kobok, a hard man to surprise, stared hard at the snarling little prisoner. "Holy Jesus, Hooper, this little Prince clown is Gilberto Rincon, probable bomber of the Green Bull and baby killer. I'll be damned."

Uncharacteristically, Kobok was stunned he had not had the slightest idea the two criminals he'd been seeking were one and the same. Somehow, he'd slept through the main feature. His present impulse was to shove Hooper aside and throttle the prisoner. The image of little Sherry, burned, tied, beaten had ignited a rage he'd never known before.

"Good God," he said aloud. "The DuPree who reported the Corvette wrecked in Denton as stolen was Homer Wayne." The coincidence had become reality.

Suddenly, Kobok's initial knowledge that they'd harvested a sack of sour lemons became a vast citrus orchard—and the crop was rotten. Good God, two maggots he'd tried for over two weeks to locate, had melded into one scrawny, weak dirtbag now sitting handcuffed in a hospital emergency room. There were enough criminal case clearances in front of him to ward off Howdy, IAD, and the common cold. But then the shattering revelation of truth—*This little rat had to be good for the murder of Sherry Kincaid! Suspicion was past. He'd butchered an innocent, full of life, child.* The words shrilled through his ears with volume he felt could be heard by others in the room.

With crushing horror, he realized the nagging at the distant edge of memory was true. If he'd pushed the Beckman case instead of dallying with Marilyn Crawford or plotting the demise of Howdy or a hundred other distractions, this sorry piece of humanity, Rincon, would have been in custody, unable to harm Sherry.

"You sick, Kobok," Hooper studied his face closely. "You're lookin' sorta green."

"Yeah…yeah, I don't feel so good." *Was avoiding a transfer to the Middle-East or the Florida swamp worth the little girl's life?* His ears continued to scream. *A disastrous trade in any dimension!* The floor was suddenly unsteady as he struggled to avoid throwing up.

CHAPTER 29:

SOME FOLKS JUST TAKE MORE KILLIN' THAN OTHERS

Homer would later be in surgery for two hours, never fully losing consciousness. Eula Jo required no treatment beyond an icepack, although the hospital had already held her for "examination" for several hours before the law woke up and handcuffed her to her gurney.

Gilberto Rincon, the now not nearly so exalted Prince of Draconia, was neither freed from handcuffs, nor laid on a cart. He remained sitting on a straight back chair, handcuffed to a rolling gurney in one of the curtained cubicles. An orderly came in to ask if Kobok or Hooper had a key to remove the handcuffs, so Rincon could be examined. Hooper produced a handcuff key and slipped the cuffs off. The orderly tried to assist removing the shirt, but macho ego forced Rincon to remove it himself.

"Now the pants big boy," the orderly said, gesturing at the greasy Levis. The Prince stood defiantly inactive.

Kobok and Hooper stepped forward to assist the orderly, a task they intended to do with whatever force necessary, hopefully bending a bone or two. They both knew the he had just been involved in a car accident and foot chase, so an additional mark or four would not be noticed. Neither would a broken rib.

Rincon, survival instinct surging to the rescue, quickly stripped off the jeans, standing at the center of the curtained room in red silk bikini underwear. He glared in princely scowl at a fixed spot on the white rear wall. Something caught Kobok's attention.

Starkly visible across his scrawny left side, about two inches above the belt line, was a three inch, very fresh scar. It was straight, die straight, geometrically straight, bullet straight, and .357 magnum wide. The wound was more scratch than injury and mostly healed, but visibly not old. In stark purple, it contrasted against the dark skin. Kobok's bullet that night behind the Green Bull had only missed canceling the scumbag permanently by inches.

Kobok and Hooper shared a look. Both knew they'd caught the fleeing man with whom Kobok had exchanged shots while running under a railroad trestle. Both realized in the absence of confession, the scar meant little on its own. But the Prince couldn't remove it. As circumstances developed, the scar might complement other evidence.

"A doctor will be in to look at him in a minute," the orderly stepped out and closed the curtain. Hooper listened as the orderly walked away. He backhanded the Prince across the chest, knocking the little man against the back wall. Rincon cowered awkwardly on the floor. The clatter of equipment broke the muted silence of the emergency room. "We better get the cuffs back on him. Looks to me like he's tryin' to escape." Hooper again smiled strangely, giving Kobok an odd chill. Hooper continued softly, "I may have to kill this sumbitch."

Rincon, the Prince of pain and dysfunction, began to sob tearfully.

Eula Jo, no stranger to violence to herself from the Prince, responded to the noise from three cubicles away. "Oh no, baby. Oh, God no," she wailed.

His Highness hunkered on the floor against the back wall, facial features locked in terror. He read death in Hooper's craggy face. Kobok was uneasy about the smile, himself.

A deputy stuck his head in. "Did you Mirandize him?" Kobok asked the deputy as the officer raised Gilberto back to his chair, using the greasy hair as a handle. Traces of fingerprint ink were still visible on Rincon's fingertips.

"Yessir, I did," replied the deputy.

"We did, too," Hooper said. "That oughta hold him." The young officer stepped back out.

Prince Rincon shivered, still clad only in red silk mini-boxers.

"Don't hurt me," he directed, voice quivering in attempted macho.

Kobok, more than aware of the limit of reasonable force allowable, visualized another glimpse of Sherry Kincaid's abused body niggling at a corner of his mind. He grasped the greasy hair hand-hold and bent the prisoner's head back over the chair rest at the most extreme angle possible without pulling off his head. "Tell me you didn't just say not to hurt you?" he whispered into Rincon's ear. The prisoner reciprocated by urinating in his silk underwear.

Hooper served dessert by leaning close and muttering, "Lemme just go ahead and kill him." But the old veteran Hooper was now well in control—his behavior was only a form of field catharsis.

Kobok allowed Rincon's head to snap upright.

"Don't hurt me, please." Rincon wasn't so tough without a belt and lighted cigarette.

"Don't worry, your Highness," Kobok interjected. "He's probably not gonna kill you, at least not right now." Again, Kobok hoped he was guessing correctly. Rincon the phony prince was an easy person to dislike.

"Tell me about the little scar on your waist." Kobok leaned back down into the prisoner's face.

"Please don't hurt me." was the only response. Prince Rincon's vocabulary was stuck on "coward". The taste revisited Kobok, sour, distant, and increasingly bitter.

"Seen Sparky from the Green Bull lately? How about Rosie Beckman" Kobok could see only Sherry Kincaid. Rincon began to sob again.

Kobok took a chair next to Prince Rincon. "We'll find out where you got the black powder because Eula Jo is too dumb not to have bought it and a bunch of other stuff on a credit card. We found parts of an alarm clock in the mess you made of Homer Wayne's bedroom. We'll find the origin and stuff it up your ass, dude. Do you wanna gamble we find the credit card receipts from ol' Eula Jo buying that crap? If you stole the blasting cap, we may not find out how, but we have snitches, wiretaps—you know the Feds. If you bought the material, we'll find out how." Kobok was on a roll. "We know you've been leading the pack trying to kill Homer. The woman down the hall, Ida Sue, is gonna finger for the whole Homer Wayne DuPree load. You, my fine Highness, are screwed. Which is exactly what you're gonna get in the joint by some alpha male...before you get the needle, that is."

The arrogant glare showed tears at the corner of his eyes. "I wanna lawyer." He sprang off his chair and partially fell. His highness groaned as Kobok assisted Hooper in up righting him, making full use of the hair as a lifting device.

"Ohh please, don't hurt him," Eula Jo wailed from her cart on hearing the clatter of scattering furniture.

"Shut up bitch," was the Princely response to pleas for mercy. "Who is that chick?"

Ida Sue, rousing from shock of the accident another cubicle away, added, "If that little rat don't die, I'm gonna kill him myself," not an intelligent threat to make in a crowded room full of cops. But Kobok couldn't disagree with her. Ida Sue, no longer the hired gun was, at least temporarily, once again the shunned whore who had offed her pimp after she'd had a bad day.

An orderly, followed by a surgeon, wheeled Homer Wayne toward the operating room. The doctor recognized Hooper from previous contacts. "Hooper, five rounds from what appears to be a .32 is not only not going to kill this old boy, he may leave to have a beer after we remove the slugs."

Emergency surgeons had dug out five .32 caliber bullets, attending to a cracked rib, and sutured damage caused by gunshot wounds to the upper chest. They weren't certain the cracked rib was the result of gunshot trauma or of a previous, on-the-job injury for which he'd declined medical attention.

Ida Sue was treated for a broken right forearm, a mild concussion, two cracked ribs, a four-inch gash on her forehead, and numerous bruises and abrasions. She would live.

Eula Jo needed only an icepack and some serious TLC. She received the former but lay in tears for want of the latter. The Prince had shouted her down twice with comments to the effect of "shut the hell up bitch." He repeatedly denied knowing Eula Jo or Ida Sue.

They decided to sweat the Prince before they interrogated Eula Jo. Kobok picked up Rincon's Levi's from the floor. Among the few items in a small billfold from the hip pocket was a bar card advertising the Green Bull with two telephone numbers scribbled across the back. Kobok would later learn one of these was the same number Eula Jo had discovered earlier.

An emergency room doctor came in. He began a preliminary examination of the prisoner, culminating by forcing Rincon to remove his soggy, silk, bikini underwear and spread both cheeks while handcuffed to the gurney. Rincon complied, but the movement required considerable exertion and dexterity. He contorted forward awkwardly, scrawny and naked in the bright light. Kobok had hoped the Prince would resist, but the little man wisely complied.

The young doctor declared Rincon bruised, but not likely to die, at least not immediately. Hooper removed the handcuffs, allowing the Prince to get dressed, and then re-cuffed him for transportation to the Sterrett Center.

His highness tossed the underwear in a trash container. In a later era, DNA from the underwear or from anywhere on his skinny body would match the semen on Little Sherry's face, earning the Prince a trip from a gurney in Parkland Emergency to one on Death Row. However, that technology would not be perfected for several more years. Kobok handed the officer the billfold to be included with his possessions when he was jailed.

"Bye baby, I love you," Eula Jo called out, receiving no reply.

Eula Jo was in the next cubicle in the traditional position of her profession, flat on her back. Hospital staff had placed an ice pack on her punched nose, obscuring her entire face.

"Like I said you've screwed yourself this time, Eula Jo," Kobok began. Predictably, she broke into tears. "This time we can prove it."

"I ain't did shit."

"Ida Sue is upstairs gettin' patched up. She won't die and I'll bet a cigar she won't go back to the joint without taking you and that sorry Gilberto Rincon Prince dork along with her," Kobok prodded.

"Why do ya' keep callin' him 'Gilberto' and...Rincon, is

it?" She looked horror movie ghastly with sagging makeup, dripping mascara, and a bloated, used up face with a swollen, probably broken nose.

"Because that's his name, Eula Jo."

"No, he's Paz, Crown Prince of Draconia."

They brought Ida Sue down from surgery after daylight. Doctors advised she had received local anesthetic only and could be interviewed. While allowing Ida Sue the opportunity to recover for a while, they harvested her criminal record by telephone. It was extensive, but aside from blowing away her pimp, it was all junior varsity. They wheeled her into a small room with solid walls.

"It's your ass in a leaky bucket, Ida," Kobok re-read her Miranda rights. "If old Homer dies up there, it's the needle for you. You been inside enough to know. Contract killin' is a death penalty case."

She responded, predictably, with tears.

"How long have you known the Prince?" Kobok said.

"Couple days. Eula Jo knew him. I jes' got outta the joint." More tears.

Then she dumped the whole load. She found Eula Jo after living on the street for several days. She included the motel liaison, the sex with the Prince at the condo, buying the pistol with Eula Jo's driver's license on Cedar Springs, the drive to South Dallas County, the shooting of Homer after turning her head, the fight with the Prince, the chase, the accident, and waking up in the hospital.

"Why didn't you shoot him with the sixth bullet?" Kobok asked.

"That Prince jerk told me to save one to put in his head. I waited, but I started pukin' at all the blood and didn't count the damned bullets." Her face contorted. "That little prick. When I recovered enough to put one in Homer Wayne's head, he was driving away in a damned garbage truck."

They conferred at length with two extremely weary, blood-spattered doctors in surgical green, who had spent tedious time, digging metal objects from Homer Wayne. "That old boy has the constitution of a water buffalo," diagnosed one of the physicians. He was early thirties, tall with dark thinning hair and thick glasses.

"He kept trying to come out of the anesthetic," laughed the second doctor, an older man, balding with remnants of black hair. "He's gonna be out here looking for breakfast if we don't beat a trail out of here."

"Does that mean he'll live?" Hooper asked.

"Live? He'll be back on the garbage truck tonight if we don't keep him sedated," remarked the younger doctor. "He kept moaning for Eula Jo."

"That's his wife," Kobok said. "She's tried several times to kill him."

"Good grief," remarked the older physician.

CHAPTER 30: THE CONSPIRATORS HAZARD:

BEING TRAMPLED IN THE LINE TO SNITCH

By noon the next day, Rincon, Ida Sue, and Eula Jo were locked up in the Sterrett Center.

Neither Ida Sue, nor Rincon, had any chance to make the $500,000 bail set by a Dallas County District Judge. Homer Wayne was alienated for all time because the Dallas County District Attorney's Office had asked the judge to hold Eula Jo without bail. Homer would have posted any bond, no matter the amount. Kobok and Hooper raised genuine concern she would murder Homer Wayne about fifteen minutes after she hit the ground.

Despite the large accumulation of evidence of violent crimes in hand, the rules of evidence, both state and federal, diluted the strength of most of the charges. Evidence can only be presented pertaining to a case for which a defendant is charged. Black powder, for instance, cannot be introduced in an attempted murder by firearms case. It was finally agreed the strongest case was to charge Rincon, Ida Sue, and Eula Jo in Dallas County for attempted murder of Homer Wayne by shooting him full of holes. Prosecutors agreed that although other egregious crimes were involved, insufficient evidence would keep them from filing anything additional.

Under the same reasoning, Jerry Kincaid was never charged for perjury in the Cutlass title case.

Kobok and Hooper re-interviewed Stephanie "Sparky" Manner. The telephone numbers Kobok had recovered from Rincon's Levi's were to the Green Bull and Sparky's home phone on Webb Chapel Extension respectively. Sparky recalled receiving a threatening call from an irate female warning her to "Stay away from my Prince" but had no idea who called.

In the next weeks, Tony Bones called Kobok several times. Kobok told him, and later explained to a high dollar lawyer Bones had hired, that although he had no doubt Rincon had bombed the Green Bull, evidence beyond a quarrel with a stripper and being tossed by a bouncer was non-existent. Kobok did not give much credence to Bones' threat, "…to pull the little baby killin' bastard's head off."

The three prisoners languished in humid squalor in un-air-conditioned-Sterrett as Summer drifted into Autumn.

On the first workday in July, an unusual occurrence crossed Kobok's path. He was working his way up the Central Parking Lot in the 5:30 P.M. traffic. To escape the usual lockdown, he exited at Northwest Highway looking for an escape route. The detour carried him past the Duncan-Frost Funeral Home and sprawling cemetery complex, which he recalled was the resting place of Sherry Kincaid. Impulsively, he turned into the well-attended driveway, flanked on either side by watered grass. He stopped by a small caretaker's office to ask directions. After several minutes of shuffling 3X5 cards, the attendant, an elderly black man with kind, brown eyes pointed out Sherry's grave on a wall map.

"That's a popular place." He smiled across the counter.

"Popular?" Kobok assumed that morbid fringes of society, drawn to bizarre situations, had visited the gravesite.

"Guy in a black car come by at least once a week. Got another guy drivin'… big ol' boy."

Kobok drove to the site, wondering what nut job he might find in attendance. No one was in sight. The grave, still freshly visible, was decorated with a vase of flowers, leaned against a modest headstone. He remained a few minutes before starting back north. The old man had obviously confused a funeral car with a morbid visitor.

Kobok contemplated stopping back by the caretaker's and asking the man to jot down the license number of the visitors in the big black car but considered the matter insignificant.

He inched home, confident Rincon was suffering as a guest

of Dallas County. Surely it didn't count in Hell to wish he was at least uncomfortable, or hopefully already selected as an alpha con's wife.

July 4th that year fell on a Wednesday, inconveniently dead center in mid-week. Bull Hooper kept a boat stored in a slip at Lake Ray Hubbard, the Eastern border of Dallas County. Hooper was on call that day, and Kobok arranged for Anne, Tad, and he to use the small outboard. After spending the day dodging drunk boaters, they watched a beautiful fireworks display over hamburgers on a public dock.

Kobok had tipped enough beers that Anne, even keeled as ever, drove home. Tad was sound asleep in her Honda back seat when they reached Spring Valley Road. Both Hooper and the ATF answering service had left calls on Anne's answering machine. When he returned the calls, both told him he needed to go directly to the Dallas County Jail and talk to Eula Jo DuPree.

He told Hooper he'd meet him at Sterrett, only after an extended cold shower for sunburn relief. In the cop world, any rookie soon learns not to allow anything to surprise. But when Eula Jo dumped the whole package, surprise had to yield to bombshell.

The Prince, Ida Sue, and Eula Jo were all in the same jail, all right. No matter who said otherwise, walls, certainly do a prison make.

She loved the little sadistic punk all right, the only thing she had ever truly loved—man, parent, dog, or otherwise. Her disclosure of the details of the plot stemmed from somewhere between a woman's love scorned and the prospects of the rest of her life in a cage. She saw Ida Sue every day in the women's quarters. She sent the Prince several notes, one or two via the approved jailhouse guard relay and many others through the illegal prisoner network. He got them all.

Eula Jo, who labored to put thoughts on paper, couldn't grasp that he didn't read so well either. She thought he was a genius. At any rate, he could never have discerned the love and sensitivity in her words, written or not. Another inmate read the pitiful pleas to him in the presence of the entire cellblock. Laughter and crude jokes were the response. A trustee sent to the women's cellblock to unstop a commode had hand carried one of her final notes to him. The trustee had overheard the ensuing ridicule of her note and the obscene guffaws shared by the Prince's cellmates.

The plumber-trustee happened by the next day and she slipped him another note. As before, she paid postage in the form of a quick blowjob through the bars with twenty onlooking female inmates cheering the effort. He knew if he told Eula Jo the truth he would dry up a source of professional, illegal mail service, jailhouse oral sex. But seeing twenty other mouths to feed, he whispered, after the postage payment by Eula Jo, of course, that the Prince not only had shared her intimate thoughts with others, he was bragging he was going to send her fat whore ass to the joint forever.

After discussing the issue with Ida Sue and several others skilled in jailhouse procedure, they universally urged her to spill what she knew. She concluded he was going to snitch. The truth was, he was too stupid and arrogant to try to snitch his way out of a tight spot. He was only talking macho, jailhouse trash. He should have snitched, because that's what she did, first in hearts, then in spades.

Homer Wayne had earlier retained an expensive lawyer. She told him to piss off. By law she had that right. A lawyer would have tried like Sunday to talk her out of a confession. But in the heat of passion, she let go the whole story.

The recorded statement would later clearly evidence she was warned repeatedly Hooper and Kobok that she had a right to remain silent and what she did say could be used against her.

Eula Jo told it the way it was, beginning with her home life, sobbing at her own bad fortune. Like most of the human race, she was unable to grasp the reality of being her own worst enemy. As she talked on. Continuing with her years as a street hooker, she discussed an array of pimps, boyfriends, arrests, and her first meeting with Homer Wayne DuPree. She told of her meeting with The Royal Prince of Draconia, of the propane bomb, the window air conditioning bomb, the Tom the cat bomb, and the chance encounter with Ida Sue Price, the wanna be hit person. She admitted buying bomb parts and purchasing the revolver for the express intention of shooting Homer Wayne to death—crucial evidence against a sneering wise ass who made sport of her affection.

She told of buying the clock used in the window bomb at a Target Store and the black powder at "some place she couldn't remember". She described him sitting at the mansion kitchen table making the bomb. She didn't know where he got the "blasting cap thingys" used in the window bomb and trash can/kill the cat incident. The term "blasting cap" was a bar drink for all she knew. She sobbed through the blotched hit-woman-shooting of Homer and the punch in the face the Prince had given her when abandoning her at the scene. She included the whippings, the cigarette burns, the perversion, the duration of sadistic love-making, and inadvertent teeth marks on the Prince's penis at the instant of the garbage can explosion.

Kobok checked his notes carefully when she spoke of the Prince's use of the Corvette, hoping to match dates with the Beckman firebombing, the Green Bull bombing, and the shots fired at Kobok. The dates were impossible to correlate. Then she dropped two nuclear blockbusters. The Prince had wrecked and totaled her Corvette in Denton on the Saturday morning before she'd been arrested. Then she admitted she'd raised the coverage on Homer Wayne's life insurance, forging his name on the application.

"Are you sure about the date the Corvette was stolen and wrecked, Eula Jo?" Kobok asked.

"The Saturday before I was arrested," she repeated. Had he followed Homer Wayne and her as they left the Condo that Sunday, they were on the way to Denton to examine the wrecked car.

A female deputy led her out, a doleful relic with 300,000 miles and a lifetime of fender benders.

"I...I'm sorry about this," she sobbed from the doorway. Her eyes hardened in narrow sincerity. "If that old bastard Homer hadda died easy like Paz said, an easy kill." The voice faltered into sobs and Eula Jo, the whore, the conspirator, the fallen, shuffled out of view in front of the deputy.

In cop-speak, the case against Rincon had just grown legs ten feet long.

They brought Ida Sue in, looking like yesterday's lunch. She could add little to her confession on the night of arrest but did confirm Eula Jo had told her after they were arrested about inflating Homer's life insurance coverage and forging his name to the application. She'd also heard the trustee tell of the Prince ridiculing Eula Jo's love letters. A veteran of jailhouse survival, she stated clearly, she would testify against Rincon and Eula Jo in return for a reduced sentence.

CHAPTER 31: And That Should Have Ended It

Homer Wayne could pay more in lawyer fees than the GDP of Sweden. He could petition the court for a reduction of the no-bail order. He could attend church and pray like Moses. He could possibly build a new courthouse. But he could not succeed in springing his Eula Jo from the slammer. He did, however, in ways Kobok and Hooper didn't understand, manage to pay enough lawyer money to enough hands willing to accept, to get her trial moved to late November.

For weeks after the Prince's cruelty had compelled Eula Jo to confess her role in the tragic comedy of errors, she'd tried her best to stick with the little pervert. Willing to risk life without parole or worse, she doggedly tried, to re-establish the twisted chemistry that had super-glued her to his cruel, psychopathic rants. Kobok and Hooper discussed the situation. Somehow, she had felt that by confessing, Rincon and she would sort of go down in flames, a la Bonnie and Clyde. Then he'd love her for eternity. For weeks, she plied him with pathetic pleas for attention by sending more love letters - a sort of form of throwing good money after bad.

The plumber-mail system again delivered news of his ridicule and rejection. Her brain trust of cellmates had multiple solutions. Bribe the plumber-mail man with an all nude girl inmate sex show. Then have him slip ground glass in the cup of tepid tea he was issued every morning. Or, hire the plumber to shank the little rat in the shower.

She could have requested a "severance", the right of individual defendants to demand a trial separate from co-defendants. Facts clearly implicated Rincon as the impetus, the driving force. With a severance, she would have gotten a manageable sentence and soon gone home to Homer Wayne and his buckets of gold. But twice bitten, broken, and shot in the ass, even the strongest weld is not immune to failure.

During the third week in November, Kobok had driven past the Police and Courts Building and fetched Hooper. They were just challenging the manager's concern of running out of food at *Lupe's Mexican Food,* a pitch 'til you win, all you can eat dive on South Industrial. Kobok and Hooper were draining the kitchen. The weather was late November cool and sunny. The North wind, the true measure of Dallas winter, had stayed home today. The Rincon and Eula Jo trial began the following Monday. Kobok and Hooper were ready. Kobok had, per instructions, radioed Tootie with his location, a common practice in those pre-cellular days.

It seemed all Mexican food restaurant managers were pudgy. The pudgy manager of Lupe's called out, "Call for Meester Kopop."

"Close enough for government work," Kobok thought and took the call. "Homicide's trying to reach Hooper," Tootie reported. "This mean you aren't gonna bring me any damned lunch, Kobok?"

Kobok, had, of course forgotten her request. He hung up, Hooper called his office on a payphone by the men's restroom and returned. Typically, his poker face held.

"Eula Jo hung herself this morning."

Kobok, in a lighter moment would have explained that things are hung, and people are hanged. He postponed the language lesson. "Should I ask, dead?"

"Deader n' hell."

"When. This time of day there are at least twenty other prisoners in her tank."

"Dunno. Happened an hour ago and they're just now transporting her to the morgue. We better go over there and have a look see."

As they left, the manager, relieved that the food stash was saved, waved them past the register.

Kobok left a ten-dollar tip, sizeable for 1984.

Kobok had parked his mostly rebuilt Plymouth on a curb

across Industrial. As he U-turned toward the Southwest Institute, Hooper asked, "You realize without Eula Jo's testimony, we're gonna have to re-shuffle against Rincon."

Hooper was citing a provision in law wherein a confession by one member of a conspiratorial case, is only admissible against the person making the confession. To use the statement against others, the person who confessed must take the stand and testify against the others. Eula Jo could not testify from the grave. The new ten-foot legs against Rincon had gotten trimmed a bit.

"Jesus Christ." Hooper's bald pate glistened in the midday sun. "Jesus H. Christ."

Eula Jo was already sprawled on a gurney, second in line for gutting and the works. Her neck contorted at a grotesque angle, bearing a nasty two-inch-wide contusion, left little doubt of the cause of death. Flat on her back, her forty pounds of mammary pride still demonstrated a tendency to stand alone. Lynn O'Hara looked over her half glasses and motioned them over. Richard Garner greeted them as cordially as the front man in an overpriced restaurant.

"Jesus," O'Hara said through her mask. "This gonna turn that ass, what's his name, the Prince, loose?"

"Naw," Hooper rolled his cigar stub. "They cut the little bastard loose and I'm gonna go ahead and perform a public service."

"Y'all can hang around," O'Hara said. "But unless you're gonna file a hot homicide charge here," she gestured to Eula Jo's corpse. "I can tell you up front she died by hanging herself."

Hooper said, "We'll go by Sterrett and try to make sure some alpha bitch didn't murder her. But suicides by hanging in a jail always... that's always, happen in the middle of the night. They serve a sort of brunch at Sterrett around ten in the A.M. The trustee pushing the food cart reported this. She's fresh meat, not a leftover from 3 A.M."

Kobok and Hooper interviewed the jail captain, the guard on duty on the floor, the food dispensing trustee and three inmates. Eula Jo had spent so much time in abject misery, crying night and day, sympathetic inmates had stood by and watched her put herself out of her misery.

Hooper declared that trying to bring charges in the matter were like stepping into quicksand barefoot.

Eula Jo was buried no more than a hundred feet from Sherry Kincaid. Hooper, Kobok, Homer Wayne, and funeral home personnel were the only ones present at her graveside service two days later. Homer Wayne gave both a thorough cussing for being a part of the demise of his Eula Jo.

As they drove away, Kobok caught sight of a black Continental pulling out of the lot on the far side. He goosed the Plymouth but failed to make contact.

"Whut the hell you doing?" Hooper complained.

"Curious who that was, dude. Just doin' my old job."

The trial lasted only half a day. Testimony of the pawn guy who'd sold Eula Jo the .32 revolver was highly contested by Rincon's court appointed lawyer before the judge reluctantly allowed his record into evidence. Ida Sue testified that she'd been present when Eula Jo bought the gun and six rounds of ammo and that she'd used it to shoot Homer Wayne DuPree five times on orders of Rincon to "shoot his worthless ass full of holes."

Kobok and Hooper were forbidden to be in the courtroom during direct testimony because of the "rule". Although neither was expected to testify, courtroom procedures prohibit any potential witness from hearing testimony of others. The idea is to keep one witness from hearing another and thus changing their own testimony. During a courtroom break, Kobok noticed Tony Bones, shadowed by Carlo in the hallway and nudged Hooper. Back in court, Bones sat quietly listening. His expression didn't waver when the jury foreman stood and announced Rincon guilty of Attempted Capital Murder.

State of Texas jury trials are a two-stage process. After the guilt or innocence finding happens to end as "guilty", the jury hears testimony for what's called the "punishment phase." Both Kobok and Hooper were among a half dozen character witnesses allowed by the system to comment on the defendant's reputation. Both, by law were limited to saying only his reputation was "bad".

Bones' expression never changed when, after the jury

foreman announced Rincon's sentence as 65 years the little Prince sprang to his feet and shrieked "Mu'fuckers".

Kobok pondered but did not comment on the depth of Tony Bones' apparent fury at bombing his strip club. Insurance had paid for the loss and the place seemed busier than ever.

Ida Sue, in return for testimony and in view of her previous confinement in prison, pled guilty the next day and was sentenced to ten years, sentence to run concurrently with her previous pimp-murder conviction. That meant she did not have to finish the pimp murder sentence before beginning the present sentence. They guessed she'd be out in five years.

Homer Wayne, waiting on the courthouse steps, gave Kobok and Hooper another cussing.

CHAPTER 32: REMEMBER, IT AIN'T OVER 'TIL IT'S OVER.

The Prince and Ida Sue spent Christmas 1984 in the Sterrett Center before both were transferred to their assigned prison units. Kobok avoided transfer to the Miami slaughter zone in next year, 1985 and again in 1986 by doggedly pursuing cases which appeared hopeless at the outset. He kept the little star heart earrings locked in his desk drawer, a constant reminder to run down all leads on all cases at all times. Each October 31st, he felt a measure of comfort that Rincon was in the joint, hopefully getting raped nightly.

Just over a year later, Special Agent Randall Bush had finished first in his academy class. Kobok was assigned as his training officer, later his partner.

In the Fall of 1989 Tad was in junior high school. He'd grown nearly as tall as Kobok and could still prevail at Monopoly or Scrabble with ease. Anne and Kobok grew closer, and he'd finally let his apartment go and moved in with her and Tad. He had discontinued his occasional visit to Lynn O'Hara's place. He still drank too much beer.

In the summer of 1988, Ida Sue had been paroled to Dallas County. Kobok heard she was homeless and living under a downtown bridge. He searched and couldn't find her. Just after the first of January 1989, Hooper called and told Kobok Ida Sue had been found dead in weeds along the Trinity River. Hooper, Kobo, and Bush, now a veteran, were the only attendees at her Dallas County funded burial. Kobok bought her a small headstone.

Then, in December 1989, Kobok and Hooper investigated a firebombing in an A.M.E. church near the Cotton Bowl. They eventually accumulated enough evidence to convince a Dallas

County Grand Jury to indict and subsequently issue a bench warrant of arrest for one Monroe "Squatty" Crockus, the avowed Skinhead and racist. They learned that Squatty, in love with a waitress at Tubby's Diner on South St. Paul, appeared there daily at 11:00 A.M. The location was difficult to surveil and the Bull Hooper in a giant pink rabbit suit situation was hatched.

After learning Rincon had not escaped, Kobok and his partner, Randall Bush, three years out of the academy had taken advantage of a sunny, late December day and decided to walk back to the Cabell Federal Building. Bush bought Italian for lunch.

They backtracked a block and strolled through *Nieman's*. The store and many employees were gaily adorned in bright Christmas colors. Christmas music drifting across the store was generated by much more sophisticated equipment than the system on utility poles outside. Kobok bought Tad a football. Now he could finish crippling his aging throwing arm playing catch with Tad with a football rather than the long-established baseball they'd always used.

Kobok stormed over to his desk in the ATF squad room, tossed the football in a drawer and called the U.S. Attorney's Office on the 15th floor. After a lengthy conference, Bush and he sat dejectedly at their desks. Chances of successful prosecution of Rincon for the Green Bull Bombing were next to zero. The federal prosecutors had said. Rincon was going to walk.

At just before 2:00 P.M. Tootie sent Kobok a call. It was Hooper.

"I gotta alibi," Hooper's gruff voice resounded through the speaker phone.

"What are you talkin' about? I was gonna call and tell you the feds won't prosecute."

"You're an hour or so late."

"Stop talkin' in riddles. I'm already at critical mass."

"Citizen called it in. Found Rincon's body in a dumpster on Harry Hines. Hadda iron pipe hammered up his fundament. I can meet y'all at the scene." Kobok jotted down the address and filled Bush in. He retrieved his football from his desk drawer.

"Fundament?" Bush asked.

"Yeah, three feet of metal pipe up his ass. That's often fatal."

"I know the word. Just impressed with your vocabulary. I gotta errand to run," Bush looked up with his soft baby blues. "I'll follow you out to Harry Hines." Bush had been assigned a year-old Ford, a vast improvement on equipment he'd driven in his first three years on the job. He had expanded into a capable, insightful street investigator.

The alley was jammed with cops and emergency vehicles. Hooper's shiny head was easily identifiable in the crowd. He'd lit a fresh stogie. The Field Agent for the medical examiner's office had already conscripted a pair of uniforms to help him lay Rincon's body on a plastic tarp next to a dumpster. The body was nude, covered with cigarette or cigar burns, with the hands duct taped behind his back. The M.E. Field Agent motioned to Kobok and Bush.

He knelt and opened Prince Rincon's eyelids one at a time. Each had a gold star earring pushed into the pupil.

Hooper bent to have another look. "Damn, he didn't go so easy."

Kobok said, "It's only three hours since we saw him at Tubby's. How the hell…?"

Hooper filled the alley with exhaled cigar smoke. "Don't look a gift horse in the mouth, dude. Looks to me like he died right nice…and won't be missed."

Kobok pointed to the works painted on the side of the dumpster, "Belongs to Homer Wayne DuPree. Now that's ironic justice."

Kobok hung with the crowd long enough to appear interested and headed back downtown to his office. With more nervous anticipation then he'd ever admit, he unlocked his desk drawer and inspected the little package. Both star earrings were resting where they had for years. He walked to the parking structure, found the Plymouth, and headed north.

It was a nice, sunny day to go home early. Tad and he could toss the new football and later Kobok could swing for pizza at their favorite joint on Belt Line road. Tomorrow he'd worry about who'd finished that sorry piece of crap Rincon. The Prince was gone. He wondered if they chalked it up in Hell that he wasn't sorry.

Central was jammed with an early rush hour pile up. Kobok detoured up Hillcrest Avenue. On a whim, he swung through the neatly manicured cemetery he'd visited regularly for over four years. Sherry's grave was just off the main path, accessible only if the visitor parked on the path and walked a hundred feet to her gravesite. He'd noted that often fresh flowers continued to be often placed against the headstone.

But today the main path was blocked by a black Lincoln Continental. The glint of the sun favored Kobok. The large man who leaned on the rear quarter panel, his image of Kobok blunted by sunlight, was familiar. Kobok stopped out of sight of the man. The big man instinctively slid a hand toward a rear pocket. Then a second figure stepped into view, also unable to see Kobok through the glare of sunlight on the Plymouth's windshield. His black hair neatly parted down the middle, Kobok knew him, but not really well at all. He was owner of a topless club on Northwest Highway with connections beyond the reach of the cops. Connections good enough to find the Prince and deal with him within three hours of the wild downtown giant pink rabbit chase.

Tony Bones stared steadily at Kobok's Plymouth as he backed down the path. Kobok realized that he had not been the only one both livid and tormented by Sherry Kincaid's horrible murder.

Kobok backed his Plymouth down the path and headed on north. If the notion struck him, he could have a chat with Tony Bones later. Right now, he had a football to give to a kid he knew.

Swinging into Hillcrest traffic, he couldn't avoid wondering if Prince Rincon had been an easy kill. Not so, he suspected. Not so.

ABOUT THE AUTHOR

Gary Clifton, forty years a cop, including a twenty-five-year career as an ATF Agent, has spent a lifetime squarely in a free front row seat to the damnedest show on Earth. Having been shot at, shot, stabbed, sued, lied to and about, and frequently misunderstood, there is no violent crime, vicious situation, nor clever criminal subterfuge he hasn't seen. Of the many tales he's written, each is based in some actual crime he's handled, with names changed only to protect the guilty. He has a master's in psychology, an invaluable tool in trying to unravel the violence human beings can inflict upon each other.

Clifton published a novel, *Burn Sugar Burn,* in national paperback in 1987. Since, he's found more fertile ground in short fiction pieces. The Toronto based magazine, *Bewildering Stories*, has published more than fifty of Clifton's stories. He has published upwards of sixty more in various venues, including *Broadkill Review, The Simone Press, Beat to a Pulp, Yellow Mama, Rusty Nail, Crack the Spine,* and numerous others.

Currently, he's retired to a dusty North Texas ranch where he doesn't much give a damn if school keeps or not.

A selection of Clifton's work is available on his blog at:

http://www.bareknucklethoughts.org.

Curious about other Crossroad Press books?
Stop by our site:
http://www.crossroadpress.com
We offer quality writing
in digital, audio, and print formats.